MALVOLLO'S
REVENGE

MALVOLLO'S REVENGE

Sophie Masson

Hodder
Children's
Books

A division of Hodder Headline Limited

A Catalogue record for this book is available from the British Library

ISBN 0 340 88364 2

Typeset in Perpetua by Avon DataSet Ltd,
Bidford-on-Avon, Warwickshire

Printed and bound in Great Britain by
Bookmarque Ltd, Croydon, Surrey

The paper and board used in this paperback by Hodder Children's Books
are natural recyclable products made from wood grown in sustainable
forests. The manufacturing processes conform to the environmental
regulations of the country of origin.

Hodder Children's Books
A division of Hodder Headline Limited
338 Euston Road
London NW1 3BH

For Rita

ACT ONE

Illyria

With a hey ho, the wind and the rain . . .

One

Toby had never seen so much rain. It poured down in great relentless waterfalls, drowning the road, the covered wagon, the horses and most of all Toby himself. Slithering and sliding in the slippery treachery of the dissolving road, he desperately tried to encourage poor Slender and Shallow to struggle on, hoping for shelter.

According to Uncle Theo's sketchy map, there should be houses not too far away. But even by the light of his hurricane lantern, Toby could barely see more than a handspan in front of his nose. Occasionally, a tree would loom out of the gloom: the strange live oaks one saw everywhere in this place, still green in winter, ghostly in the pale lantern-glow, the moss hanging from their drenched black branches like the tattered rags of criminals on the gallows. Far above the sunken road was the levee which held back the huge swollen Mississippi, whose muffled but still menacing roar could be heard even through the din of the rain.

Water, water everywhere, thought Toby, sneezing violently. Water – this damned country is only an excuse for land, it's just a floating island on a huge black current. Our wagon's a frail little ship, and soon enough we'll be wrecked, swept away like so much flotsam, drowned by water above and below!

Some New Year's Eve this was! Some 'gala tour' it had turned out to be! His gullible Uncle Theo, director and manager of the Trentham Troupe of Players, had been promised riches and fame by a con man named Roland Batiste, who called himself a 'theatrical agent'. Batiste had promised to find them a good theatre in New Orleans, a substantial crew, big audiences, fat takings. Instead, when the troupe reached the city, Batiste had disappeared, with all the considerable money Theo Trentham had paid him. There was no backstage crew waiting for them. And there was certainly no theatre able or willing to take them. No one in New Orleans had heard of Uncle Theo's play, *Malvolio's Revenge*. Twenty years ago, it had been a modest success in the West End of London, but since then, it had fallen into obscurity, along with its author. Besides, theatre managers wanted light things in the festive season: pantomimes and musicals and variety shows. *Malvolio's Revenge* was none of these.

Things looked bleak indeed for them all. And then ever-optimistic Uncle Theo had a 'brilliant' idea. They'd take the play out into the countryside. There were rich, educated planters out there, starved for culture, who'd pay good money to see a show that had once been a West End hit.

Alas! The Louisiana countryside, if it held people who hungered after culture, certainly hid them well, maybe drowned in the swamps or the marshes or the blessed little bayous that covered so much of the place. Oh, sure, in a miserable little town or two, they had played Uncle Theo's pride and joy. But audiences, and takings, had been very poor. What Uncle Theo had not banked on was the fact that many country people spoke French, rather than English, and that they couldn't care less about some long-forgotten English play. As to the rich planters, most of them had shut up their houses for the Christmas and Carnival season and moved into New Orleans.

Toby sighed gustily. Oh, how he longed to be warm and dry in New Orleans! Images of the city crowded in his mind this horrible night: large, comfortable houses; warm fires; cosy, noisy taverns; brightly lit, never-sleeping streets . . .

The wagon lurched violently as the horses skidded to a sudden stop. Toby was flung sideways, and fell sprawling in the mud, the lantern flying out of his hand. He groped for it, swearing loudly. Alarmed faces peered out of the stalled wagon.

'You idiot boy!' shouted his uncle, clambering out. 'What

the Devil do you think you're doing? Are you trying to get us all killed?'

Scrambling to his feet, Toby glared at his uncle. 'It's the dratted horses! They just stopped dead!'

'Why the blazes did they?' said Uncle Theo, snatching at the lantern.

'How should I know?' retorted Toby, but Uncle Theo was not listening. 'Now, Slender, now, Shallow,' he crooned, squelching through the mud to the horses standing stock-still in the road, 'what's up with you, boys, eh?'

In the dim light of the lantern, the horses' mild, stubborn faces appeared. They had stopped hard against what looked like a gatepost. The light swung up as Uncle Theo raised the lantern, revealing an archway, and a name, painted on it in fading letters. Toby didn't have enough time to read it before his uncle lowered the lantern.

'I do declare!' Uncle Theo exclaimed. 'They've got good sense, this pair.' He swung the lantern in Toby's direction. 'Wait here, and hold the horses. I'm just going up the carriage-way a little to see if there's any sign of life at the house.'

He didn't wait for Toby's answer, and his portly figure was soon lost to sight in the darkness.

'Toby!' A plaintive voice came from the wagon.

Toby smiled to himself. 'Yes, Madame Leonard?'

'In the name of the blessed Virgin, what's happening? Why have we stopped?'

'We've been shipwrecked, ma'am,' said Toby, jokingly. She was so easy to tease. He would not have done so, mind you, if his uncle had been in earshot. Uncle Theo treated leading lady Matilda Leonard as if she was a rare jewel, or perhaps an unexploded bomb. She had pretensions to being French, and so felt entitled to put on artistic tantrums, though everyone knew well enough she was born in London.

She gave a little cry. 'Shipwrecked? Is the river coming down on us? Is that why there is so much water?'

It had been her greatest fear ever since arriving in Louisiana. She did not like the look of the Mississippi. It was too big and the land was too flat, and she didn't trust the levees. One day they would burst and the big booming river would sweep everyone away.

'It could be,' Toby muttered gloomily, enjoying his moment of power. 'It could be.' And squealed in outrage, as his ear was twisted.

'Stop it, you rascal!' It was the light Irish voice of Gabriel Harvey, who played villains and character parts. His dark, rough-cut face with its grey-green eyes under a shock of coal-black hair was not handsome or stupid enough to qualify him to play the parts of romantic leads. 'You're not the one has to calm Matilda's hysterics. Where's Theo?'

'Down there,' said Toby, crossly, rubbing at his ear.

'Down there? In the darkness? Has he lost his wits?'

'House,' explained Toby, sullenly. He could see the dim

glow returning, the vague shape of his uncle behind it. 'There's a plantation house down there somewhere. Horses saw it first.'

'Well, thank their good horse sense. Or whatever.'

'Much good it'll do us, if there's no one there, or they won't let us in.' A gloomy voice from the wagon.

Gabriel laughed. 'Trust you, Old Fate, to raise our spirits!'

Toby couldn't help grinning. Jacques La Fete was the company's clown – and in real life so morose and pessimistic that Gabriel had nicknamed him Old Fate, a play on the English sound of the clown's name, which in French actually meant 'the festival'. He really was French, though from Canada.

Theo Trentham squelched back up to them, his red face glowing in the pool of light. 'It's our lucky night, friends! Not only is there a house down there, but they'll take us in for the night and set us on our way tomorrow. It's only a few hours to New Orleans from here, apparently. There's soup and bread and bacon, and a good fire! We'll have a good New Year's Eve, after all.' He paused. 'You'll never guess what the name of the house is!' Not waiting for anyone to speak, he hurried on, 'It's called Illyria! Just like the setting of our play! Isn't that a good omen, now?'

Gabriel said, lightly, 'Illyria, is it? I would not care if it were Hell itself, opening its gates to us this wicked evening, and the Devil himself who was to be our host!'

Matilda Leonard gave a little gasp, her face paling under its layers of rouge. Crossing herself, she said, 'Have a care, Gabriel Harvey. You will bring bad luck down on us, with such words.'

'Couldn't be worse than the luck we've had already,' retorted Gabriel, trudging off to help Toby lead the horses down the drive of Illyria.

Two

Toby never forgot his first sight of Illyria, rising out of the rage of rain like a down-on-her-luck beauty clad in the tatters of splendour. The house had clearly once been beautiful indeed. It was large, three-storeyed, white, with graceful Grecian pillars, ironwork balconies and French doors. But now the balconies were rusty and missing bits, the pillars were no longer white but grey, and seemed to totter under the weight of the house rather than support it. Most of the French doors had been shuttered and nailed shut, giving the house a look of missing teeth and blind eyes. And much of the white stucco work had fallen off, leaving ugly blotches and stains like skin blemishes.

The avenue of trees that led to the house had also been elegant, once; but now the evergreen live oaks had tangled together. The grey Spanish moss hung from their branches like ghostly rags, brushing at the sides of the wagon as they squeezed down the track. The whole thing was rather gloomy and sinister, and for a moment Toby shuddered, gripped by a premonition of disaster.

But it *was* a house; it was shelter from the weather. Besides, the Trentham Troupe were used to making do with some very unfortunate accommodation. Ever since they'd arrived in the United States on what Theo Trentham had hopefully named a 'gala tour', they had had to stay in a succession of miserable boarding-houses and seedy hotels. This at least had some class, even if that class was more of a memory than anything else. Best of all, as Theo had said, there would be soup and bread and bacon and a fire to sit and warm up by.

And the place was called Illyria, after all. Despite Gabriel Harvey's sarcasm, the coincidence did count for something, especially for superstitious actors. Not only was it the setting of *Malvolio's Revenge*, but also the much more famous play it was based on, Shakespeare's *Twelfth Night*. On the other hand, Illyria was obviously down on its luck; but then, so were they. Two bad lucks might cancel each other out and, together with the omen of the name, create good luck, after all, thought Toby, hopefully.

The wagon creaked to a halt in front of the house. Out came the relieved troupe. First came Matilda Leonard, creaking as much as the wagon in her damp stays; then Toby's pretty, auburn-haired eighteen-year-old cousin, Olivia, who played the younger female parts; then leading man, handsome, vain Henry Smallwood, brushing at his golden waves; then came lowering, gloomy Old Fate; and finally, grubby, sleepy eleven-year-old Will, Olivia's brother, who played urchins and children.

'Well!' said Henry Smallwood, opening his baby-blues very wide. 'Here we are, then.'

He had a habit of stating the obvious, and it never failed to rouse Gabriel. 'We are indeed, Harry, old man,' he said flippantly. 'We are arrived at the—'

He broke off as the front door abruptly opened. An old woman stood on the threshold, candlestick in hand. Dressed all in black, she was small, rather shrunken, with a face like a withered brown apple under silver hair neatly pinned into a bun. She would have been quite unremarkable if it had not been for her eyes: of a startling green, they were rather unfocused, almost as though she were going blind.

'Good evening,' she said, in a soft voice, with a singsong French accent. Her eyes roved over them all. 'Welcome to Illyria. I am Marie Laroche, last retainer of this house.' She raised the candle so that they could see to go up the steps. 'Mademoiselle Isabelle de Castelon is awaiting you in the dining-room, for supper.'

Toby didn't hear his uncle's effusions in return, for at that moment, he happened to look at Gabriel. The actor was staring straight ahead, at a point in the darkness of the hall beyond the old lady's shoulder, with a strange expression on his face. What was wrong with him? He looks as though he's seen a ghost, thought Toby, with a little shiver.

'There's a stable around the back,' the woman went on. 'You can unhitch the horses, stow the wagon, give them hay. Good hay it is, too,' she added, with a note of pride in her voice.

Toby knew what was coming. And indeed, on cue, his uncle turned to him and said, firmly, 'Off you go then, boy. Give those poor beggars a bit of a rubdown, while you're about it.'

'I'll help you,' said Gabriel, lightly. He seemed to have quite recovered. 'Come on, lad. Nothing to it.'

Gabriel was a good sort, even if he could be hellishly moody at times. He wasn't much older than Toby – twenty-one to Toby's seventeen – but sometimes he gave the impression he had lived several lifetimes, all exciting and dangerous. Toby wasn't sure if he believed all of Gabriel's stories, but what the deuce, they were entertaining enough to deserve being true, even if they weren't. And they more than made up for the actor's occasional bouts of black moodiness.

'I tell you what,' said Toby as they reached the stables, 'this place gives me a strange feeling.'

Gabriel shrugged. 'Does it?'

'And that strange old woman,' went on Toby. 'She looks like a witch, with those weird eyes.'

'Bah,' said Gabriel, shrugging, 'you read too many penny dreadfuls, Toby.'

Toby laughed. 'I saw your face, Gabriel, back there! You looked spooked! What did you see in that hall?'

Gabriel looked at him, a startled look on his face. 'What do you mean? Oh . . . that. It was nothing. Just my own distorted reflection in a mirror. There was a tall mirror, just beyond the old lady. Didn't you see it?'

'No,' said Toby, a little dashed.

Gabriel laughed at his discomfiture. 'Sorry, Toby.'

The stables were as down on their luck as the house, but they were dry, large, and easily accommodated the wagon. Once, they must have held many horses and carriages; now there was only a sulky and a couple of horses.

Gabriel and Toby worked quickly, unharnessing, rubbing down and feeding Slender and Shallow. The other two horses watched, timidly flicking their ears. Soon, it was all done, and the relieved and exhausted horses comfortably settled in for the night. Then Toby changed out of his wet clothes into a clean, dry, warm set from the wagon. He towel-dried his wild ginger hair, brushed it back, scrubbed at his freckled face, and suddenly felt a lot better.

Gabriel and Toby set off for the house again, but the front door was closed and no one answered their knock. So they went around the back and at last found a door which pushed open to the touch. Beyond was a narrow, dark passageway, which in turn led to a scullery, and then to a darkened kitchen. Feeling their way, they went through that, down another narrow passage, and into a dimly lit hall lined with portraits, heavy gold-framed paintings of elegant people in period costume.

'Well, well, the ancestors, eh?' said Gabriel, softly. 'We have fallen amongst high class indeed, my friend Toby.' He looked thoughtfully down the line of portraits. 'Class down on its luck, mind you: neglect everywhere, and only one servant, it appears. But class nevertheless. Creole aristocrats, you know – the descendants of the original French and Spanish who were the first Europeans to settle in Louisiana,' he explained as Toby looked blank. 'You know,' he went on, striking a pose, 'the old maid Mademoiselle de Castelon is probably the last melancholy relic of her noble Creole race. What'll she be like, I wonder: ruined glamour, like this house? Or fierce old bat with a peremptory French voice? Or silvery ghost, tended by that strange old coloured woman?'

'Hmm . . .' Toby was not interested. His stomach was growling too urgently. Supper, supper, supper, it demanded. Supper, by the fire! He looked around. There were three doors leading off the hall. Which one? He went over to one, turned the knob, and stopped. 'What the . . .?

Gabriel had reached him. He, too, peered in. 'Jumping Jehoshaphat!' he breathed. 'That's something, all right!'

Inside the little room beyond was an open wardrobe, filled to bursting with clothes. No, on second thought: not with mere clothes, but *costumes*. Shimmering falls of satin, velvet, lace, silver and gold thread, organza, sequins: there were glorious gowns and doublets, embroidered coats and worked shawls of great delicacy and splendour, robes and waistcoats, veils and all kinds of other wonders. On a shelf above, there were also wigs of various sorts and styles, from a towering silver confection that looked like a great cake, to a mass of little corkscrew curls in the deepest black and a pigtail in eighteenth-century style, all stiff white horsehair and black grosgrain ribbon.

'What *have* we come into, Gabriel?' breathed Toby.

Gabriel shook his head. 'Illyria? No, I think the storm has landed us on Mystery Island, lad. Well, I think at the very least we've got an interesting time ahead of us! But right now, let's find that supper your uncle was telling us about.'

Three

The dining-room was just what Toby had dreamed of on the rainy road. Cosy, shut off tightly from the outside world, it must once have been just an informal family breakfast-room, but now it was one of the few rooms that bore little sign of dampness or neglect. A roaring fire blazed in the grate; slender white and red candles burned in silver candlesticks on the table; the good smell of rich onion soup and bacon filled the air. All the other members of the troupe were already seated.

'Ah! Toby! Gabriel! What took you so long? We were about to start without you!' Theo Trentham, seated at the head of the table, looked very happy indeed. But Toby had no eyes for his uncle, or even, more surprisingly, for the food on the table. For at the other head sat . . . not a mad old maid in crumbling lace and a ruined face, as they had imagined, but the most beautiful young woman Toby had ever seen.

She was about his age, or a little older. She had long, wavy dark hair, large brown eyes flecked with patches of hazel, set in a cream-and-honey face, and full soft red lips. Though she was dressed in a simple, plain white dress, with no jewellery, she was the most sophisticated, glamorous person he not only had ever seen, but also imagined. He could not take his eyes off her, quite forgetting how hungry he was. Beside him, he heard Gabriel make a little sound in his throat, then the older man said, lightly, 'Sorry, all. We were delayed. The horses – they just wouldn't let us go!'

The young woman laughed. 'I know just what you mean,' she observed. Her eyes sparkled, giving extra light to her beautiful face. 'They can be very hard taskmasters indeed, our so-called dumb friends. Welcome to my poor home. You have already met my darling nurse, Marie Laroche, whom I call Maminou. I am Isabelle de Castelon, last of that name, last owner of Illyria.'

'Now, then, Isabelle.' It was Marie Laroche speaking, gently reproving. 'It is New Year's Eve, and our friends have had a hard road.'

Isabelle smiled suddenly, very sweetly. 'Forgive me, friends. One becomes a trifle gloomy and inward-looking, in Illyria.'

'Oh, there is nothing to forgive, Mademoiselle,' said Uncle Theo, warmly. 'Nothing at all. We are more than grateful, all of us.'

Isabelle motioned to Gabriel and Toby. 'Come, sit down. You must be very hungry.'

'That we are for sure,' agreed Gabriel, thumping down at the table with a sigh of relief. 'Ah. Mademoiselle, excuse me – my name's Gabriel Harvey,' he said, nodding in the young woman's direction, but not looking at her, 'and I surely am grateful for your hospitality, Mademoiselle.' Toby was puzzled by his casual, almost flippant tone. How could Gabriel not have been struck dumb by such a vision of beauty?

'Pleased to meet you, Mr Gabriel Harvey,' said Isabelle, pertly. 'Are you an actor too? I have been hearing such fascinating tales from your colleagues! What parts do you play, if I may ask?' Her English, though most charmingly accented with French intonations, was perfect.

'You may,' said Gabriel Harvey, ladling himself out a generous bowlful of soup. 'I play villains and characters – you know, the eccentric, the mad, the bad, the loopy, the unmarriageable – who come to a sticky end.'

Isabelle smiled. 'Oh, but you must tell me more about that! When you have eaten and drunk your fill, of course . . .' Now she seemed to properly notice Toby for the first time. A mischievous smile tweaked at the corners of her lips. 'Aren't you going to sit down? You make me feel a trifle nervous, towering up there!'

Toby flushed to the tips of his ears. He had always been self-conscious about his long thin frame. 'Sorry,' he muttered, and pulled out a chair rather too quickly, so that it fell over and he nearly fell over with it. Everyone laughed, even Isabelle, and Toby felt mortified, especially after Uncle Theo said, 'That flummer-foot's Toby, Miss Isabelle, my dear nephew Toby. He does his share of things, I must say, despite his sadly unimaginative disposition.'

'You are an actor too?'

'No,' murmured Toby, 'I—'

But his uncle broke in. 'Toby's our set carpenter, bill-sticker, stage hand, prompter, runner-around, errand-boy, general dogsbody! We are severely depleted as to crew, and so we've all had to double up as both cast and crew, at various times. Toby's been our only consistent crew member, you see.'

'Invaluable indeed,' said Isabelle, glancing over at Toby then away.

'We couldn't do without him, that is so,' Theo Trentham said, and Henry added, nodding his head wisely, 'He makes himself useful.'

'Oh yes, that he does,' said Olivia, languidly. 'He's always there when you need him – and even when you don't!'

'Tobe's a norphan,' said Will, importantly.

Toby blushed. They were talking about him as if he weren't there, making him look ridiculous in the eyes of this girl. He couldn't bear it.

He was about to get up to flee the room when she said, gently, 'An orphan? Why, so am I.'

Their eyes met. And in that moment Toby, who'd been wishing the earth could swallow him up, felt strength and courage and hope come rushing into him again. He said, squaring his shoulders, 'I lost my parents many years ago. Uncle Theo was kind enough to take me in and bring me up alongside his own. For that I will always be grateful.'

He'd meant the words for Isabelle, but to his alarm, it was Uncle Theo's pop-eyes which filled with sentimental tears. 'No need to be grateful, dear boy,' he said, patting Toby's hand. 'You are family, after all.'

Despite himself, Toby felt warmed by his uncle's words, and by the wistful smile Isabelle directed at him. Uncle Theo saw it too, and taking back the initiative, he said, hastily, 'But enough of such personal matters, Mademoiselle. We are most grateful to you for taking us in; we, who are strangers to you. Would we be able to repay you in a small way, after supper, by performing some extracts from our play?'

Well, isn't that just like Uncle Theo, thought Toby, ruefully. Losing no opportunity to inflict his play on any audience that came to hand! But it seemed that Isabelle did not share his dismay.

Her face clearing of all melancholy, she clapped her hands and cried, 'Oh, Mr Trentham, if you would, it would be just the best New Year's gift of all! I do so love the theatre, though I have little opportunity to go! What is your play named, sir?'

'It is called *Malvolio's Revenge*,' said Uncle Theo, proudly. 'It continues the story of Shakespeare's famous *Twelfth Night*. You know how at the end of that play the pompous steward Malvolio promises vengeance on all the people who have ridiculed and humiliated him? Well, my play tells how he does indeed take his revenge.'

Marie Laroche gave a little gasp. Her face had lost colour. Isabelle reached over to her and touched her gently.

'Maminou is startled,' she explained softly, 'because, you see, *Twelfth Night* is a bit of a tradition in this house. My parents . . . it was their favourite play.'

'Ah!' said Uncle Theo, beaming. 'I thought, when I saw the name of your estate . . . I thought to myself, why, we have fallen amongst Shakespeare lovers, the omens are good indeed for us!'

Isabelle smiled. 'My father certainly loved Shakespeare and especially that play, sir,' she said, 'but the estate was actually named by my great-grandfather, who had been on campaign with Napoleon's forces in the land of the Slovenes, which they called Illyria. When my father, who was partly educated in England, took over the plantation, he started a tradition of mounting a production of *Twelfth Night* in the house, every actual Twelfth Night, on January 6, to mark the opening of Carnival season. And my parents themselves took on the roles of Sebastian and Olivia.'

The costumes, thought Toby. That's what they must have been for.

'Why, this is most marvellous!' exclaimed Theo. 'Most marvellous!'

'My mother Violette used to say *Twelfth Night* had its own magic, which drew good things to you. It seems that is certainly the case tonight! I am so glad the storm blew you to us! Oh, may we have this rendition from the play as soon as possible, dear Mr Trentham?'

'Why, of course.' Uncle Theo was in seventh heaven, thought Toby. And no wonder, with such an enthusiastic auditor for his play . . . At that moment, Toby happened to glance over at the old woman, and was startled by the fixity of her expression. She was staring not at anyone, but into the shadows beyond the pool of light cast by the candles: staring as if she'd seen something that shouldn't be there. It made him feel prickly all over.

'Maminou!' said Isabelle then, making the nurse jump a little.

'Yes, *chère?*' Marie Laroche spoke calmly, though there was still a certain fixity to her gaze.

'I was just saying to Mr Trentham that you used to be wardrobe mistress, when my parents put on the play.'

'Yes,' said the old woman gently.

'Everyone in the staff had a role, didn't they, Maminou? Either on stage or backstage, you see, Mr Trentham. We used to have a lot of servants, you see, quite enough to mount a full production.'

'That is so,' said the old woman. She got up. 'I will go and make us all coffee.' She picked up some plates, but her hands were shaking. Gabriel got up. 'Allow me, Madame,' he said, lightly, taking the plates from her. She looked at him, seemingly startled, but nodded.

'Don't be long, Maminou,' called Isabelle, as they went out. 'Mr Trentham wants to start immediately after we've had coffee.' She turned to Toby. 'And you, sir . . . what is your role to be?'

'Er . . . nothing,' stammered Toby, looking quickly at Uncle Theo. 'That is . . . there are no sets to get ready, here, are there, Uncle?'

'No, boy, of course not. Don't be a fool. We are just doing extracts. But here . . . the table needs to be moved back, the chairs arranged in rows. Come on, Toby . . . what are you waiting for?'

Four

Everything was ready, and the coffee – good, hot, strong –
had been drunk. Uncle Theo coughed importantly, smoothed
down his glossy moustache, patted at his glossy brush-cut
hair, and stroked his waistcoat, straining over his belly. 'This
is the story of my play, ladies. We are twenty-five years from
the action of *Twelfth Night*. Malvolio, who left Illyria at the
end of Shakespeare's play, promising revenge on all and sundry
for the tricks that were played on him, has become a rich and
important personage in the neighbouring country of
Moldonia. In fact, he has become the confidant of its king,
who is a sworn enemy of Illyria. He has persuaded the King
of Moldonia to invade Illyria, subjugate its inhabitants and
disinherit its noble families. He has been given the post of
viceroy, and in that capacity has been able to pursue his
vengeance against his old enemies. His main tormentors, Sir

Toby Belch and his wife Maria, have died in prison; the Countess Olivia, whom once he pursued, has died of a broken heart after her only child Lydia was stolen from her home and never seen again. Her husband Sebastian has been outlawed, and roams in the hills of Illyria with his nephew Lysander, son of his twin sister Viola and Count Orsino. Orsino himself died in battle, and Viola has taken the veil.'

Told like that, thought Toby, it sounded like the most depressing mishmash you could imagine. No wonder the theatre managers had wanted nothing to do with it! He caught Marie Laroche's eye and thought he saw in there a reflection of his own dismay. But Isabelle's eyes were sparkling.

'Goodness, Mr Trentham, it does sound like a most dramatic and exciting story! I hope it ends satisfactorily?'

'Oh, indeed, I assure you it does, Mademoiselle,' said Uncle Theo, hastily. 'All ends most happily – with all Malvolio's schemes confounded, and everything back in its proper place – and a wedding between Lysander and Lydia.'

Isabelle clapped her hands. 'Excellent! Just as I hoped! Well, Mr Trentham, now we know the story, may we begin?'

'Right away, Mademoiselle,' said Uncle Theo eagerly. 'In honour of your own parents' roles, Mademoiselle, my colleagues and I have decided to perform two special extracts from the play. Our first extract is the prologue, which is a speech by Count Sebastian. I play him in our production. He is a man old before his time, and bowed down by care. You will have to imagine me in full make-up and costume, Mademoiselle, Madame – I assure you, it makes me look a great deal older and more worn.'

Toby met Gabriel's eye, and grinned. Uncle Theo was almost as vain as Henry Smallwood.

'We promise we will imagine it, Mr Trentham,' said Isabelle pertly.

Theo beamed. 'Now then, here is the setting: a lonely night-time beach, bathed in starlight, and Sebastian, quite reduced, wandering like a lost soul. There should also be soft sad music playing . . . Goodness me, what's that!'

'That' was a great hollow banging that resounded throughout the room. 'Someone must be at the front door,' said Isabelle, frowning.

'Some other poor traveller must be abroad on this unpleasant night,' said her nurse.

'Well,' said Isabelle, 'we cannot shut our door to those in need. Go and see who it is, Maminou.' She turned to Uncle Theo. 'Please excuse us, Mr Trentham.'

Uncle Theo was quite flustered at being interrupted. 'Er . . . well . . . of course . . .'

'Your play sounds a most artful work,' said Isabelle, skilfully easing him around. 'What is its history, sir?'

Oh lord, thought Toby, settling into his chair, she's only hit on Uncle Theo's favourite subject! He could keep going on this till the cows come home!

Uncle Theo looked quite happy again. 'I wrote it twenty-two years ago,' he said, 'when I was a struggling actor in the provinces in England. By great good luck, a friend of mine knew a London theatrical agent, and persuaded him to look at it. Well, it just so happened this agent loved it – and passed it to one of the best West End managers. It premiered a few months later, and was a great success with audiences, though the critics – jealous men all – were not kind to it. With the money I earned during that time, I was able to set up the first incarnation of the Trentham Troupe. I wrote many other plays. But none quite captured the imagination of the public as *Malvolio's Revenge* had done. That is widely acknowledged to be my masterpiece.' He paused. 'Later, alas, Mademoiselle, fashions changed. Audiences are not as well-educated as in the past – begging your pardon – and true art has to struggle against the brash and vulgar. Yet I have never lost hope that one day, the true value of *Malvolio's Revenge* would be seen again. And so I decided a couple of years ago to reform the troupe. We have been touring many parts of the world – Britain, Canada, and now the United States.'

Poor Uncle Theo, thought Toby. How could he tell Isabelle the unvarnished truth – about the doors slammed in his face, the unkind laughter of managers telling him the play was hopelessly old-fashioned, the shabby provincial halls they'd played in, the miserable Christmas dinner of beans and tinned sardines, on this grand international tour? Nobody else in the company would breathe a word of it, though – how could they? The play's failure reflected on them, too.

'I really do not know how—' began Isabelle, but whatever she'd been about to say remained unsaid as the door opened and a newcomer entered the room, Madame Laroche behind him.

He was a handsome young man, quite small, but wiry and graceful, with a pair of dancing brown eyes under a thatch of wet, pale hair. He was dressed shabbily but tidily, and under one arm carried a violin case. In the other hand, he had a small carpetbag.

'Good evening, ladies and gentlemen,' he said, into the hush that greeted his arrival. 'Thomas Nashe, travelling fiddler, at your service.' He bowed over Isabelle's hand. 'Mademoiselle, I thank you from the bottom of my heart for taking pity on a lost traveller.'

'You are welcome, sir,' said Isabelle brightly. 'This is the home of lost travellers tonight. And what's your story, sir? Why is a travelling fiddler abroad on New Year's Eve?'

'Well, I thought I had an engagement to play at a party at a plantation a few miles from here. But when I arrived this afternoon, I found the house boarded up and deserted. So, hey-ho, I thought, no New Year's jollifications and supper for me.'

'My dear sir!' said Theo, warmly. 'I do believe we are brothers in misfortune!'

'Oh, and fortune, I would say, now we have found shelter with you, Mademoiselle,' the fiddler said, bowing to Isabelle.

'You are welcome, Mr Nashe,' said Isabelle, smiling. 'Do sit down. We were just about to be entertained with a rendition from *Malvolio's Revenge*, Mr Trentham's famous play.' Surprisingly, Uncle Theo seemed hardly to notice the compliment. His eyes were shining with a light Toby recognised all too well. It was a 'brilliant idea' expression.

'Why!' he exclaimed. 'Mr Nashe! You are just the very fellow we need for our rendition. We could do with a little music, sir, to create atmosphere. Would you be willing to provide it?'

'Gladly,' said the fiddler, taking his instrument from its case.

'Capital! Now then, sir, what we need is a melancholy air of some kind – the first scene is of heart-rending sadness . . .' Drawing the fiddler aside, he rapidly explained the scene. It didn't take long.

'Right, then,' said Uncle Theo, briskly. 'Everyone take your places again. We will start. Ready, Mr Nashe?' He moved into the space right in front of the firelight. Softly, the violin began to play.

The fiddler was good. Really good. The tune that came sweetly from his violin's strings was so lovely, so sad, that Toby, to his shame, could feel tears starting in his eyes. But looking at the other faces around him, he could see the others felt the same, even cynical Old Fate. His cousin Olivia had a rapt look on her face as she gazed at the handsome young musician. She had probably fallen for him already, Toby thought. Only Gabriel seemed not to fall under the spell of the music.

The tune ended. Uncle Theo began his speech, gently, brokenly:

> '*In vivid strips, the skin of evening*
> *Peels off into the dark of night.*
> *Stars of sharp, salt-rinsed radiance*
> *Tumble on black seas of light.*
> *Sail-sigh of night-wind blowing*
> *In stippled islands of cloud and bright!*
> *I search for treasure on the beach of memory*
> *And find there only dross and wrack;*
> *Flotsam and jetsam, rejected and weathered:*
> *No profit in going on, no joy in going back.*
> *My wife gone, my lands taken*
> *My only child lost to life:*
> *Oh God, why did you not end my days?*
> *Why am I not with my child and my wife?*'

Toby had heard it so many times before. He couldn't even begin to count the number. It had never really moved him before. For his taste, the speech was a bit too wordy, a bit too

31

literary. Besides, Uncle Theo was not a good actor. He was far too self-important, he was always just himself playing a part, he didn't melt into it, like the others did, especially Gabriel. But as the fiddle began to play softly again under the last lines, Toby found himself biting his lip, and a lump came to his throat. Suddenly, the tragedy of Count Sebastian made sense to him, real sense. In his mind's eye, he could see a broken man, once proud and confident, reduced to a pitiful wreck by treachery and cruel revenge . . . Oh my lord, he thought, astonished, the hair rising on the back of his neck. Even Uncle Theo's voice has changed, it's gone deeper, slower, less fussy and whiny, as it usually is in this scene. This is how it should be! This is how it *should* be!

There was another hush when Theo had ended. Then the sound of vigorous clapping, and Isabelle's voice. 'Excellent! Wonderful!'

'You think so, Mademoiselle?' said Uncle Theo, in his normal voice. He shook his head, as if puzzled by his own performance. He looked at Thomas Nashe. 'That was a lovely melody, Mr Nashe. So sad, so rich, so haunting. What is it called?'

But it was Marie Laroche who answered. Her luminous eyes fixed on the young fiddler, she said, quietly, 'It is an old French song, "Le roi Renaud", and it's about a king who is fatally wounded, and on the point of death, but who nevertheless is determined to reach home . . . It's about love conquering death.'

'You are quite right, Madame,' said Thomas Nashe, bowing. 'I learned it from an old Cajun fiddler, out in the bayou.'

The Cajuns were poor country people of Louisiana, descended from exiles from French Canada who had trekked thousands of miles to their present home to escape persecution by the British. Their musicians were renowned throughout Louisiana.

'He was the greatest fiddler I ever met,' went on Nashe, lightly. 'And no wonder, for he'd sold his soul to the Devil at the crossroads, in return for a very long life and perfect pitch. I must confess I have thought of following his example.'

There was a little gasp from Matilda Leonard. She crossed herself. 'You should not jest about such things, Mr Nashe,' she said faintly. 'Twice tonight people have invoked the Evil One's name. It is more than enough. You will bring very bad luck on us.'

'Bah, Matilda,' said Gabriel harshly, 'we're actors – haven't we sold our souls to the Devil many times over? As to bad luck, well, Devil or no Devil, it's been following us like a mangy dog for a long time. Now then, Theo,' he went on, turning his back altogether too deliberately on the fiddler, 'are we going to do that other scene, or not? For I confess I am weary of talk.'

There was an indrawn breath around the company at Gabriel's rudeness. Theo, colouring, said, 'Perhaps Mademoiselle and Madame might wish to . . .'

'Oh no, do go on,' said Isabelle, seemingly unperturbed by the tension in the room. 'I really want to hear more, Mr Trentham.' Her smile at them all was so dazzling that it made Toby's knees feel weak, yet it only seemed to make Gabriel scowl. What was wrong with him, for heaven's sake?

Five

Usually, Gabriel was by far the best actor amongst them. In fact, he was really much too good for a down-at-heel travelling company. They all knew that, except for vain Henry Smallwood, who never saw anyone else's talent. There was no telling why Gabriel hadn't chosen to go chasing fame and fortune. Though he told so many colourful stories about his past, he discouraged all direct questions on either his antecedents or his future, saying the present was quite enough for him. The only token he carried from his previous life was a little leatherbound copy of the famous children's book, *Lamb's Tales from Shakespeare*. He'd once told Toby that it was this book which had made him decide to become an actor. But Toby wasn't sure if that was true, or just another one of his stories . . .

* * *

Despite his youth, Gabriel usually made an entirely believable, rather frightening and finally pitiable Malvolio. But tonight was quite different.

The scene was one at the end of the play. Malvolio is confronted by Lydia, finally returned from exile. She and her nurse Dame Vera, accompanied by Lysander, have burst into Malvolio's rooms, looking for Sebastian and his faithful friend, the clown Feste, who have been captured by Malvolio's forces. Malvolio, who has not seen Lydia since she was tiny, is thunderstruck by her resemblance to her mother Olivia, and driven to a terrible moment of self-revelation. The impact of the scene, if played properly, was quite dramatic; the whole cast on stage, and many dark secrets coming to light. But though the rest of the cast played valiantly on, they were quite let down by Gabriel's stiff, almost wooden performance.

Toby could see the puzzled, irritated looks they were all directing at Gabriel, Uncle Theo most of all. As to Thomas Nashe, he looked quizzical: even he could see something was wrong. Madame Laroche was quiet, still, her green eyes unreadable. Only Isabelle did not appear to know any different. When the scene ended, she clapped as vigorously as before, her eyes shining. 'Bravo! Bravo!'

There was a pause, then Uncle Theo, his eyes warily on an impassive Gabriel, said, rather uncertainly, 'Er . . . there's still Malvolio's final death scene . . . and the wedding scene, after that, but I think perhaps it'll do, for tonight, if you don't mind, ladies.' Toby knew that his uncle would dearly like to reprove Gabriel for his astonishing lack of professionalism tonight, but also that he didn't quite dare to, not in the mood the actor was obviously in.

'You were all quite wonderful!' said Isabelle, warmly. 'Oh! I think you will be the toast of New Orleans! Which theatre are you to play in?'

'Er . . .' began the director of the Trentham Troupe, colouring, 'that is, you see . . .'

'Theo was tricked,' said Old Fate, gloomily.

'Swindled by a wicked con man,' agreed Henry Smallwood, patting at his hair to make sure its waves were still in order.

'He promised us fame and fortune, but we haven't seen the inside of a single New Orleans playhouse, nor are we likely to,' said Matilda Leonard, crossly. 'No one would even look at us there, and then Theobald' – she always called Uncle Theo by his full name – 'had the grand idea of a rural tour, when rich planters would be sure to want us. Bah!'

Marie and Isabelle's eyes met. 'A rural tour at this time of the year!' exclaimed Isabelle. 'Why, most everyone who's everyone is in town!'

'We know that now,' put in Toby suddenly, 'but we didn't then. It's not fair, to blame Uncle Theo for everything.'

'That's right,' said Olivia, defending her father. 'How was he to know? We've come from England; we can't be expected to know. But Mr Smallwood's from America, and—'

'Not from Louisiana, girl,' said the leading man, with great distaste. 'Benighted part of the— I beg your pardon, miss,' he went on hurriedly, even his thick skin suddenly registering the freezing light in Isabelle's eyes.

Thomas Nashe had been listening to all this with an amused smile. 'I know just how you feel,' he said. 'That phantom party wasn't the only failure I've had here. When I reach New Orleans, I think I'll catch the first train out of there.'

'Perhaps we should do that too,' said Uncle Theo, despondently.

'Certainly not,' said Isabelle, vigorously. 'It is prime theatre season in New Orleans. It is there you should be!'

The actors looked at each other, the same weary expression in their eyes.

'Dear Mademoiselle,' said Theo, uncertainly, 'that is indeed where we would like to be. But the doors of the playhouses are closed to us.'

'Nonsense!' said Isabelle sharply. She leaned towards her nurse and whispered something in her ear. The old woman's green eyes flashed. She nodded, very slowly, and, it seemed, resignedly.

'Mr Trentham,' went on Isabelle, 'what if I told you I could get you into a playhouse – one I know very well, the Terpsichore in the French Quarter? It's in a not very fashionable part of town, but it is a good theatre.'

There was a silence. Then Theo said carefully, 'But,

Mademoiselle . . . we were told all the theatres were fully booked.'

'Not this one! It belongs to my father's second cousins, Blanche and Bruno Biche, and it's been closed for restoration for a while. I know they were planning to open again in the spring; but I believe the renovations are finished, and that they would be delighted to open early, with a guaranteed good show like yours.' She looked at their dumbstruck faces, and seemed to suddenly lose her confidence. 'I assure you, it's a good theatre – small, but perfectly formed. Would you care to consider it?'

'Oh, Mademoiselle,' said Toby's uncle, his eyes nearly popping out of his head. 'Consider it? I would be . . . we would be . . . your devoted slaves for ever, if this could happen!'

Too late, as he heard a hiss of indrawn breath, he realised his *faux pas*. Slavery had only been abolished in the United States thirty years or so ago, after a terrible civil war; there was every likelihood that Marie Laroche herself had been a slave, or at least a descendant of slaves. Flushing brick-red, he said, 'Forgive me . . . I didn't mean to give offence . . . A figure of speech . . .'

'And no offence taken,' said Madame Laroche, absently. Her attention was not on Theo's words, Toby saw, but on the faces of those around her. There was a tension in her expression which he couldn't quite figure out. Did she not approve of what Isabelle was saying? She caught his eye, at that moment, and he looked away, quickly, half afraid those strange eyes of hers would search out something in him, something hidden even from himself . . .

Uncle Theo was talking again, eagerly. 'Truly, Mademoiselle, if you could do a thing like that for us . . . I don't know, we would give you . . . a share of our proceeds, whatever you wanted, whatever we could afford.'

'No need for that either,' said Isabelle hastily. 'I will make a bargain with you, Mr Trentham. I get you into the Terpsichore. You allow us to come with you.'

'Of course,' said Theo, after a moment's puzzled silence. 'You must come with us, Mademoiselle, if we are to gain entry to—'

'That is not what I meant,' said Isabelle. Two red spots appeared in her cheeks, and she clenched her hands together, as if nervous. She cast a quick glance at her impassive nurse. 'We . . . we want to go with you as members of your troupe. We want to be part of *Malvolio's Revenge*, Mr Trentham.'

There was a dead silence. Then Gabriel spoke for the first time. He spoke lightly, as if the dark mood had never been. 'And why not? You can always write in another couple of female parts, eh, Theo?'

Theo glared at him, then turned to Isabelle. 'Mademoiselle,' he stammered, 'are you sure? Er . . . would it be er . . . socially suitable . . . ?'

It was Isabelle's turn to laugh. 'I am the last of the Castelons,' she said. 'I don't give a fig for what's socially suitable any more. I have no money, and no estate except for the few acres this house stands on. What do I have to lose? Besides, the Castelons have never been priggish, Mr Trentham. We have always lived life to the full. And my family has always loved the theatre. Not only do my father's cousins own the Terpsichore, but I told you, my parents themselves acted in the productions of *Twelfth Night* they had here in Illyria. I should love to be part of that tradition, sir.'

'But . . . people in New Orleans . . . will they be as open-minded?'

'Oh, I don't give a fig for them either. In any case, they won't know it's us, except for people we trust, like the Biches. To keep malicious tongues from wagging, we will come incognito. In disguise, sir. We will begin to play roles before we even leave Illyria. What do you think of that?'

'Um . . . a capital idea,' said Uncle Theo, weakly.

Isabelle smiled. 'Don't look so worried, sir. It will not cause you any trouble. I'm eighteen; I've never had much fun or adventure in my life. Will you allow me this small indulgence?' She laid a hand on his arm and looked soulfully up into his eyes. 'Please understand, Mr Trentham, despite Mr Harvey's kind suggestion, we do not need speaking parts, we can just be part of a crowd, or work backstage if you'd prefer. And if you are thinking that you will have an extra

couple of mouths to feed, do not concern yourself. We have
. . . a little money set aside, if necessary.'

'Oh no, that won't be necessary,' said Theo, hastily. 'If you
can get us successfully into the Terpsichore . . . all our
problems would be over. We would be more than glad to put
you on our company's pay-roll, Mademoiselle.'

Isabelle's face lit up. 'So we're agreed?'

'Most heartily,' said Uncle Theo, his face clearing. He
looked around the company. 'I think I can speak for us all,
yes?'

There was a chorus of agreement from everyone, including
Gabriel. Toby's heart thumped with excitement. Definitely,
this was proving to be the best New Year's Eve of his life!
Delightful prospects of the days ahead flitted through his
mind.

'Could you maybe use another member?' Thomas Nashe
broke into the general rejoicing. 'I can provide the best music
this side of Old Nick's crossroads. And I have independent
means too, so I shan't be a drain on your finances.'

Her black eyes narrowing, Matilda tutted crossly at this
renewed mention of the Devil, but a beaming Theo said, 'The
more the merrier . . . and we certainly do need a good
musician if we're going to do this properly. Are we all agreed,
then?' he added, turning to the rest of the troupe. Everyone
nodded, cheerfully. Gabriel raised his eyebrows – but no
objections, at least.

'Well then, tomorrow morning we shall all set off for New Orleans,' said Isabelle briskly. 'Maminou and I will take you in the sulky, Mr Trentham, as we will get there much more quickly than your wagon. We need to see the Biches, and organise a place for you all to stay, before the rest of the company arrives. Now then, we should toast our agreement, don't you think? Maminou, will you get the last bottle of champagne from the cellars? Oh, one more thing, Mr Trentham — could you perhaps do with more costumes?'

'Why, yes,' said Theo, a little faintly. 'Always could do with more . . .'

'We've got a few old costumes packed away, from the *Twelfth Night* productions, and also costumes from Carnival balls,' said Isabelle. 'Let me show you. I think you'll be pleasantly surprised.'

Watching them go, Toby felt an odd feeling agitating in his chest. It was something he couldn't put a name to: made up of excitement at the possibilities ahead, but also of something else, something that made him feel uneasy. The events of the night had been like a play in themselves — a real-life play directed not by Theo Trentham, but by Isabelle de Castelon. Yet it was like a play begun in the dark, without lines. What was this play going to prove to be about? What was really going on? What roles would they all play? Was it really only for 'fun and adventure' that Isabelle was so keen to go with them? And what was wrong with the old woman? Why did she look so . . . haunted? Toby hated secrets. Or at least, he hated not knowing, and usually tried to ferret them out. Well, perhaps he would!

'Mark my words,' said Henry Smallwood, speaking loudly into the pensive silence, 'our fortunes have changed this day!' He patted at his hair. 'New Orleans!'

'Pleasure! Balls! Lovely ladies to impress, sweet nothings to whisper in their ivory ears,' said Gabriel, with a crooked smile. 'Eh, Harry? You can trot out those tired old lines of yours for all the Creole beauties and the Yankee lasses and the Cajun girls . . . You can pass a hundred mirrors and make sure you're still as handsome as you were yesterday. Ah! Bliss in New Orleans for the Handsomest Man on the Planet!'

'You're just jealous, Harvey,' shrugged the leading man, unperturbed. 'You're too bitter and sardonic to attract any woman, that's your trouble. As to your acting, dear fellow, you'd better look smart about it! You were dreadful tonight.'

Toby held his breath. But all Gabriel said was, 'And you're a judge of acting now, Harry the Ham? Well, wonders will never cease.'

'I'll have you know, Gabriel Harvey, that I have a reputation from coast to coast in this land—' began Henry indignantly, but Old Fate cut him off. 'Shut up, both of you! You make my head ache!'

'Ah well,' said Gabriel lightly, 'better prepare yourself for a few more headaches, old-timer, in this set-up. What

Mademoiselle Isabelle really has in her head concerning us doesn't bear thinking about, I'd say.'

Toby burst out, 'Mademoiselle Isabelle is a gently bred young lady, and you'd do well to remember that, Gabriel Harvey!'

'Friends, friends,' said Thomas Nashe, placatingly, 'I think we should be celebrating, not fighting.'

Gabriel's face darkened. 'We're not your friends on such short acquaintance,' he said, striding out of the room.

Olivia burst out, 'Don't worry, Mr Nashe, Gabriel can be most fearfully rude and hard, you need to ignore him, sometimes!'

'I'll take that advice most gratefully,' said the fiddler, not at all crushed, his eyes dancing.

Blow Gabriel, thought Toby, crossly. Let him stew in his own bitter juice. And let the rest of us rejoice!

Six

Toby woke with a jump out of a fitful sleep. For a moment he couldn't work out where he was. Then he remembered. He was in the Illyria stables, lying on a bed of straw, in the company of Gabriel, Nashe, Old Fate and Henry Smallwood. Theo, his children and Madame Leonard had been found beds in the house.

As his eyes got used to the darkness, he could make out the sleeping figures of the others, sprawled on the lumpy straw. Through a window he could see a pale, windswept sky, lit by moonlight. It must have stopped raining.

He got up, stretching. Not far behind him, Shallow gave a deep, gusting breath. 'Well, old fellow, things are looking up for us at last,' Toby whispered. Shallow shifted his feet and blew down his nose again, in the stoical, non-committal way of draught-horses.

Toby went to the door. He opened the top half and looked out. Everything was still and silver under the moon: trees glistening wetly, the Spanish moss like soggy ectoplasm; the house, or what could be seen of it from here, unlit by candle or lamp but windows silver-squared with moon. Toby gazed out at the peaceful but rather desolate scene. He thought, well, it's New Year's Day. No sign of snow, but there was a kind of blessed hush; or at least, an expectancy . . .

It was then he saw the light flickering among the trees. The feelings that had assailed him earlier that day – the mixture of fear and thrill – came rushing over him. Something odd was going on in Illyria, and he meant to find out what it was . . .

As he slipped into the night, a little wind sprang up. It made a funny little whistling sound in the live oaks, like a tuneless melody, a silver thread of sound. The Spanish moss brushed at his face as he went past, probing fingers of living mist. Toby's pores seemed individually alive, open, each bit of skin pinpricked by sensation, the back of his neck sweating, his hands clenching.

He came to a sudden stop. He had come to the source of the light: tall candles burning inside two red and gold glass lamps. They stood on the steps of an extraordinary white building which at first sight looked like a miniature model of the house, but which Toby soon realised, with a small shock, was an elaborate mausoleum tomb.

There was a huge, graceful stone angel guarding the great carved metal door of the tomb. In one hand, the angel held a long stone scroll, on which names were inscribed. Toby edged closer and peered at the scroll. The family name was all the same: Castelon. Isabelle's ancestors were buried here . . . He looked at the two most recent names: Armand and Violette de Castelon. They must be Isabelle's parents . . . He peered at the dates. Heavens, they had died within a week of each other, fifteen years before!

Then his eye was caught by something odd, just beyond the angel, at the very door of the tomb. He crept closer: surely that wasn't . . . yes, it *was*! He stared down at two crude dolls, dressed in what looked like scraps of silk and velvet – one an approximation of a gown, the other clothed in bits of black and white, like a man's evening suit. Their stick arms were crossed over their chests, their eyes were painted shut, there was a tiny cross at their feet and at their heads. A shiver rippled over him. There was something really frightening about those dolls . . .

Suddenly, he heard a rustle in the trees. Someone was coming down the path. Instinctively, Toby leaped for a hiding-place, behind a tree at the side of the tomb. Carefully, he peered out. Soon, he could see a hurrying figure, coming closer. It was slender, small, wrapped in white: Isabelle! Without looking to right or left, the girl came to the tomb steps, ducked her head before the angel, kneeled, crossed herself, and murmured something which Toby strained to hear but could not.

After a moment, Isabelle lifted her face and looked up at the doorway. But she did not come any closer. On her face was a look Toby would never forget – a kind of fierce longing. It made his neck prickle.

Isabelle spoke. He heard the words properly this time. He thanked his stars that Uncle Theo had insisted they have French lessons before they came to Louisiana, because he could understand her, so clearly did she speak. 'I will not rest till you are *really* at rest, dear Mother and Father.'

The expression on her face was watchful, listening. In his hiding-place, Toby crouched, shaking, the hair standing up on his head. For it seemed to him all at once that in the voice of the wind breathing through the trees, he could hear the ghostly echo of voices, answering her. And the dolls . . . the dolls . . . was that his imagination, or had they moved, ever so slightly? Were their painted eyelids fluttering, opening? No, surely . . . surely not . . .

He did not know how long he stayed there, not daring to move, as Isabelle stood, staring at the tomb as if she thought it might open and her dead parents walk out.

Nothing happened, though; and his heartbeat soon went back to normal. He'd imagined the voices and the dolls moving, he thought to himself. He'd been spooked, just like Gabriel, by nothing at all, just sinister atmosphere.

Finally, Isabelle gave a sigh, a great melancholy sigh, whispered, 'Farewell, Mother and Father,' and turned away, back the way she had come.

Without hesitation, Toby followed her, ducking from shadow to shadow so she wouldn't catch sight of him. But Isabelle never looked back. She went into the house by a side door. Toby slipped in after her. She headed up some stairs, still hurrying, her step quick and nervous. He followed, hoping the stairs wouldn't creak. When he got to the top of the stairs, she had disappeared. There was a door along the corridor; it was closed, but he could see a thin sliver of yellow light under it. He crept to the door, and put his ear to it. He could hear the murmur of Maminou's voice. He tried to listen, but though this time he could make out no clear words at all, he could hear that the old nurse's tone was one of reproof. He pressed his ear closer to the door.

'What the Devil do you think you're doing, Toby?'

Toby jumped. 'For heaven's sake, Gabriel, why do you creep up on people like that?' he whispered, crossly.

'I could ask the same of you,' said the Irishman, eyebrows raised.

'Have you been following me, Gabriel Harvey?'

'So if I have?'

'Oh. Then you saw . . .'

'I saw the girl at the house of the dead, and the voodoo charms, yes.'

Toby gasped. 'Voodoo?' Images culled directly from penny dreadful magazines leaped into his brain: black roosters with their throats cut, mad trances, weird rites, calling-up of the dead . . . He stammered, 'What do you mean?'

'Voodoo's just the name they give charms and witchcraft around here. The little dolls, those were voodoo talismans, *gris-gris* as they call them: in this case, to stop the dead from walking.'

Toby's flesh crept as he remembered what he'd thought he'd seen and heard. But he spoke briskly. 'All that's just superstition, surely.'

Gabriel smiled faintly. 'You know that's not true. Even in your dear old sensible England, there are ghosts and witches. And most people are afraid of the dead, especially the restless dead.'

Before Toby could find the wits to answer, the door handle rattled. Someone was about to come out. With one accord, Toby and Gabriel fled.

Outside, Toby turned to Gabriel. 'Tell me more.'

'About what?' said Gabriel, absently.

'Oh, Gabe, stop it! You know – the witchcraft, voodoo, or whatever you called it.'

'I told you. Someone's afraid of those dead ones walking. I'd wager it was the old lady made those dolls to keep the dead in their proper place. She looks as though she has a healthy respect for the power of the dead to reach out from beyond the grave. But our young Mademoiselle's a different matter.'

Toby stared at him. 'How do you know all this?'

Gabriel shrugged. 'I've read a fair bit about that sort of thing. It's by way of a minor interest of mine. Never mind the *gris-gris*, though: what interests me is what the girl said. It's not just fun and adventure she's looking for, with us.'

'No,' said Toby, uneasily. 'What do you think she's after?'

'I don't know,' said Gabriel. 'But you heard her – she says she won't be at rest till her parents *really* are. Something happened, back in that family's past. You saw the dates on the scroll, Toby. Her parents died when they were quite young – and within a week of each other. Violently, perhaps? Or through disease of some sort? It's not a very healthy country, this water-land.' He paused. 'Perhaps I should tell Theo.'

'No!' said Toby, sharply. Flushing at Gabriel's surprised expression, he went on, more calmly, 'I'm sure Isabelle's family business is nothing that need concern us, or that will do us any harm. And you know this is our only chance to get into a New Orleans theatre. Uncle Theo would scarcely thank you for cruelling that for him.'

'That's true,' said Gabriel, laughing. 'Still, there's something about this house – these people – that troubles me.'

'You said there wasn't, before,' Toby couldn't resist saying.

'So what did you really see, back there, in the hall, before we came in?'

'I told you,' said Gabriel, calmly, outstaring him. 'Just my reflection in the mirror.' He paused. 'The oddest thing of all, anyway,' he said, 'is that Nashe fellow turning up when he did . . .'

'I saw that you didn't take to him.'

'There's something insincere about him. And his coming was altogether too opportune,' said Gabriel, a little evasively. 'Besides, we saw no lone travellers behind us, did we?'

'I couldn't see anything behind or in front of us, frankly,' said Toby. 'It was raining too hard.'

'Yes, but did you notice, he was damp but not soaked, like you were. He had no carriage, no horse. If he'd been walking in the rain, he should have looked like a drowned rat. He must have been here already, waiting under the trees. Maybe even waiting *for us.*'

'But why on earth . . . ?'

'Your uncle would say it's because he heard of our great reputation, and wanted most earnestly to join our company,' said Gabriel, flippantly.

'Or maybe it's just a coincidence,' said Toby, hesitantly.

Gabriel snorted. 'Like hell it is. Anyway, he may not have been waiting for us at all . . . but for an opportunity to get into Illyria itself.' He gave one of his rare, sweet smiles. 'Frankly, Toby, old boy, I think this place harbours more secrets

53

than the depths of the Mississippi. I think we should keep an eye on all our new friends – but discreetly. We don't want the Terpsichore and our gala tour to vanish into the mist!'

'That we don't, indeed,' said Toby, fervently. But what he really thought of was not the gala tour, but the chance to have Isabelle in their midst, every day . . . Nothing must be allowed to spoil that wonderful prospect.

Seven

In the morning, Toby's head was thick and heavy from lack of sleep. But he had no time to rest, being kept very busy preparing for the day's journey, including packing all the new costumes. In the weak sunlight of a new day, the events of last night seemed too melodramatic to have any sinister meaning. After all, this was the twentieth century. No one surely really believed in witchcraft or raising the dead. He'd seen or heard no ghosts; his imagination had only run riot in an atmospheric setting, that was all, just as Gabriel had been fooled by a twisted reflection in a mirror. The dolls were just an old woman's superstition; a bit distasteful, maybe, but harmless. And Isabelle's words could just as easily have referred to an ambition to do well in the theatre and thus honour the memory of her parents, as to any dark secret or devious plot. As to Tom Nashe, despite what Gabriel assumed, it was likely his coming had indeed been a coincidence. After all, the night had been foul, and the shelter of Illyria very inviting to anyone who was wandering the roads. Besides, *he'd* done no prowling last night, when Gabriel and Toby had been up . . . he'd been sleeping most peacefully on his bed of straw . . . which surely proved he had no ulterior interest in either this place or the troupe.

What mattered was none of that nonsense, but the fact that they were setting out into a new day, new hope – and Isabelle would be there with them, every day!

He was just checking that the wagon's load was evenly distributed when someone tapped him on the shoulder. He spun around. A ragamuffin of a girl stood there: a street urchin with tangled black hair under a dirty scarf, and a dirt-streaked face browned by the sun. She was dressed in a ragged jacket over a faded print dress, and her feet were shod in dirty, cracked boots.

'Chiquita, your honour,' whined this vision. 'Norphan, like you. Goin' to N'awlins to take up job as scullery maid.'

Toby stared at her. 'Good lord! You are changed indeed!' he said, with great feeling. 'I hardly recognised you, Mademoiselle Isabelle! Amazing to see you so transformed!'

'I told you I was used to the theatre,' said Isabelle, with great satisfaction. 'I'm glad you approve, Toby!'

She sounded bright, cheerful, and approachable. For an instant, an image of the girl before her parents' tomb, and

Gabriel's words, leaped into Toby's mind. He brushed it aside. 'I certainly do, *Senorita* Chiquita,' he said, happily. 'I do reckon we are going to have a great deal of fun, all of us!' He looked around. 'What about your nurse? What is to be her disguise?'

'Oh, Maminou is being difficult! She doesn't approve of the disguise I had thought of for her – I thought she could come as a nun, Sister Mary of the Angels. She says that's disrespectful, she doesn't want to attract the wrath of God by pretending to be a nun. She'll only consent to wearing glasses, and a shawl over her head. Ah! She has no sense of adventure, my poor Maminou, she's too old. She doesn't really approve of my own disguise, either, but she'll go along with what I say, because she always does. And she has at least consented to the story I've invented – that I'm going to New Orleans to take up the post of kitchen servant in a house where her cousin is the cook.'

'That's a good story,' said Toby, admiringly. 'Why, Miss Isabelle, I do believe you have the manner born to be an actress.' Hesitatingly, he added, 'Will you not be sorry to leave Illyria behind?'

She looked at him, her face clouding. 'I cannot do otherwise,' she said at last, and turned and went out of the stable. Toby cursed himself for his clumsiness – and just when he had been getting on so well with her!

* * *

57

The company set off very soon afterwards. When the wagon reached the end of the carriage-way, Toby looked back. In the watery sunlight, the house seemed more pitiable than it had last night, with an abandoned look to it. He thought of the tomb, lonely now under its canopy of trees. For a moment, a solemn, almost fearful feeling gripped him. The last of the Castelons was leaving Illyria, and he couldn't help feeling that it was, perhaps, for ever. But would the ghosts of the past give up their hold on the girl so easily?

He shook himself. Whatever strange thing was there, he thought stoutly, would stay there. Only in such a gloomy and weird place could witchcraft or ghosts have any meaning. The dead would stay dead; it was Illyria they haunted, and perhaps the mind of the old lady. In the bright city lights of New Orleans, all that would seem like another planet. Yes, he was glad to turn his back on Illyria, and head for the future. The future, where anything might happen . . . where a proud and beautiful girl made suddenly approachable by circumstances, might become his true friend – and much more beside! Filled with swelling hope, he began to whistle as he guided Slender and Shallow past the potholes.

ACT TWO

Terpsichore

Any thing that's mended is but patched: virtue that transgresses is but patched with sin; and sin that amends is but patched with virtue . . .

Eight

New Orleans is one of the most beautiful cities in the whole of the United States. In the spring and summer, it is lush with greenery and the rainbow colours of thousands of exotic flowers. But even in the cold season, which is milder here than most other places in the federation, it presents a smiling face to the world, with its graceful white-pillared mansions, quaint terraced houses decorated with elaborate ironwork balconies, elegant squares and magnificent churches. On this bright New Year's afternoon, it was festive indeed, packed with people in their best clothes, promenading in the squares, spilling out of churches and houses, sauntering on sidewalks, sitting on balconies. There were musicians and jugglers and organ-grinders and all kinds of street performers, and stalls selling the fragrant doughnuts called *beignets* and hot roasted chestnuts.

Toby nudged Gabriel, trudging beside him. 'Isn't it great to be back amongst folks?'

'Aren't we folks, Toby?' said Gabriel, laughing. 'But yes, I know just what you mean!'

At that moment, a group of noisy young revellers went past. They called out, '*Joyeux Nouvel An! Joyeux Nouvel An!*'

'And a happy New Year to you too!' said Toby and Gabriel in unison.

Olivia poked her head out of the wagon. 'Who are you speaking to?' she demanded, then blushed happily as one of the young revellers looked back at her, doffed his hat, bowed deeply, and said, in strongly accented English, 'One who falls in admiration at your feet, Mademoiselle!'

Down the street towards them came a familiar figure, gesturing and waving, smiling and out of breath. Uncle Theo, dressed in his Sunday best. He gave an absent-minded glare to the young gallant who had so boldly addressed his daughter, but his heart wasn't in it. He was bursting with news, glowing with gladness. 'Glad you're here at last. Everything's set. And we've got a show on in two days' time.'

Toby, Gabriel, Tom Nashe and Old Fate, who had climbed out of the wagon, stared at him. 'So soon!' said Gabriel.

'Well, it's by way of a preview, really. But I expect everyone to be in tiptop form, of course. Big rehearsals tomorrow and the next day.'

'Of course, you always expect miracles,' groused Old Fate, but his heart wasn't in the grumbling either.

Uncle Theo babbled on. 'You'll see, the theatre is charming, perfect, and Mademoiselle's father's cousins – Madame Blanche and Monsieur Bruno – are even more charming. Damned fine woman, Madame Blanche, damned fine, so capable yet so feminine, and her brother is a true gentleman, in every sense of the term.'

The rest of the company looked at each other a little warily. Theo was prone to sudden and great enthusiasms, which weren't always shared by those about him. Still, they were all disposed to feel most kindly towards those who had rescued them from the country mud.

'We will go to the theatre as soon as you are settled in your quarters,' Theo went on. 'You'll see, the boarding-house we have organised, the Magnolia, is most pleasant. It's owned by a friend of the Biches, a charming widow named Madame La Praline. Olivia and Will and I are to stay with Madame Blanche and Monsieur Bruno, but Toby, you're to stay at the Magnolia with the others. The Illyria ladies are also staying there, in the servants' quarters. The cook has been with Madame La Praline for a long time, and will keep the secret of their true identity from the other servants. Now then – take a right turn here.'

They had come into a short dead-end street, with only a few houses in it. At the very end, behind a tall white wooden fence, stood a ramshackle but most attractive narrow two-storey house, painted in faded blue. It had wooden balconies painted with delicate traceries of white flowers, and a sign above the door reading, '*Pension Magnolia, prop. Madame Alice La Praline*'. To one side was a cobbled passage leading to the stables at the back.

'Hmm,' said Matilda Leonard, rather peevishly, 'I do not think that it is very fair or right that I, who have been with the troupe for much longer than anyone, should be put up at a mere boarding-house while Miss Olivia—'

Theo interrupted her hastily. 'Matilda, my dear, please come with me, I will introduce you to the mistress of this establishment, whom I think you will find much sympathy with. She was a milliner in Paris, my dear!'

'A Paris milliner!' said Matilda Leonard, the jealous frown leaving her face at once. Hats were her especial love; the wagon was full of her hatboxes, which she cherished as though they held the Crown Jewels.

'Mr Trentham . . .' began Tom Nashe, hesitantly, 'perhaps I ought to go and find myself some other accommodation. I do not want to trespass on—'

'Don't be silly, friend,' said Uncle Theo, expansively. 'You're part of our company, now, while we're in New Orleans.'

Toby caught Gabriel's eye. The actor looked a little cynical. But he said nothing.

Theo pushed open the gate, a fanciful affair, decorated

with iron carvings of pitchforks. 'In we go, then. No, not you, Toby, go and help Gabriel with the horses. Be in the lobby in ten minutes, we mustn't keep Madame Blanche and Monsieur Bruno waiting.'

Ha, thought Toby sourly, trudging into the stables after Gabriel and the wagon, why aren't I surprised that Uncle Theo doesn't bother mollifying *me*? Good old Tobe, dogsbody, harmless old thing you can just brush aside, no bother, send off to the stables with the horses. Of course, there was Gabriel too, but then Gabriel did his own thing, always. No point trying to mollify *him*. Really! Sometimes he felt like running away. That would show Uncle Theo! It would show him how much he, Toby, was necessary to the smooth running of the troupe, even if he wasn't an actor and had no wish to be. Maybe he would, one day. Maybe he would, now! He could just melt away into New Orleans, into the merry crowds, enjoy life instead of being taken for granted. Well, so he would, if it wasn't for the fact that now Isabelle was here, too . . .

'Hey, mister!'

Toby spun around. A small, ragged black boy was regarding him curiously. Barefoot, wearing an old jacket over a grubby shirt, suspenders and trousers, he dangled a cheap little tin horn in his hand. He grinned impishly. 'Hey, mister, can I ask you a question?' He had come running from a delivery wagon which Toby could see parked near the hotel entrance.

Karnofsky Brothers, Scrap and Coal Merchants was painted on the side. It was driven by a fair, bearded young man with long sidelocks, dressed all in black. Another man, smaller and darker, was just carrying a sack of coal into the hotel.

'Go right ahead and ask,' said Toby.

'We heard from the Magnolia servants that you were actors from England,' said the boy breathlessly. 'Is that true?'

'Well, some of us are,' said Toby.

The boy's bright eyes opened wide. 'What's your show called, mister?'

'*Malvolio's Revenge*,' said Toby.

'Does it have any music?'

'There's a fiddler,' said Toby, 'plays a few tunes.'

'No horn, mister?'

'No – why? You fancy playing for us?' said Toby, grinning.

The boy laughed uproariously. 'You a funny one, mister!'

And he was running off after the disappearing delivery wagon, blowing on his little horn, an outlandish yet somehow pleasant sort of tune such as Toby had never heard before. Quite put in a good mood by the little encounter, Toby waved after him and went to attend to the horses.

Nine

At first sight, Toby thought that Madame Alice La Praline, owner of the Pension Magnolia, looked just like a superior kind of French china doll. Her hair was set in brittle spun-caramel waves, her pale, rather protuberant blue eyes were set in a white-powdered face and her mouth was painted on with bright red strokes of lipstick. She wore a pale blue coat over a blue and white striped dress, and her feet were shod in pale blue kid shoes. Her voice was like a little girl's, breathless and high. But there was a steely efficiency in her eyes and a briskness in her manner that suggested that she was much more formidable than her looks suggested.

She was sitting with Uncle Theo in the cosy, rather overstuffed parlour of the pension when Toby and Gabriel walked in. Her eyes assessed them shrewdly as Theo made introductions.

'Welcome to the Magnolia,' she said. 'I hope you will be happy here.'

'Oh, I am sure they will,' said Theo, pompously speaking for them. 'Madame La Praline was telling me a great deal of most important information about society in New Orleans,' he went on. 'She has been most kind and helpful.'

Alice La Praline smiled discreetly. 'Now, now, Mr Trentham, don't compliment me until you have proper cause. You see,' she said, turning to Gabriel and Toby, 'as I was telling Mr Trentham, I still keep my hand in making hats occasionally for society ladies. They like to attend artistic entertainments, and will, I think, be especially glad to attend such a famous play. I will spread the word amongst them.'

'As I said, most kind of you, dear lady,' said Uncle Theo, effusively. 'We are much obliged.' He jumped up, rubbing his hands with great satisfaction. 'Now, my dear lady, we really must go. Madame Blanche and Monsieur Bruno are waiting for us at the Terpsichore.'

'Of course. I will see you at dinner,' smiled Madame La Praline. 'I hope you care for ham and chicken?'

'Care for them?' said Uncle Theo, grandly. 'We pay homage to them! Especially when served in such a charming establishment, Madame!'

'Oh, Mr Trentham,' smiled the pension keeper, 'you will make me quite giddy with your compliments, you know.'

'Dear Madame, I hope I will,' said Uncle Theo, gallantly

bowing over her hand. Gabriel's and Toby's eyes met, in mutual amusement. The director of the Trentham Troupe was obviously in grand old form, bounced back from bad luck like an irrepressible rubber ball.

As Uncle Theo had said, the theatre was only a short distance from the boarding-house. It was tucked in between a rather flashy dance-hall and – Toby was glad to see – a poky little Nickelodeon, where for a nickel you could watch newsreels and filmed stories of bank robberies and love affairs. Uncle Theo thought films were an abomination, but Toby did not share his uncle's bad opinion of them, and hoped to spend a nickel or two in that den of modern barbarity sometime soon!

Between these two shabby representatives of the modern age, the Terpsichore was like an exotic relic from a fabled past. It was two storeys high, its wooden façade lavishly painted in red and gold, and covered in fantastical decorations: scrolls, whorls and carved lyres, picked out in white and black. When they entered the foyer, Toby saw it was just as splendid as outside: red and gold wallpaper, long thin mirrors lining the walls, a few paintings, and red velvet armchairs. Behind a pretty gilded desk in the glassed-in box-office sat a most formidable-looking lady.

She was statuesque, tall and solid, the strength of her body apparent under the delicate cream lace dress she wore. She had a magnificent head of pure white hair, tinged with a most becoming hint of silver, piled up on her head. Her eyes were very dark, very direct, fringed by great long eyelashes, her nose straight and her mouth determined. On her fingers glittered many rings.

Behind her stood a man who so strongly resembled her that Toby thought the two must be twins. Bruno Biche had the same height and build as his sister, the same dark eyes, and the same magnificent head of hair, though his was shaped in old-fashioned but charming waves, just a little too long. He was dressed like an old-fashioned dandy, in an impeccable if old grey silk suit and pure cambric shirt, with a black velvet ribbon at his throat. He, too, wore several rings, though not as many as his sister. Brother and sister wore identical dazzling smiles.

'Welcome, ladies and gentlemen of the Trentham Troupe! How very good it is to see you all!' Madame Blanche's voice was soft and musical. 'You must be impatient to see the stage and the facilities,' she said, going straight to Old Fate, recognising in him both the oldest and the grumpiest member of the troupe. Thus appealed to, the clown raised an eyebrow and growled, 'Glad to hear something sensible being said. All very well, Theo making arrangements, but there's more than him in the company, and that's a fact.'

'That is a fact indeed, Monsieur La Fete,' said Madame Blanche smoothly, earning herself points at once by already knowing the clown's name, and pronouncing it right, what's more. She went up even further in his estimation by saying, 'A classic comedian like yourself, Monsieur, knows how important it is that timing is exactly right; and that timing depends on knowing the stage and its peculiarities . . .'

'That's so,' beamed Old Fate. Madame Blanche, with an exquisite eye as to pecking order, had already moved on to Henry Smallwood, and was busy expertly buttering him up, while her equally expansive brother flirted with old-fashioned gallantry, with a fluttery Matilda Leonard. They knew exactly how much time to spend with each; the right jest, the right word to flatter vanity, calm nervousness, or allay doubt. Even Gabriel seemed quite taken with them, and as to Tom, he was positively beaming.

Toby wandered away to have a look at some of the pictures on the walls; portraits of once-famous actors and actresses, framed testimonials, and painted scenes from famous plays. He was peering at a picture labelled, '*From* Twelfth Night: *Malvolio in Yellow Stockings, Cross-gartered, Seeks Countess Olivia's Love*', when Madame Blanche's calm voice said at his shoulder, 'It's a little artless, isn't it, but it was painted by my dear Violette – Isabelle's mother. And so, you see, I have a sentimental attachment to it.'

Toby's mind leaped to the white tomb. He stammered, 'She painted that?'

'Why, yes. She had so many gifts, Violette. I wish you

could have known her. She was such a lovely girl, so gentle and sweet too. Isabelle looks a great deal like her. It is so sad, what happened. So unfair.' Her voice hardened a little. 'But then, they say the good die young, don't they?'

Toby said, impulsively, 'Madame Blanche, what happened? I . . . I saw the mausoleum at Illyria, and the dates on which they died . . . only a week apart.'

'Violette died of a broken heart,' said the woman, simply. 'She died a week after her beloved husband Armand was found in his study, dead of a self-inflicted gunshot wound. Though he's my cousin, I have to say Armand was rather a selfish rascal. He had lost everything – fortune, estate, honour – to his incessant gambling and frequenting of bad company. After his suicide . . . well, you can imagine the reaction of New Orleans society.' She paused. 'So you see what hangs over their poor daughter. Marie Laroche has done a very good job, protecting her from malicious gossip; for even now, the whole scandal has not been forgotten.'

'Oh, my lord,' said Toby, faintly. 'I had no idea . . . I am so sorry . . .'

Madame Blanche smiled sadly. 'You understand why Isabelle preferred to come disguised?' Toby nodded. 'And you must understand that it is best not to talk about this.'

'Of course not, Madame,' said Toby, fervently.

'You are a fine boy, Toby, I can see that. My dear young cousin was quite right about you.'

'She spoke about me to you?' whispered Toby.

'She did indeed. She feels a kindred spirit in you, Toby.'

'Oh,' said Toby weakly, his legs like jelly, heat flaming up the back of his neck, incredulous joy filling his whole being. Isabelle cared enough to speak of him thus to this lady! Perhaps there was, then, a chance for him . . .

At that moment, the girl herself came into the hall. Toby's heart lurched painfully. He stared at 'Chiquita' as she sidled over to Madame Blanche. She was acting exactly like a half-starved orphan brat, half-cunning, half-pitiable. She took no notice of Toby, but after speaking to Madame Blanche, went to crouch in a corner of the room, from where she regarded the company with hard, glittering eyes. She made as if to count out money in her palm, then began crooning to herself. Finally, she shuffled to her feet and slunk out, casting suspicious looks over her shoulder. It was an extraordinary little scene, and closely watched by more than one person there.

When they'd left, Gabriel said, in a rather peremptory tone, 'She should be in the play. You should write her in some parts, Theo.'

'My dear fellow——' Theo began, a trifle indignantly, but Madame Blanche interrupted him, in her soft voice. 'I think that's an excellent idea, Theo dear.' (*Theo dear*! Already!) 'It would add to the pathos of the scene on the beach . . . We could have the gypsy child scuttling along, meeting Count

73

Sebastian . . . I can see it now . . . And at the end of the play, the orphan child can be taken in by the Count himself, and transformed into a beautiful young lady for the final scene of the ball. Oh, Mr Trentham, do say yes! It would be so romantic and play so well, sir!'

There was a loaded silence. 'Really, I . . .' Theo began, weakly, then he forced a smile. 'I could certainly think about it, dear lady. It is a most excellent notion, if it can be fitted in without—'

'Nonsense, of course it can,' said the dear lady, briskly, and Toby hid a smile as he met Gabriel's amused eye. Poor Uncle Theo — normally he would have rather fried in hell than change an iota of his precious play. But he could hardly refuse to please his benefactors. Besides, Toby thought, it would do the play good, to be shaken up a bit. After all, it had long fallen out of favour since its famous debut decades earlier. Changes like this might make the whole thing more exciting to modern audiences.

'Now then, let us show you all the stage, the wings, the dressing-rooms,' said Madame Blanche. 'May I take your arm, Mr Trentham?'

'Of course, dear Madame,' said Theo hastily. He'd better watch out, thought Toby, amused. He'll have to dance attendance not only on Madame Blanche, but also Madame La Praline! It might well cause jealousies! Well, at least he wouldn't have to worry about Matilda Leonard — she seemed very happy indeed, leaning on Monsieur Bruno's elegant arm, smiling coyly up at him as if she were a mere fifteen, instead of nearly fifty.

Ten

The theatre itself was small, but perfectly adequate. Red and gold striped wallpaper decorated the walls, a large crystal chandelier hung from the ceiling, and the floor was covered in imitation Persian carpet, in deep reds and blues. There was enough red velvet seating, on tiers, for about two hundred people, as well as a few polished wooden benches on the sides, and a small gallery. The stage was compact but quite deep, and certainly big enough for the action of *Malvolio's Revenge*, while the dressing, wardrobe and prop rooms beyond were also small, but perfectly functional. The whole thing had a smell of fresh paint and wallpaper glue; the restorations must have been very recently completed.

Uncle Theo was giving the company his usual pre-show pep talk. Toby didn't listen. He'd heard all this a thousand times before. He knew, too, that there'd be precious little rest for him, because he'd have to start putting the sets back together again, check all the props, run errands for his uncle, and generally act as the dogsbody he was. Uncle Theo had explained that until the show broke even, they'd not be able to employ any other crew, except casually; the Biches, who had agreed to put up money for the show, would not want any more outlays until it was sure the show was a success. So that meant Toby would be even busier than usual, even with the help of Gabriel and the occasional help of Old Fate and Henry.

While Uncle Theo wound on and on, Toby let his eyes, and his attention, wander around the theatre, not really looking at it, but thinking about all Madame Blanche had told him about Isabelle's parents.

She must have been only about three when the double tragedy happened, he thought: three years younger than him when his own parents died in a coaching accident on their way to Bath. It had been meant to be a romantic holiday away; Toby had been left behind in London with his nurse.

His Uncle Theo was his only living relative; but it was to his credit that though his wife had recently died giving birth to Will, he took his nephew in without protest. It was especially creditable when it was revealed that Toby's parents had left him utterly penniless – their fine train of life entirely bought on borrowed money. Accident was one thing, though;

but how much more horrible must it be to lose your parents in such a way as Isabelle had lost hers? A self-inflicted gunshot wound; a broken heart; a scandal that even fifteen years later would not die. What would it do to you, deep in your soul? How could a person have these things in her past and not be touched by them? A sudden shivery image of her at her parents' tomb came to him. Poor Isabelle.

'Toby!' Uncle Theo's voice startled him back to the present. 'I've got a job for you to do. Go quickly, because when you come back, we're all going to church together, to give thanks to God for our good fortune.'

'Yes, Uncle,' Toby answered obediently, though he was a little surprised by his uncle's enthusiasm on the subject of church. Perhaps he was hoping to impress Madame Blanche, or Madame La Praline, or both of them.

'I'm having playbills printed,' went on his uncle. 'A special job, a good friend of Madame Blanche's is doing it for us, especially – I want you to take the copy to him right now. You're to go to the office of the *Louisiana Bugle* and ask for Joe Horn. Tell him we must have it done by noon tomorrow. And then come back here straight away. Here's the address, and the deposit for the printing job. Mind, don't linger.'

'No, Uncle, I won't,' said Toby, with a sigh. He had to listen to a few more unnecessary instructions from his uncle before he could at last make his escape.

* * *

He emerged into the street with a distinct sense of relief, but also unreality. All theatre people are nervous as cats at a sudden break in expectations and routine, even if that's the routine of failure. Though they were all excited about the possibilities, they were also superstitious about sounding happy or pleased, because you never knew when those jealous theatre gods might just choose to pull the wings off you and crush you in their heavy fists. Theatre was a chancy business, pure magic when it worked, pure torture when it didn't, heaven with one audience, hell with another, and no certainties given. The Terpsichore was a gift from the theatre gods; but you had to be careful, you never knew if the gift might turn out to be a trick of the gods, instead.

What a world I'm in, he thought, sauntering along the street, what a weird fantasy world of greasepaint and costume and real, bloody and panting emotion! Lucky for him that he'd had no yearning, ever, for strutting the stage himself. He was quite happy to be backstage, thank you very much . . .

'Where's you going, that's wrong way, if you goin' to *Louisiana Bugle*,' said a voice near him, and Toby turned to see a grubby little face under a mop of tangled chopped hair, regarding him fiercely. He gulped. 'Er . . .'

'Chiquita show you,' said the supposed gypsy, and firmly took him by the arm. 'You come.'

'Er, very well,' said Toby, weakly. It was wonderful to have the girl's fingers on his arm, the warmth of her washing through him. Yet at the same time, it was an odd situation to be in. Nothing in his experience had prepared him for it. He cast a cautious look at the girl's face. She stared back boldly, perfectly in character. He muttered, 'This is all a bit strange for me . . .'

'You just don't know N'awlins, that's all,' said Chiquita, firmly. 'That's why I come to show you.'

'Please,' said Toby, blushing, so that his freckles stood out more than usual. 'I don't know if I can keep this up, it's just I wish you could er . . . be yourself.'

'Many strange things in N'awlins,' said Chiquita, pulling him into the next street with firm hands. 'Many strange people, dangerous ones too. I am always myself, besides . . .' She looked at him full in the eyes. 'Don't be afraid.'

'I'm not afraid,' said Toby heatedly, stopping, 'or at least not for me, that is, I . . .' He broke off abruptly, for in a fluid movement, Chiquita had reached up to him, and planted a kiss on his cheek. He could not speak or move for a moment, the touch of her cool lips on his hot cheek stinging, burning, his heart jolting. But she stood looking at him with a mischievous smile on her face. 'Cat got your tongue, Tobe?'

'It's not fair,' he said thickly, after an agonised moment, then angrily, 'it's not fair, I'm not a little boy, you know, I can't be just bought off, just taken for granted . . .' He couldn't finish, he was too choked up with things he could hardly put a name to. 'I mean,' he went on, miserably, knowing she must hate him, now, 'why don't you trust us? Why haven't you told us what it is you really want? It's not really fun and adventure, is it?'

'Trust is earned,' she said, coldly. 'Haven't I delivered on my end of the bargain? Or isn't the Terpsichore good enough for a travelling company down on its luck?' Her voice was no longer the gypsy girl's, but the voice of a haughty, self-confident aristocrat.

He winced. 'You may think of us thus, miss,' he said, softly, 'but trust is a two-way thing, wouldn't you say? And we have trusted you enough to take *you* into our company, without real questions, though we had a right to ask them, too. We're not your servants; we won't just do as you say, like your poor nurse.' He turned away from her, and walked away, heart wrung with a mixture of pain and anger.

Then he heard her light footsteps behind him, and her voice saying quietly, 'Forgive me, Toby. It was very wrong of me, to treat you so disrespectfully. Maminou says pride will be my downfall, as it was my poor father's.' She paused. 'Toby . . . look at me. Please.'

He turned, reluctantly. 'Yes?'

She looked him straight in the eye. 'Toby . . . if I tell you something, will you promise to keep it a secret?'

He nodded. 'Of course.'

'Promise to tell no one, not even your uncle? Because

what I'm about to tell you . . . no one knows this, except for Maminou.'

'I promise,' he said, heart thumping.

She searched his face, then dropped her eyes. 'My father shot himself, and my mother died of a broken heart a week later. My father shot himself because he'd accumulated so many debts, through gambling and bad living, that he'd lost everything.' Toby made as if to say something, but she cut in, harshly. 'At least, that's what everyone believes. Everyone, except Maminou and I, and . . . You see . . . there are elements of my father's supposed suicide which Maminou and I have never understood. Things that don't make sense at all.'

Toby stared at her. 'What do you mean?'

'I mean we suspect he was *murdered*.'

Toby went cold. 'Oh, my God,' he whispered. 'But why didn't the police . . .?'

Isabelle's eyes glittered. 'My father had a bad reputation. He had been utterly ruined. He had lost land, fortune, honour. He was found dead in his study. He'd been shot with his own gun. It was found in his hand. There were no other prints on it.'

'Oh,' said Toby, uncertainly. It all sounded conclusive to him, though of course he didn't want to say so.

Isabelle shot him a baleful look. 'Yes. That was quite enough for the police, as well as for most other people, who thought my father was a decadent man who let the side down. But Maminou had her suspicions from the start. She knew my father would never do such a thing. He was not a saint, my father . . . he was not always faithful to my poor mother, and yes, he gambled . . . he knew some pretty shady types. And he had big debts. But he was not a coward! He would never have taken the coward's way out. He would never have left my mother and myself to face the shame alone. Maminou knew all this. She also knew he had enemies in the city; my father had a biting tongue, Maminou told me, and he had little patience with hypocritical pieties. But she knew the police would not listen to the half-baked theories of a coloured servant. And she had not a shred of proof as to who might have done it. But things changed, recently.'

'What happened?'

'Someone who had left Louisiana just before my father's death came back – someone who might well know the truth about my father's death.'

Toby's skin prickled. 'You mean the murderer?'

'No . . . but an important witness. Someone who knew the ins and outs of my father's affairs; someone who might be able to give me some very useful information.' She paused. 'The Biches and Madame La Praline think I've come disguised because of the family scandal. But it's not really that, Toby. See, I can't be seen talking to this witness in my real identity

– it's not safe.' She looked at Toby. 'You see, this man, he is from the underworld. He is a gangster, Toby.'

Toby gulped. Imagine if Uncle Theo heard this!

Isabelle saw his expression. 'Don't worry, Toby. Nothing will happen to any of you. Like I told you, this man is definitely not the killer, just a witness.'

'But are you sure of that?'

'He was in Alaska when it happened,' she said, quietly. 'There is no chance it was him.'

'Do you know then who the killer—?'

'No, of course not,' she said, a little too quickly. 'You see, that's why I need to speak to Klondike – yes, that's the name he's known by, because he was on the goldfields of the Klondike, in Alaska, for so long. I'm certain he has information that will help me to pinpoint the killer.'

Toby was beginning to get over his shock, and to feel excited instead. 'What will you do when you find out the truth?'

Isabelle looked at him. 'I don't know,' she said, quietly.

'It won't do much good telling the police, will it, after all this time?'

Her eyes flickered. 'I don't know. Perhaps. I haven't really thought about it, Toby. I just want to know the truth. I want to save the good name of my parents . . . even if only in my own mind. Do you understand?'

He nodded. 'I understand,' he said gently. He paused, then

hastened on, 'Please. Let me help you. Let me come with you when you go to speak to this man.'

'Well . . .' she said, hesitantly. 'It might not be a good idea. You see—'

'It would be safer if we went together,' he broke in eagerly. 'Please. I really want to help you.'

Her face cleared. 'Thank you, Toby. You are very kind to me.' Again, she reached up and kissed him on the cheek. Toby felt as if his very bones were melting in a confusion of delight and excitement. He wanted to take her in his arms, to kiss her again and again, but he did not dare to. Instead, he blurted out, 'I . . . forgive me, but I saw you . . . at the . . . at your parents' tomb, in Illyria.'

Her expression was forbidding, but he hurried on. 'I didn't mean to . . . to snoop. It was just . . . I couldn't sleep . . . and I saw a light.'

'I see,' she said.

'I understand now why you . . . why you made that vow to your parents. I understand it all now. Despite what Gabriel said, I—' Too late, he realised his mistake. She said, sharply, 'Gabriel was there too?'

'He followed me. I didn't know, I swear.'

'I see,' she said again. Seeing his expression, she gave a small smile. 'It's all right. Don't worry. It doesn't matter. Tell me, what did Gabriel say?'

Toby swallowed. 'He said . . . he said you had charms

on the tomb, to stop the dead from walking.'

'Maminou put the *gris-gris* there,' she said, unblinking. 'Don't misunderstand . . . she loved my mother – whom she also nursed – very dearly, and she is convinced my father was killed. But she's an old woman now, and afraid of so many things. She's afraid of what might happen to me if I probe too far; she's afraid of the evil of the man who destroyed my family; and she's afraid of the restless spirits of my parents. She believes the charms will protect us from all that.'

'But do they . . . do people believe those things really work?'

She looked at him, surprised. '*Believe* they work? We *know* they do.'

'Oh,' Toby said in a small voice.

'Don't you wonder why we were not surprised to see you last night? Why we had enough food for you?' said Isabelle. 'It was because we expected you. Maminou saw your coming in a dream, a week ago. She knows those sorts of things; it's a gift she has. It runs in her family; she's descended from Marie Laveau, you know, the one they call the Voodoo Queen of New Orleans. Maminou knew you were fated to come to our gate, and that it was for a reason.' She smiled at Toby's expression. 'You look shocked, Toby.'

'But surely . . . you can't believe . . .' he stammered.

She cut him off, gesturing towards a house. 'Do you see that gate?'

'What?'

'They're very popular here – do you know why, Toby?'

He shook his head.

'Because those decorations at the top . . . they're not just decorations, they symbolise devils' pitchforks, and they're made of cold iron. They are there to protect the house from the Devil, and from other evil spirits. Louisiana is an old place, Toby, with an old, dark, secret and bloody history.' She paused, and crossed herself, swiftly. 'The Devil, and other evil spirits, have walked here; *still* walk here. And you'd do best to believe in evil, and protect yourself from it, at least while you're here, or heaven knows what'll happen to you.'

There was a silence. Toby felt chilled all over, as if the evil she talked about had breathed coldly on his face.

'You still want to help me, Toby?'

'Of course,' he said thickly. 'Of course I do.' He looked up at her. 'I'll do anything you want,' he said simply.

Something flickered in her eyes. 'What will you tell Gabriel?'

He stared at her. 'Nothing. You said to tell no one.'

She turned away a little. 'I don't mind if you tell him,' she said, softly. 'I think he would understand.'

He felt a sudden spasm of jealousy. 'There's no need to tell Gabriel anything. We don't need him.'

'As you wish,' she shrugged. 'Now then . . . you had to get to the *Bugle* office, didn't you, Toby?'

He'd completely forgotten Uncle Theo's errand. 'Oh, heck, yes. I'd best hurry, or he'll be steaming.'

'It's just around the next corner,' she said, smiling. 'I'll have to leave you there, Toby . . . I was supposed to be on an errand myself, for Maminou. I will see you at dinner-time, at the hotel.'

'We can talk then of when we can go and see Klondike together,' said Toby.

'Sure,' she replied. 'But remember, say nothing.' And she was gone before he could follow, her small figure disappearing down the street so fast he didn't even have any time to call after her. Shaking his head happily, grinning like a Cheshire cat, Toby hurried to the *Bugle* office, his head full of excited plans and dreams.

Eleven

The *Louisiana Bugle* office was small, shabby and noisy, with printing machines rattling away, and several clerks, or journalists maybe, pounding away on typewriters. Toby asked a harried clerk for Joe Horn, and was waved away to a wizened little fellow with thick glasses, an almost completely bald head and ink-stained fingers, and a cheerful manner. Toby had to shout to make himself heard above the noise of the machines, but Joe Horn seemed to understand him anyway, taking the proffered copy with a smile.

'Tomorrow noon, sure,' he said. He jerked a thumb at a pile of papers stacked near one of the machines. 'Here. You can take four copies of the paper back to Madame La Praline, for the hotel.'

Toby did as he was told. He glanced at the front page, which under a proudly emblazoned motto, 'The Bugle – Truth

Much Better than Fiction!' bore the headline, 'Clarence Wilson III to Host Twelfth Night Carnival Ball'.

'That's our esteemed new owner,' said Joe Horn, looking over his shoulder. 'California hotshot, millionaire, and owner of a string of newspapers in the South and South West, including the *Bugle*, and our big competitor, the *Southern Star*. This is his first visit to New Orleans. He's rented a big mansion in the Garden District. It'll be a glittering occasion, son, that ball! Wouldn't mind being there myself!'

'I thought Carnival was later,' said Toby, scanning the article, with its excited descriptions of just how 'glittering' the occasion would be.

'No, Twelfth Night marks the beginning of the Carnival season. From then on it's party, party, party, for six weeks, till the finale of Mardi Gras.' Joe Horn adjusted his glasses and grinned. 'You players have picked a good time to come here. Everyone wants entertainment, in this season.'

'Yes,' said Toby absently, his thoughts returning to what Isabelle had told him. 'I'll come back for the playbills tomorrow,' he added, seeing Joe Horn's quizzical look.

'Very well,' said the old newspaperman. 'They'll be ready at noon tomorrow. And you say howdy to everyone at the Terpsichore and the Magnolia, you hear?' Whistling, he strode off back to his work. Toby shoved the folded newspapers under his arm and hurried out.

* * *

Dinner that night at the Magnolia was a cheerful affair. Plans for the play were discussed with great animation over ham, roast chicken, champagne and chocolate cake. It was a large and noisy party. Both the Biches were of the company, as well as Madame La Praline, of course. The only flaw, for Toby, was that the Illyria women stayed in the kitchen with the other servants. They had to play their parts, of course, but it was annoying. He would have to wait till later to speak with Isabelle and make their plans for going to see the gangster Klondike. He could hardly wait!

He did not notice that Gabriel's eyes rested on him speculatively more than once. And nor did he notice the actor getting up to leave the table soon after the cake had been served. He had much more to think about than the comings and goings of Gabriel Harvey. After all, he was right in the middle of a most extraordinary adventure, one you might read about with great pleasure in some serial in a magazine. It'd be headlined in big splashy letters: **Romance! Mystery! Danger! Murder! Gangsters! Revenge!** He listened to the excited talk around him and thought, rather smugly, why, they're getting so thrilled about putting on a bit of make-believe, and they have no idea a real-life drama is going on around them. And it's me, the company dogsbody, who's been chosen to help in the unmasking of a murderer and the unveiling of a dark truth buried for fifteen years!

He managed to slip into the kitchen, carrying a stack of

plates, a little while later, while everyone else was busy with coffee and liqueurs. After a bit of searching, he found Isabelle in a little broom closet of a room, just off the kitchen. Her nurse was nowhere to be seen.

Isabelle smiled at his dismayed expression. 'Don't worry. I don't mind being here. It's best this way.'

Toby said, his words tripping over one another, 'I thought . . . tomorrow . . . Uncle Theo will be keeping me busy a lot of the day, but there's a time I can slip off legitimately. That's when I have to go and get the playbills from the *Bugle* office, at noon. Everyone else in the company will be busy – there's a big dress-rehearsal on at that time. No one will notice if I'm away a bit longer than normal.'

'Perfect,' she said. 'I've found out that Klondike will be in a saloon in Rampart Street – that's not far from the *Bugle* office – not long after noon; he's always there at that time, playing cards. It'll be better than going to his house, safer probably. We'll meet in the street tomorrow, at fifteen minutes to twelve, sharp.' She smiled. 'And thank you again, Toby.'

'No need for thanks,' he said, a little choked. 'I am just so very glad that I can do something to help you.'

Isabelle said hastily, 'Well, I do appreciate it. But you'd better go, now, Toby. Maminou might come back any moment, and I don't really want her to know we're going to see Klondike tomorrow.'

'But I thought you said she was the one who first suspected your father's death was . . . was not self-inflicted. Wouldn't she be eager to know if she was right?'

'You would think so, wouldn't you? I don't understand Maminou any more. It must be old age, changing her, making her timid. I'm not sure she'd approve of what I'm doing.' She paused. 'I'm so glad you're not scared, Toby.'

Eyes shining, Toby said, 'I most certainly am not! I'll be there tomorrow, exactly as you said. Sleep well, Mademoiselle de Castelon.'

'And you too, Mr Toby Trentham,' said Isabelle, pertly, with a smile that made his knees suddenly feel weak.

True to his expectations, Uncle Theo kept Toby extremely busy the next morning. There were costumes to unpack, put on hangers and check for rips and tears, sets to be bolted together, backcloths to be unrolled and hung, parcels to carry, the stage to be swept and readied, the curtain mechanism and lights to be tested, and a thousand and one other things that kept him busy from six o'clock that morning. He was helped by Monsieur Bruno, Gabriel, Old Fate and even Tom Nashe, but he did not have time to sit down for a breather, let alone anything else. So busy was he in fact that when at last he contrived to look at the theatre clock in the foyer, he saw to his horror that it read nearly ten to twelve.

'Uncle Theo!' he shouted desperately above the uproar. 'I have to go and fetch those playbills from the *Bugle*!'

'What?' shouted Theo. 'They can wait a few minutes; come here, Toby, there's this light to—'

'No, Uncle Theo! Ask Gabriel to look at it! Joe Horn said most particularly to pick them up at twelve sharp, and it takes ten minutes to get there!'

'What nonsense! Oh very well. We've got to have them – Madame La Praline has kindly offered to deliver a great many to people of her acquaintance from this afternoon.' He beamed. 'She's even thinking of delivering one to the mansion of that visiting newspaper mogul – that Clarence Wilson fellow. Apparently his wife adores Shakespeare. Now then, Toby! Be sure to be back soon.'

'Yes, Uncle,' said Toby, making good his escape. He knew that once rehearsal started, Uncle Theo would forget about him for a while.

He ran as fast as he could into the next street. Damn! Isabelle was not there. She must have got tired of waiting. He reached the *Bugle*, and still he hadn't caught up with her. She must be walking devilishly fast! He didn't linger, but walked rapidly on. She'd said the saloon was in Rampart Street, he remembered; but he'd looked at a map of New Orleans at the hotel last night, and Rampart Street was a long one. Which direction should he go in? He'd have to ask someone.

'Hey, mister!' The familiar tones made him spin around. It

was the bright-faced little boy from the coal delivery wagon. He was with a gang of other boys.

'Oh, good morning,' said Toby, a little uneasily, noticing for the first time that this was really a rather dodgy neighbourhood. Some of the boys in the gang didn't look half as friendly as the wagon-boy; and many of them were considerably older.

'You look lost, mister,' said the child. 'This ain't the way back to the Terpsichore, you know.'

'Oh, I know,' said Toby. 'I'm . . . I'm looking for a place in Rampart Street. A saloon.'

'There's many saloons in Rampart Street,' said the boy. He came closer to Toby. 'Which one do you want, mister?'

Yes, definitely, a couple of those boys had knives; and their eyes were flat, unfriendly.

Toby gabbled, 'I'm not sure which one, but I have to . . . to find Klondike . . .'

At the mention of the name, the gang, which had been pressing forward, fell back. The delivery boy's eyes opened wide. 'Did you say Klondike, mister?'

'Yes,' said Toby, emboldened by the scared look on the boys' faces. 'I have an appointment with him.'

His words were obviously too much for most of the boys, who scampered off. Only the little boy remained. He said, 'They're all scared of Klondike, mister.'

'I can see that,' said Toby, casually, as if it really didn't impress him in the least. 'Do you know then where he can be found?'

'Sure thing,' said the boy. 'He'll be at the Rising Sun Saloon, playing cards.'

'Can you show me where that is? I can pay you a bit for directing me,' said Toby, rummaging in his pockets for a few stray coins.

'Sure I can, mister,' said the boy, pocketing the coins. He looked up at Toby. 'You sure you got an appointment with Klondike, though, mister? 'Cos he don't like strangers fronting him, you gets my meaning?'

'Yes,' said Toby, swallowing, but determined to sound unfazed. 'Don't worry – I know what I'm doing.'

'That's good, mister,' said the boy, gesturing him on. ' 'Cos I wouldn't like to see you in trouble.'

'Don't worry, I won't be,' said Toby, lightly. He held out a hand to shake. 'Listen – I don't even know your name. Mine's Toby.'

The boy stared at him a minute, as if Toby had done something odd. Then, giggling, he took Toby's hand, a little gingerly, and dropping it almost at once, said, 'You're a funny one, mister! I'm called Louis. But folks hereabouts call me Dippermouth, or Satchelmouth, on account of this . . .' – and here he stretched his lips, and made as if he were mouthing a trumpet. 'I've got the biggest mouth of anyone I know,' he added, proudly.

'I can see that,' said Toby, smiling.

* * *

They soon found the Rising Sun Saloon, a big, brassy, sprawling wooden construction that was jumping with people and noise. Coming into the warm, wine-smelling dimness of the interior after the brightness outside, Toby could hardly see a thing. He peered around, trying to find Isabelle in the heaving crowd of merrymakers. It was a colourful sight – all shades of skin tones, from the palest cream to the darkest brown; all shades of clothes, from the brightest mustard yellow and shrieking scarlet to the palest pastel blue and pure white. There was a scrum of drinkers at the bar; dandyish gamblers seated at tables, fiercely concentrating on their games; gaudily attired girls sitting on men's laps; and on a makeshift stage, a group of musicians playing a strange, pulsating, melancholy, exciting sort of music. It seemed to jump and fizz in Toby's veins like the taste of another world, as thrilling as the adventure he was in right now.

He felt a tug on his sleeve. Louis squeaked, 'That's Bunk Johnson!' His face was rapt, staring up at the trumpet player. 'He's just the best. One day, I want to play just like him . . .' He put his fingers to his mouth in a trumpet shape and blew softly through them, imitating the trumpeter, lost in his own private ecstasy.

'What do they call that music?' said Toby. 'I don't think I've ever heard anything like it before.'

'That you won't have, mister!' said the boy, proudly. 'You only gets it in N'awlins. And it's called jazz. You remember that, mister. One day it's goin' to be me, on that cornet!'

Toby, smiling, listened for a while, before remembering what he'd come for. He said, 'Louis! Can you see Klondike?'

But the boy didn't hear. He moved closer to the stage, still staring at the man he had called Bunk Johnson. Toby sighed, and looked around. He wished he'd asked Isabelle what Klondike looked like. He moved gingerly through the press of people, scanning the faces but trying not to look like he was staring, for some of the men – and indeed a few of the women – looked like they might take exception at that. He'd no wish to find himself with a gun barrel or a knife-point in the ribs!

He came up to the bar, intending to ask the barman if he knew where the gambler might be. But the unfriendly faces of the drinkers made him hesitate. Timidly, he raised a hand. 'Excuse me, sir, but can I . . . ?'

'Don' you know nothing? You can't drink here, boy,' grated the barman, a big man with a hatchet face that looked as though he had at least some Indian blood. He jerked a thumb at a sign behind him, which read, 'Only Coloured Served'.

'I . . . I don't want a drink,' said Toby hastily, flushing to the roots of his hair.

'You're a Limey, kid, right? Looking for a pretty young lady, perhaps?' sneered the barman. 'Halfway up the stairs, take first landing, turn right. Have a good time, son. You look like you need it.'

'No, no,' stammered Toby, feeling like he was on fire. 'I don't want . . . er . . . a lady. Er, at least, I mean . . .'

The drinkers around the bar burst out laughing. Toby blushed even more scarlet. Looking down at his toes, he swallowed and said, desperately, 'I . . . I'm just looking for Mister Klondike. Can you tell me where I might find him?'

The hush around him was intense. Everyone was still, staring at him, even the band had fallen silent. Toby could feel the pressing crowd around him move back. Then he heard a quiet voice, just a few steps away from him.

'Who needs to find me?'

Toby spun around . . . and saw, in the sudden space that had been created behind him, a table, discreetly positioned in a dim corner. There was Isabelle in her Chiquita disguise, poised uneasily, as if for flight. Flanking her were two big, burly, stone-faced men in black suits and crumpled hats. Seated at the table was the owner of that quiet voice – quite the most extraordinary personage Toby had ever seen. Slighter and smaller than his henchmen, he had skin the colour of milky coffee, eyes the washed out blue of a summer sky, fine features, and full lips, above which reposed a jet-black pencil moustache. His brilliantined hair was of the same colour, parted in perfect twin waves on either side of his face. He was dressed in a butter-coloured suit, with a pale blue shirt and a yellow silk cravat with an opal crucifix pin on it, and wore pale kid gloves on his hands. On the chair behind him was hung a beautiful camel hair coat, and on the hatpeg nearby reposed a Panama-style hat in pale cream, with a yellow and blue band. On the table in front of him was a beautiful silver cardcase, and what Toby, who had an interest in such things, recognised as a brand-new Smith and Wesson handgun, in a smart leather holster.

'Forgive me, sir,' said Toby, gulping, but trying to brazen it out. 'I . . . I did not mean to be late.'

The man raised his eyebrows. 'Late?' he enquired, politely.

'For our appointment, sir.' Under the scrutiny of all those pairs of eyes, Toby did the most difficult thing he'd ever done in his life. He walked casually, trying to control the shakes, right up to Klondike's table. 'Good afternoon, Mr Klondike. Toby Trentham at your service.'

The black-suited men left Isabelle and moved towards him, but Klondike held up an exquisitely gloved hand, stopping them at once. Surveying the curious crowd, he made another gesture; and instantly, they all obediently turned away, back to the activities they'd interrupted. The band struck up again, louder than ever.

Klondike's pale eyes regarded Toby thoughtfully, then he turned to Isabelle. His mouth stretched in a wide smile; and Toby could not help staring. For the man's mouth glittered with gold teeth: a souvenir of his gold-mining days in Alaska, perhaps?

'Friend of yours, Chiquita?'

He laid the faintest ironic stress on the name. Toby's heart thumped. Klondike's already seen through her disguise, he thought. What would happen now?

But Isabelle did not falter. Holding her head high, she said, 'Yes. I can vouch for him. He is one of the company, sir.'

'An actor,' said Klondike, raising his eyebrows.

Toby stammered, 'No, Mr Klondike. I'm crew: the general dogsbody, really.'

'Good. I'm not overly fond of actors. Vain men, in my experience.' His tones were precise, cultured, almost pedantic. Toby thought, I'll bet *you're* vain, with those clothes, and the gold teeth and all – but he said nothing, merely smiled.

'I'll say this for you, Toby Trentham,' said Klondike, gently. 'You've got courage coming here on your own. It's not the most congenial of neighbourhoods for a soft English boy.'

'I'm not a soft English boy,' said Toby, indignantly. 'I've lived in a lot of hard places, sir. Life with a company of players is none too easy.'

'Don't you know you could be arrested just for being here?' said Klondike, negligently, signing to his bodyguards to get him his hat and coat. He picked up the gun and holster, strapped it on nonchalantly, and took the cardcase. 'Jim Crow laws, boy – coloured people and whites aren't meant to mingle, and certainly not to drink or have fun together.' He smiled faintly. 'Not that the police would really want to raid a place like this. They know better.' He stood up and shrugged on his coat. He took his hat from the bodyguard.

'We will talk again,' Klondike went on, turning to the girl. 'Tell my aunt I bid her good day, and good health.' He looked at Toby. 'And I am pleased to have made your acquaintance, Mr Toby Trentham. Perhaps we will meet again.'

'I hope so, sir,' said Toby, boldly. Klondike flashed his golden smile again, then walked out, flanked by his bodyguards. Toby and Isabelle lost no time in following him out, pursued by the curious stares of the crowd. Toby looked for Louis, but the child had vanished.

Out in the street, they watched as Klondike stepped into an elegant motor car, a cream and silver saloon that made Toby's eyes pop. The goons jumped up on the running-boards, one on each side of the car, the driver started up the engine, and the whole equipage took off sedately down the street.

'Well, well,' said Toby. 'He must have made some money gold-mining, this Mister Klondike.'

Isabelle laughed. 'Not him! He certainly made his fortune in Alaska, but by fleecing rich gold-miners in high-stakes games of cards, not grubbing around in the dirt. When he came back here, he had more than enough to buy up a great deal of property – that saloon, for instance, and several other places.'

'Oh. Why did he ask you to bid his aunt good day and good health? Do you know her?'

'Didn't I tell you?' said Isabelle, casually. 'Klondike is Maminou's nephew. She looked after him and his younger brother when their parents died. But he fell out with her when he was a teenager; he was too wild. I won't give her his message, of course; she's completely disowned him.'

'Oh,' said Toby, amazed, thinking how odd it was that the respectable old nurse should be related to the flamboyant gangster. He stared at Isabelle. 'But I thought you said he was a witness to your father's murder . . .'

'I did not say he was a witness to his murder, only that he had information that would lead me to the killer,' said Isabelle, quietly. 'My father was a gambler, Toby. And Klondike started off as a card-sharp. They played many games together; they were, believe it or not, good friends.' She laid a hand on Toby's arm. 'You're looking shocked again, Toby. You are wondering how I could associate with . . . with a coloured criminal. Don't you see – Klondike might be a bad lot in many ways, but he's on our side. He would not let me down. I can *trust* him.'

'I hope you're right,' said Toby, soberly. 'I should think Klondike would make a bad enemy.'

'He certainly would,' said the girl, her eyes glittering strangely.

They nearly went right past the *Bugle* office, when fortunately Toby remembered the official reason for his absence. He dashed in, picked up the bundle of playbills, paid the rest of the money, and was out in a couple of minutes flat – helped by the fact the talkative Mr Horn did not seem to be at work today. As they walked back down the street, he said, 'Did Klondike have anything useful to tell you?'

'A little,' said Isabelle vaguely, 'but not enough.'

'So you'll see him again?'

'Of course. You heard him, Toby.'

'You must wait for me next time,' said Toby, anxiously. 'You could have been in great danger. He knew who you were, despite the disguise.'

'Of course he did,' said Isabelle, surprisingly. 'It's not him I wanted to fool – but everyone else. He'll play the game I want him to – I tell you, Toby, he has a great fondness for our family.'

'Really?' said Toby, as non-committally as he could, but thinking, I only hope that fondness is not like the crocodile's for his prey . . .

'Let's talk about something else,' said Isabelle now, a little pettishly. 'Show me one of those playbills, Toby.'

Obediently, he pulled one out from underneath its

wrappings. She took it from him, and scanned it avidly. *'Malvolio's Revenge — the Terrible Story of Vice Triumphant and Virtue Cast Down,'* she read out loud. *'Thrill to the mystery, the love, the danger! Watch how the avenger is himself destroyed! See how dark secrets rise up from the grave to vanquish evil!'*

'Goodness,' said Toby, startled, 'that's a bit different from the usual thing Uncle Theo writes on the playbills.'

'It was my idea,' said Isabelle, rather smugly. 'And Madame Blanche agreed with me. Do you think it's good, then, Toby? Do you think it will bring in the crowds?'

'I surely think so,' said Toby, stoutly. He was amazed that Uncle Theo had agreed to the copy; he was usually so careful to avoid what he called 'vulgarity'. This playbill made *Malvolio's Revenge* sound like one of those great crowd-pleasing boo-hiss melodramas Uncle Theo loved to hate. Well! It was all to the good. They'd have to make sure that they could deliver on the promise, though.

'I think it will bring in big crowds,' he went on, more definitely.

'We want everyone, you see,' said Isabelle jauntily. 'Cheap seats and expensive seats; society ladies and working men. That's what we need – all of New Orleans at the Terpsichore.'

'Madame La Praline was even talking of sending a playbill up to the mansion of that Californian millionaire,' said Toby.

'Wilson, you mean?' Isabelle spoke absently again. 'Yes,

people like him would be good. Perhaps he might even buy the company?'

'I should think not,' said Toby, indignantly; but he stopped, startled by the look in her eyes – a look that reminded him of her expression, back in Illyria, when she stood before her parents' tomb. Her mind was obviously on quite other things than dubious jokes about millionaires and actors.

He was about to say something when all at once a familiar voice made him turn around.

'There you are. Your uncle's screaming blue murder, Toby. You've been gone an hour. You'd better get along as fast as you can.'

It was Tom Nashe, arms folded, smiling at them. Toby flushed. 'I was just a little . . . er . . . detained,' he said, with great dignity, but hurrying his pace, just the same.

'Explain that to him,' said the fiddler, genially. He looked at Isabelle. 'And your nurse was looking for you, Miss Chiquita,' he said, doffing his hat. 'Best get along, both of you. As to me, I'm not needed for the moment, I'm just going to go and take the air.'

Doffing his hat again, he set off in the opposite direction, rapidly vanishing down the street. Isabelle looked after him for a moment. 'That man – he's a strange one. Deep, if you get my meaning.'

Toby nodded. 'I know what you mean. He's a bit of a mystery, isn't he? Gabriel thinks—'

Toby broke off. Isabelle said impatiently, 'Oh, do go on!'

'He thinks he's a suspicious character. He thinks he was prowling around Illyria before he knocked on the door. He thinks Nashe might be . . . interested in you, or Illyria, for some reason.'

Isabelle stopped dead. She had gone pale under her walnut-juice tan. 'He said that, did he?'

'I doubt it's true,' said Toby. 'Why should he be interested in . . . Oh, no!' he exclaimed, as a thought came belatedly to his head. 'Do you think . . . he's not the murderer, is he?'

'Don't be silly,' snapped Isabelle. 'He looks about the same age as your Gabriel.'

'He's not *my* Gabriel,' protested Toby, but Isabelle went on, relentlessly, 'He'd have had to be about five or six when my father died. No; he's not the murderer.'

'But maybe he's a spy, or an informer for him?' said Toby.

Isabelle's eyes widened; then she shook her head. 'I don't think so,' she said, slowly.

'We'd better keep an eye on him, make sure he doesn't follow us around,' said Toby, eagerly. Isabelle nodded, rather absently. She seemed to have lost interest in Tom Nashe.

They were back at the Terpsichore by now. At the door, Isabelle paused and said, 'Now remember, Toby, not a word to anyone.'

'Of course,' he said, a little crossly. After all, he'd promised several times already – didn't she trust his word?

'Not even to Maminou,' she said. 'She has ways of putting things that make you want to tell her secrets. Say nothing, Toby.'

'Then you're not even going to give her the message from her charming nephew?' he joked, but he spoke to thin air. Isabelle had already gone. Toby sighed, and went in to face his uncle's wrath.

Twelve

The rest of the afternoon, Toby laboured over putting together sets; and by the time he'd finished, it was well and truly time for him to retire to the Magnolia and go to bed absolutely exhausted. He thought he'd be far too excited and anxious to sleep, but in the event was asleep almost as soon as his head hit the pillow.

Uncle Theo certainly didn't let him sleep in the next morning. This was the final day before the show started, and everything had to be in perfect working order. There would be one more dress-rehearsal, complete with music cues, that day. All the actors were on tenterhooks, and more difficult than usual. Jacques La Fete, full of pre-show nerves, had drunk a whole bottle of wine to himself the night before, and was so fragile he snapped even if you looked at him sideways. Olivia and Will kept squabbling over nothing. Henry

Smallwood threw a tantrum because he had not been able to buy another bottle of the hair oil he normally used. Matilda Leonard had hysterics when she discovered that her favourite lace handkerchief, which she used in one split second of one tiny scene, was missing, and Toby had to turn the whole hotel upside down looking for it, finding it at last scrunched down in the bottom of one of her hatboxes. Gabriel brooded, becoming Malvolio, all the light and sparkle gone from his animated face. As to Uncle Theo, he was in a right old state, shouting at this person and that, tearing his hair out over minor details, unfailingly courteous to the Biches, but turning a great deal of his pent-up anxiety on his unfortunate nephew. Only Tom Nashe was unflappable, cool as a cucumber, lounging in a chair waiting for his cue, observing it all with a wry, amused eye.

It seriously began to annoy Toby, that wry amusement. As he went past the fiddler for what seemed like the hundredth time, he could not help throwing him a baleful look.

Nashe laughed. 'Goodness, Toby, you look angry enough to kill someone!'

You, if you're not careful, thought Toby crossly, not bothering to answer. Rotten old informer or snoop or busybody or whatever the hell you are, you could at least look busy while everyone else is full of frantic activity!

He hadn't had a chance to speak to Isabelle all morning. As he worked on his many jobs, his mind kept jumping back to the day before, what he'd learned, what he'd seen. He could not help swelling with pride at the fact she'd chosen him – not Gabriel, not his uncle, not any of the adults – to help her. As God's my witness, he thought, I'll do whatever I can. But he couldn't help wondering about Klondike, and his association with her father, Armand. It must be yet another element of the scandal surrounding her family. Poor Isabelle! She had a great deal of spirit and courage to cope with things that would have destroyed many lesser beings.

Whom did she suspect of her father's murder? She hadn't said a name, but he'd got the distinct impression she had a suspicion, someone in mind. She hadn't told him what Klondike had said; she was keeping her cards close to her chest, but that was understandable. He hoped that soon she'd let him into her full confidence . . .

It was when he'd had to run back to the hotel on yet another errand for Matilda Leonard (this time she must, at all costs, have a fresh roll of bread warm from the hotel kitchen), that he came across Madame Laroche, sitting alone, reading the *Bugle*. She looked up at him as he came in, and smiled faintly.

'You're looking hot and bothered today, child.' Behind the disfiguring thick glasses, her green eyes looked huge, like a magnified insect's.

'There's a lot of work to do, Madame, just before a show.' Uncle Theo had told him the old woman had, in the end, decided against going on stage; she got stage fright, he'd said. He wondered why she wasn't at the theatre, though; you'd have thought she'd want to see her charge appear in that first little scene. But quite likely it was Isabelle who was stage-struck, and not her nurse at all. She'd just gone along with things – because she was an old family servant; because, as Isabelle had said, she always did.

He gathered up a couple of rolls and wrapped them in a clean napkin. 'For Madame Leonard,' he said lightly. 'She gets very hungry, just before a rehearsal.'

Marie Laroche nodded. He had an awful feeling that those seemingly unfocused eyes saw a great deal. She'd looked at him and Isabelle very thoughtfully indeed, the previous day, on their return to the theatre. He wished he'd had time to consult with Isabelle as to what the official story of their absence was.

She seemed to read his mind. Tapping the newspaper, she said, 'Isabelle told me you'd been to the *Bugle* office together, and Mr Horn gave you a tour of the machines.'

'That's . . . er . . . that's right. It was very . . . er . . . interesting, very interesting indeed, and Lord, what a racket those machines make, Madame. Have you ever been in a printing shop? I have never heard so much noise . . .'

'Toby,' she said, cutting into his gabble, 'take care. My little Isabelle – she has not lived a normal life.'

He stared at her. 'I don't know what you mean, Madame.'

'Isabelle feels the loss of her family's honour and property like a deep wound. It is more than a concern — it is an obsession, Toby.'

Toby swallowed. The woman's eyes were fixed on him in a baleful stare. He said, mustering as much courage as he could, 'Why are you saying this to me, Madame?'

There was a silence. Then Marie Laroche said, gently, 'You are a kind and honest boy, Toby. But not everyone is like you.' She leaned towards him, her eyes searching his face. Suddenly, her hands began to shake, her eyes to roll back. 'Get back! Get back! Get back where you belong!' Her shaking hands groped for the crucifix around her neck. She held it up, her eyes fixed on something unseen, just beyond Toby's shoulder. 'Get back!' she croaked. Her body convulsed, a madness came into her eyes. She gave a great cry, and fainted right off her chair, her glasses flying off her nose.

Toby had been paralysed with terror. He had seen nothing, yet he'd felt the definite presence of something: *something* that drenched him in a cold sweat breaking out all over the pores of his body. Something bad, he knew; something that shouldn't be there . . . When the old woman fainted, though, the spell of horror broke. He rushed over to her, kneeled beside her, and lifted her head gently up. 'Ma'am! Madame Laroche! Are you all right? Ma'am!'

For an awful moment, he thought she was dead. Her face was the colour of clay, and she did not move. Then her eyes, that had been closed, flew open. In their green depths was a despairing sorrow. She said, brokenly, 'Oh, Toby! It has begun, and I can do nothing to stop it . . .'

His heart beat wildly. 'What has begun, Madame? What?'

But she shook her head. She closed her eyes again. Slowly, the colour returned to her face. Her hand stole back to her crucifix. She held it tightly for a moment, gave a sigh. 'It's all right, Toby. Help me up, will you?'

He did as he was asked, settling her back into her chair. He picked up the glasses and gave them back to her. 'Madame . . .' he began.

She raised her head and looked at him. 'Don't worry about me, Toby. Just . . . just make sure you stay close to her, won't you? I can't do anything any more; she doesn't listen to me. But you . . . you might be able to help. You . . . and that other young man.'

'Who?'

'Gabriel,' she said. 'He knows the world of shadows. He does not carry his name for nothing.'

'What do you mean?' said Toby, staring.

'He carries the name of an archangel, who sits at the left hand of God. His name means *hero of God*; the angel of revelation, and mercy. He knows the pain of this world, Toby. He knows the world of shadows. You could do with his protection.'

Toby's stomach lurched. Had the old woman gone mad?

Madame Laroche read his expression. She smiled, faintly. 'He has fought it for years, Toby. But it's there. Ask him.'

Toby swallowed. 'I'm sure I don't know what you mean, Madame.' The shock of the incident was receding now, leaving only unease at being in the old woman's presence. He looked surreptitiously at the kitchen clock. He said, through a rather dry throat, 'I must take my leave, Madame. They are waiting for me at the theatre. If you're sure you're all right . . .'

'Of course you must go,' she said, sighing a little. 'Don't forget what I said, though, Toby.'

'No, Madame,' he said, and fled, feeling like a coward, but desperate to get away. Isabelle was right, he thought. Her poor nurse was confused, afraid of everything. Worse still, she no longer thought rationally. She had literally gone mad . . . And her madness had even infected Toby, who had believed, if only for an instant, that something . . . *something* terrifying, unnatural, had been in there with them, when in fact it had only been the shock of seeing her have such a horrible fit. It had all been self-suggestion, he thought confusedly, as he hurried along. He'd read about that somewhere. Isolated at Illyria, believing in all kinds of evil spirits and magic, full of grief for what had happened to the Castelons, the nurse had quite simply lost her grip on reality. And her fears had been so real to her that they'd even become real to Toby . . .

As to what she'd said about Gabriel, it only proved how

mad she was. It was almost blasphemous, if it wasn't ridiculous, what she'd said about him being like the angel of mercy and revelation. He gave an involuntary giggle as he imagined Gabriel Harvey, black-browed, bad-tempered Gabriel Harvey, with wings sprouting from his shoulders. Should he tell him? The Irishman might even see the joke in it, if he was in a good enough mood!

Sobering, he thought, Isabelle should be warned. She obviously wasn't aware quite how far her poor Maminou's mind had disintegrated. A sudden image of Marie Laroche's strange green eyes shot into his mind, making him shudder involuntarily. Those eyes had not seemed mad, but instead to have a bright, intelligent clarity, seeing right inside him, fixing him with a glance that was not quite of this world. Stop it, he told himself sternly, stop it, she's just a mad old woman, not a witch or a seer at all. She has no power, it's just that her personality is strong, especially in insanity. He'd do best to forget the whole episode; except for the one thing that had made sense: when she told him to look out for Isabelle. Hell, he was going to do that anyway, no matter what!

Thirteen

The dress-rehearsal was just about to start when, puffing and panting, he reached the theatre and raced into the dressing-room, delivering Matilda's bread rolls just in time to forestall a storm of angry tears. She devoured the bread, her teeth ripping into a soft roll. She was always like that before going on stage. Everyone had their own eccentric way of coping with the start of a new show. Gabriel had to have his *Lamb's Tales from Shakespeare* in the top pocket of his coat; Henry had to have what he called his 'lucky comb'; Matilda had to have her treats; Old Fate had to stroke the right side of his nose seven times before he could step on to the stage! Only Uncle Theo and Olivia seemed to have no particular talismans or rituals, but plodded on, repeating lines.

Toby grabbed the prompt-book and went to sit in the wings. The audience consisted of Madame Blanche, Monsieur

Bruno and Madame La Praline, all three sitting in the red velvet seats, looking expectant. The Biches had watched the rehearsal yesterday, of course, but this was the first time for the hotel-keeper.

The curtain rose. And there was Uncle Theo, solemnly wandering along the painted strand. He wore one of the costumes from Illyria. It was perfect, giving him an aura of faded splendour, of patched glory.

> '*In vivid strips, the skin of evening*
> *Peels off into the dark of night . . .*'

began Uncle Theo, as the Count, in a booming voice. A soft violin air began; Tom Nashe, playing in the wings. Then, at stage left, a curious little figure entered – Isabelle/Chiquita, looking like a ball of fur on legs in an old, rather short fur coat. She advanced towards the Count, and made a dumb show of giving him something in her palm. He shook his head, and moved sadly on.

> '*Stars of sharp, salt-rinsed radiance*
> *Tumble on black seas of light . . .*'

The girl followed him, insistently, clutching at his cloak, but he walked determinedly on, still declaiming. Toby watched it with a thrill of mingled delight and confusion. The girl certainly could act, there was no doubt about that. She was a natural.

'No profit in going on, no joy in going back,'

ended Uncle Theo's speech, and he bent over the child then, and patted her head, as she kissed his hand. It was absurd but curiously touching, and Toby found his eyes were smarting with tears, which he tried to brush away without anyone looking.

A conviction grew in him. How could he add to Isabelle's burdens? How could he tell her Madame Laroche was insane? It would be too much for her. He would say nothing to her about what the nurse had said. He would pretend it had never happened, at least until Isabelle had been able to find out more about her father's death. She should not be distracted from that. And he would help her in any way he could. As to speaking to Gabriel . . . well, he'd rather not. There was no reason why the actor should know anything. It was none of his business. It was he, Toby, who had been chosen by Isabelle to help her. She needed no other help, he thought, jealously, as Gabriel came on stage for his first scene.

Whatever had caused his bad performance that night in Illyria, it seemed to have no more effect on him now. He was superb – so good that after an instant, Toby even forgot about his worries, forgot even that he'd watched Gabriel performing a hundred times. He watched, spellbound, from the wings, as the actor became possessed by the spirit of Malvolio. So intent was he that he failed at first to notice that Isabelle was standing beside him.

'I have never seen anything like it,' whispered the girl, suddenly. Toby started.

'What? Oh, Gabriel,' he said, trying to sound casual, but flushing to the ears. She was staring at Gabriel on the stage, her eyes full of some expression Toby didn't much care for at all. He said, a little roughly, 'He's good when he's good, if you know what I mean.'

She looked at him, smiled a little distantly, and nodded. He was mortified. She had looked at him as though he'd been a foolish child. Damn Gabriel, he thought, angrily. Damn all actors. It's all just self-suggestion, just like that mad old woman. It's not real; it's all just illusion. He said nothing of all this, of course, though it burned fiercely in him as he watched the girl he loved stare like a thunderstruck fool at a rough Irishman who just happened to know how to act. Look at me! he felt like shouting. Look at me! It's all surface with Gabriel; there's nothing there but what he shows on stage. Not me, not me, I'm not like that; Isabelle, look at me, I *love* you!

As if she'd felt the strength of his feeling, she turned and looked at him. 'I think this play is going to be a success, Toby,' she whispered. 'Isn't that wonderful?'

He nodded. That was all it had been, he told himself. She

had just been impressed by Gabriel's acting, which was good enough, it had to be said. He whispered back, 'It's all thanks to you, getting this theatre for us. Everyone's had new heart put in them.'

'And it's thanks to you I've had new heart put back into me,' said Isabelle, smiling so warmly that the last scraps of his anger vanished. What a fool he'd been! How lucky it was that he'd said nothing about what had just gone on in his foolishly impetuous heart! She'd not have taken it well, he thought . . .

'Why isn't that man on the West End or Broadway?' Tom Nashe's whisper made them both jump.

Toby said, 'We've often wondered the same thing, Mr Nashe. But then, you're good enough to be in one of those big theatre orchestras yourself.'

'Ah, no thank you,' said Tom Nashe, casually. 'I like my freedom too much.'

'I guess it's the same for Gabriel,' said Toby, looking challengingly at Nashe, who grinned and spread his hands. 'I guess you're right,' he agreed, watching as the actor finished the scene and walked off-stage. A small storm of clapping followed him.

The play went on. Everyone was indeed in very good form, though, true to form, Olivia forgot some of her lines and had to be prompted by Toby – though not as often as usual. Even Henry Smallwood managed to inject some passion into his portrayal of Lysander. There were no extra new scenes, except for a bit right at the end. After Malvolio's death, and the wedding of Lydia and Lysander, Tom Nashe appeared on the stage and played a rousing tune, and the whole cast appeared on stage to dance, including the gypsy girl, now wearing a lovely ball-gown. Toby only heard that scene, he didn't see it, because Uncle Theo had most annoyingly sent him off to check the bolts on part of the first set, which he thought had not been securely fastened.

But he heard how good the music sounded, the loud applause at the end, and the shouts of 'Bravo!' from the small audience. He smiled to himself. It was on! It was really on! It was a live thing, this play!

Everyone seemed reasonably happy with the rehearsal, afterwards, though no one spoke about it very much – you didn't, after all, want to tempt fate. Rehearsals were all very well; but it was the real thing, tomorrow. That was the acid test. Who knew what might happen? Toby had put up playbills all around the district; and Madame La Praline had gone in her own carriage to deliver more, around the town, to her best clients. Joe Horn had also promised to send a reporter to cover the first night. But would the audiences come? Or would they have to face the shame of empty seats yawning back at them? Or would they come, but hate the play, boo and hiss, walk out, or worse still, laugh at the wrong moments? Such fears would be gnawing inside every

Trentham Troupe heart, but not one would be spoken out loud.

Of course, Toby had no time to sit and relax, after the rehearsal, or to talk with Isabelle. Uncle Theo did not let the pace slacken for the unfortunate Toby. Luckily, Gabriel helped him constantly. The Irishman was looking a good deal more cheerful than he had that morning. Indeed, he seemed full of verve, of a lightness that was all the more charming for not being frequent. Toby was glad Isabelle was not in the vicinity; she'd gone back to the hotel, for a rest. In this mood, Gabriel could charm the birds off the trees, let alone a girl who admired his tremendous talent.

Yes, Toby was glad she wasn't there; but he was also glad Gabriel was like this, too. After all, the actor was probably his closest friend. It did not do to become estranged from your friends. You needed them, on the road, or you wouldn't easily survive.

They had been working pleasantly for a little while, when Gabriel said, 'Well, our self-satisfied friend the fiddler didn't completely ruin the play.'

'He played very well, I thought,' said Toby, fairly. 'Whatever we might think, he is a real fiddler.' He paused. 'And he said you were good enough to be on the West End or Broadway.'

'He did, did he?' said Gabriel, laughing. 'Wonder what he'd know about that, eh?'

'Perhaps he's really a scout for some big theatre company,

working incognito,' suggested Toby, laughing in his turn. 'Perhaps he'll reveal himself at the right moment and hand us a big fat contract!'

'Hmm. Perhaps.' Gabriel's voice changed. 'Toby, where did you disappear to, yesterday – you and our lovely little gypsy girl?' His voice had a hard, unfriendly edge to it.

Toby stared at him, then snapped, 'I can't see that it's any of your business, Gabriel Harvey.' After a pause, he added, 'We just walked around New Orleans, that's all.'

'Toby, you're transparent. Be careful. There's much more to that girl than meets the eye. She's trouble, with a capital T.'

In a strangled voice, Toby said, 'You shouldn't say such things. You shouldn't!'

'Toby,' said Gabriel, 'you're a fine lad, but you don't know how the world can be.'

'Don't I?' said Toby, exasperated. 'I don't see why not! And you're hardly much older than me, Gabriel Harvey. What makes you the great expert in the ways of the world?'

Gabriel gave him a bleak look. 'Don't say I didn't warn you, that's all.'

No, assuredly he would never tell Gabriel anything about what was happening, thought Toby, furiously stalking off. The actor was just a gloomy misanthrope, interpreting everything and everyone in the worst way possible. Isabelle was a brave, spirited, beautiful girl, and he would go through hell and high water to help her, and if Gabriel wasn't happy

. . . well, *he* could go to hell and stay there! And good riddance too!

Fourteen

Toby chafed all the rest of the day and the evening, wanting to plan the next move with Isabelle, but unable to get a moment alone with her.

At dinner, Uncle Theo was in high, but nervous good humour. Tomorrow would see first night of the play; and though it wouldn't make or break the season, it was still important, psychologically. Madame Biche was quietly confident; she had, she said, spoken to many people about it, and they'd all promised to come. True to her word, Madame La Praline delivered playbills to the houses of all her best customers, and even to the mansion where the millionaire Wilson and his wife were staying. 'I spoke briefly to his wife,' she was saying now. 'As good fortune would have it, she's an ex-showgirl herself, from New York, considerably younger than her husband, and only recently married. She says she loves *Twelfth Night* and will persuade him to come, as a present for her birthday. She says he'll do anything for her.'

'Nothing like the fondness of an old man,' beamed Theo. 'Well done, Madame La Praline!'

'A New York showgirl, eh,' said Henry Smallwood, thoughtfully. 'Wonder if she has any acquaintances on Broadway?'

'Now, then, Mr Smallwood,' said Madame Biche, roguishly, 'you aren't thinking of deserting the Terpsichore already, are you?'

Henry flushed. 'No, no,' he stammered.

'Mind you,' said Madame Blanche, 'as long as *Malvolio's Revenge* has premiered here, cementing the reputation of our theatre, there's no reason why Broadway shouldn't be allowed a season.'

'Oh, Madame!' said Uncle Theo, laughing proudly. He's well away in pleasant dreams of fame again, thought Toby. Let's hope they're not confounded. Again.

At that moment, a servant came in with a letter, which she handed to Madame La Praline. She turned it over to look at the seal and gave an exclamation.

'Well, speak of the Devil, and he shows his tail! Monsieur Trentham – the visit to Mrs Wilson has paid off more swiftly than we might have hoped for. Mrs Wilson will be at the first night tomorrow, along with several of her friends. And she says that if she likes it, her husband has promised to come and see it too. And if he likes it, why, he'll promote it in all the newspapers he owns!'

There was a general chorus of delight at this. Uncle Theo had gone pale. 'Goodness me,' he said, weakly. 'Goodness me.' Recovering a little, fanning himself, he went on, 'A good fairy is watching over us, I'm convinced. We have been blessed with good luck since stumbling at the gates of Illyria. Well! Trentham Troupe, we will have to give more than our very best tomorrow night. All our futures may well depend on it.'

Everyone started talking at once now, totally absorbed in this new development. Toby looked swiftly around. Isabelle was in the servants' quarters. Now was his opportunity to talk to her; no one would notice. He slipped out and went looking for her. She wasn't in her room, or in the kitchen, and he got curious and not altogether friendly glances from the scullery-maid and the cook as he went past. Where could she be?

He went to the back door and looked out into the street. In the light of a gas lamp, he caught a glimpse of scarfed black hair, bobbing on ragged shoulders. Where was she going so fast? Without thinking about it, he slipped out in his turn, hurrying after her. Some instinct, though, made him stay a few paces behind her. There was a strange hollow feeling in his stomach. Was she going to see Klondike again, without him?

Then he almost screamed as a hand fell on his shoulder. He

spun around. Gabriel! 'What are you doing, following me around?'

Gabriel jerked a thumb up the street. 'What are *you* doing?'

'Leave us alone.'

'Seems to me you're following her, not walking with her.' Gabriel's face was set. 'This time, I'm coming. Forget arguing. Get a move on, or we'll lose her.'

'She's doing nothing wrong,' said Toby, desperately, as they walked on. 'Leave her alone.'

'Why are you following, then?'

Toby didn't answer. There was no reason he could give without seeming to distrust Isabelle. He didn't; he had just, instinctively, been struck by the way she hurried, by the furtive way in which she kept in the shadows. He was afraid for her, for the situation she might put herself in, by her rashness. Why had she gone at that moment? Then he thought he had the answer. There was so much noise, so much commotion going on; even her nurse was blocked from view by the milling, excited people. She had her chance to slip out unnoticed, and took it.

Isabelle stopped. She looked behind her. Gabriel and Toby fell back, outside the range of the light. The girl looked anxious. She rubbed at her face, as if unsure. She looked one way, then the other. Then she took a deep breath, and plunged into an alley. Gabriel and Toby followed, soft-footed. She hurried down the alley, and was just about to turn into an arched passageway, when all at once, a shadow detached itself from the wall of the alleyway and spoke to her. Together, they moved in under the archway. Before Gabriel and Toby could react, two burly men appeared on either side of them.

'No further, friends,' grated one of them.

Gabriel spun around; only to fall back. Another man, even bigger than the others, was standing behind them, immobile, a gun levelled straight at them.

'Turn around, both of you,' said the man who had first spoken. He had a flat, pock-marked face, with little piggy eyes and a boxer's nose. He also had a switchblade open in one hand and a knuckleduster on the other hand. His companion was similarly armed. Neither he nor the giant gunman said a word, and their faces stayed impassive, the eyes not even flickering.

'You will walk straight out of here,' said the flat-faced man. 'You will walk straight back to your hotel, and you will stay there. You are trespassing on what is not your business.'

'But we—' began Toby, but the man gave him a push. 'Move!'

There was nothing for it but to walk, humiliated, outgunned and outwitted, back up the alley, into the next street, and back the way they'd come. Though the men followed them closely every step of the way, they had taken care to hide their weapons, so the whole group of them looked merely like a group of friends out for an evening stroll. Toby thought once or twice of trying to make a run for it, but the thought of the blades and the gun was enough to kill the idea at once. These men wouldn't hesitate to use them, he knew that for sure.

In silence, they reached the back door of the Magnolia. 'Get in,' said the flat-faced man. 'And mind your own business.'

Toby found his voice. 'But I know Mister Klondike!'

The flat-faced man laughed. 'Kid, you got guts, I'll say that for you. Don't worry. The girl will come to no harm. But you got to get back inside. Go to bed. Forget it all.'

'But I—' Toby began, but this time it was Gabriel who stopped him. 'Shut up,' he said, in a rough voice, and dragged Toby in by main force. He slammed the door behind them, bolted it, and pushed Toby up against it. 'Now, tell me where you went yesterday, Toby,' he grated. On his face was a look of such black fury that it made Toby feel quite scared, though he tried not to seem so.

'We just went to see Klondike,' he shrugged, looking into the dark passage to see if help was coming. But everything was silent, and still. No one was about.

'*Klondike*,' Gabriel repeated, looming over Toby. 'Who is he? And don't even think of lying, Toby. Out with it.'

Toby hesitated. Gabriel said, 'If you don't tell me, Toby, exactly what happened, I'm going to go to Theo, tell him the girl freely associates with the kinds of people who employ

131

armed thugs, and that it's best if we pull up sticks and move out of New Orleans immediately. And that if he doesn't, I'll pull up sticks myself. I'll walk out of *Malvolio's Revenge*.'

'You wouldn't do that!' gasped Toby. 'It's first night tomorrow!'

'Try me,' said Gabriel, harshly.

'You wouldn't dare . . .' repeated Toby, eyes wide.

'Easily,' said Gabriel. His eyes drilled into Toby. 'Well, what's it to be? Do you want to take the chance? Do you want to be responsible for destroying your uncle's dreams?'

'You're a bastard!' burst out Toby, almost in tears. 'How can you do such a thing?'

'Easily,' echoed Gabriel. 'You're in the middle of something very dangerous, Toby. I don't want to see you hurt – or worse. Now come on, tell me.'

Toby looked away. His throat was thick with fury. He said, reluctantly, 'Klondike is a gambler. A gangster, actually.'

'I see.' Gabriel folded his arms. 'Go on. I want to hear it all.'

Mutinously, Toby explained, as sketchily as he dared to. When he'd finished, Gabriel said, 'So you believed what she told you.'

Toby stared angrily at him. 'Why shouldn't I? It's the truth. Isabelle is looking for her father's murderer, and she'll stop at nothing to find him, even going into the very mouth of danger. Can't you understand that, Gabriel?'

Gabriel's lips were pale, his eyes bleak. 'I was speaking to Madame Laroche this morning. She never said anything about suspecting Armand de Castelon had been murdered. I think the little Mam'zelle has been telling you fairytales.'

'That's rubbish! Madame Laroche probably doesn't want to tell you,' said Toby, indignantly. 'Anyway, she's mad as a hatter! She said that—' He broke off, but too late.

Gabriel seized him by the shoulder. 'What happened? What did she say?'

Toby told him. Gabriel dropped his arm.

'She told you that?' he said in a still, strange voice. He had gone quite pale.

Toby nodded.

'You don't want to listen to that,' Gabriel said, thickly, after a while.

'I know,' said Toby, staring. Gabriel looked ill.

'You should—' began Gabriel, but just then, Uncle Theo's booming voice floated down the hallway towards them. 'Gabriel! Gabriel Harvey! Where are you? I need to run over one more thing with you, for tomorrow . . .'

Gabriel looked at Toby. 'Wait here,' he hissed. 'I'll be back right away.' Toby nodded, trying to look as cowed as possible. Gabriel hurried off.

As soon as he was out of sight, Toby unbolted the door, trying to make as little noise as possible, and slipped outside. He looked quickly up and down the street, then back at the hotel. No one was about, and no one came in pursuit.

He set off at a jogtrot for the Rising Sun. He'd go and beard Klondike in his den, make him tell him what was going on. Gabriel would be furious when he found out he'd gone, and he might well guess he'd gone to see Klondike, but he didn't know about the Rising Sun. Toby would have a head start on him, anyway.

He had almost reached the saloon when he came across Louis, the boy from the Karnofskys' wagon, larking around with some other boys.

'Hello, mister!'

Toby stopped. 'Hello, Louis. I'm looking for Mister Klondike again. Is he at the saloon?'

'No, mister! He's gone home, now!'

'Where does he live?'

'A few streets away, mister. A fine house, he has.'

'Does it have an entrance archway?'

The boy stared. 'No.'

Toby thought hard. If it wasn't Klondike's house Isabelle had gone into, then whose was it? Klondike would know, he'd bet on that.

'Can you take me there?'

'Sure thing. Come on, mister. It's quite a walk from here.'

Fifteen

After a brisk walk which left Toby puffing, Louis stopped, in the shadow of a big tree. They were in a prosperous district, in a street full of fine houses. Louis pointed at a large house across the street. 'That's it. I go no further, mister.'

Toby glanced at the house. It was a big pink-washed building, with beautiful ironwork balconies, freshly painted. Several very smart motor cars were parked outside, the uniformed drivers watching over the expensive vehicles. There were lights blazing inside the house, and a couple of windows were open, loud music spilling out into the street.

'He's havin' a party, sounds like,' said Louis.

Toby looked at the front door. A couple of beefy men stood guard. He said to Louis, 'Is there a back way?'

'There's a garden wall, out the back, but I think he's got

dogs,' Louis whispered. 'I've got to get goin', now, mister, or my mamma will be worrying. You take care.'

Toby fished in his pockets. He could find only a couple of meagre coins. 'Sorry.'

'That'll do fine, mister.' The boy was off, with a wink and a grin, and Toby was left alone in the shadows, staring at the house, wondering if he dared to go to the front door and ask for Klondike. Probably not: the goons would never believe he had an invitation. They'd throw him out directly. But maybe there was an opportunity to get into the house, and find out what he could?

He looked speculatively up at the house. One of the French windows opening on to the first-floor balcony was ajar. If he climbed up the side, there where the dead creepers would hide him from the sight of the goons at the door, he might get in unobserved. He could climb well enough, as he had to do a lot of it, in the theatre. Heart in mouth, he crept slowly around to the side of the house, taking care to keep out of the light. He needn't have worried: the goons were relaxed, smoking, laughing, chatting. They were obviously not expecting any uninvited visitors.

Toby climbed up the balcony post, taking care not to make the creepers rustle. He reached the balcony and jumped down. He pressed against the wall, taking a deep breath, listening intently. No one to be seen. He could hear music, but it came from downstairs. The room beyond the French window was perfectly quiet, and quite dark.

Cautiously, he crept to the window and pushed it. He stepped in. He waited. Silence. Darkness. He looked around him. His eyes were getting used to the dimness, so he could see it was some kind of drawing-room: there was a divan in the French style, and several large armchairs, and surprisingly, a graceful bookcase with fretted doors. He peered at the books behind their grille: they looked old, leather-bound, with gilded lettering on them. Hardly what one would expect to find in a gangster's den. Indeed, to his unpractised eye it looked more the sort of thing one might associate with a gentleman's house . . .

He made his way to the door, and looked warily out into the dim corridor beyond. No sound, no movement there at all, though downstairs the party was going full swing. He sidled along the corridor and came to a set of stairs leading up to the next floor. Up the stairs, and still it was quiet and dark up here. He opened the first door along the passage, and looked into the room. It was a bedroom, with a dressing-room opening off it. Toby slipped in. A vast four-poster bed, decorated with blue brocade hangings, dominated the room. A Persian carpet of the most beautiful blue covered most of the floor, but there was little other furniture, except for a bedside table, and a chair, on which was draped a black velvet cloak, lined with white silk, and a white top hat. Klondike's bedroom, surely; and yet this room, with its feeling of serene luxury, was again not at all what Toby might have expected of such a flamboyant man.

There was a big fireplace too, with a carved mantelpiece on which stood a large sepia photograph in a gilt frame. Toby gave an exclamation. Was that Isabelle? He came closer to look properly.

Like Isabelle, the girl in the photograph had a cloud of black hair framing an ivory-coloured face and large dark eyes. But though it was so like her, it wasn't Isabelle. It wasn't only the old-fashioned clothes that gave that away, but also the soft, almost timid expression in the large eyes, and a slight weakness to the chin. It must be Isabelle's mother, Violette de Castelon! Now why would a man like Klondike have a portrait of a dead planter's wife in pride of place on his mantelpiece? Perhaps it was just to remember his supposed friend Armand by . . . but in that case, why have a portrait of the man's wife, and not the man himself?

A cold suspicion awoke in Toby. Had Klondike been in love with Isabelle's mother? Did Isabelle know that — and was it she who was using Klondike, not the other way around? But why would she — after all, such a relationship could never have been. Violette was not only a married woman, but a white Creole aristocrat, and Klondike a coloured hustler and gambler of dubious antecedents and occupation. It would have been impossible. Yet perhaps, if Isabelle knew that Klondike had loved her mother, no matter what the impossibility of the situation, it gave her a kind of hold over him – the hold of reflected affection. Toby swallowed. He could never have imagined feeling sympathy for the man. But the portrait, along with the unexpected quiet beauty of the room, had made him begin to reassess Klondike.

He looked around the room. He'd like to find out more. He opened the drawer of the bedside table. There was nothing in there except a crumpled packet of cigarettes, and some bottles of patent medicines. Closing the drawer again, he went to the dressing-room and opened the door.

Klondike sure had a nice wardrobe, he thought, whistling softly to himself as he looked in at the racks of smart suits, beautiful coats and shiny shoes displayed there. There were some shelves along one wall, which held neatly folded sweaters. Under these shelves, though, were a couple of cardboard boxes which looked as though they might hold documents. Toby went into the dressing-room. He kneeled down and pulled out the first box. The flaps were not closed; he opened them gingerly. There was something in there, wrapped in dusty velvet. Carefully, he lifted it out.

It was a photograph album, a very elaborate if old-fashioned one. Dust flew in the air as Toby opened it. There was nothing on the first page, only the thick black paper of the album. Obviously, though, there had been pictures in there – the corners to hold them were still there. Toby turned the next page. There was only a small photo left on that one. He prised it from its corners and peered at it. It was a photograph of a house. He recognised it immediately, though it looked much more youthful than when he'd last seen it. Illyria!

He turned the page. Another blank one. But the next one was a picture of a whole group of people, standing under some spreading live oak trees. There was a well-dressed family, a man, a woman and a small boy, surrounded by people who were obviously servants, some black, some white. They were all dressed in very old-fashioned clothes. Toby peered at them. Perhaps these were Isabelle's grandparents, and their son, Armand? He looked at the boy's face. Yes, he thought he could see Isabelle's fire and determination in the long-dead eyes, gazing out at him from the photograph. He turned the page, only to find another blank; and then, finally, another picture. This time, it was quite big, and it had been hand-tinted, with a caption in curly writing under it. '*Twelfth Night, 1893*', it said. It must have been taken after one of those productions of the play Isabelle had told them about, Toby thought. He stared at it.

It was of a big group of people in fancy dress, with bright, laughing faces. In the first row, Toby recognised Violette, beautifully dressed as Olivia; and what must be her husband Armand, dressed in flamboyant black and gold, with a black silk cloak thrown over one shoulder. He was indeed a handsome devil! There were many other costumed people there – friends of the Castelons, no doubt. And oh . . . there behind them, in the third row, a much younger Marie – he'd know those eyes anywhere – wearing a neat cap, her gaze direct at the camera. There was a baby in her arms. Toby looked at the baby, counting back. 1893. That was the year he'd been born. Seventeen years ago. Yes, he thought, heart lurching, that baby must be Isabelle, an Isabelle less than a year old . . .

Was there anyone else here whom he recognised? He looked at all the other faces, thinking maybe Klondike might be there, somewhere, but there was no sign of anyone remotely like him, man or boy. He touched the photo gently with a forefinger, melancholy welling up inside him. Violette and Armand looked so happy, bright and cheerful, surrounded by their family, their friends, their staff. And yet, just two years later, they would both be dead, and everything they'd known would crumble into ruin . . . Only faithful Marie and Isabelle would be left, at the last . . .

Time had destroyed that glittering past, smiling up at him from the photo. Time – and the murderous malice of one man. He peered at the faces. Was any of them the one responsible? Was any of them the one who had pulled the trigger and killed Armand de Castelon? None of the faces bore the mark of Cain, as far as he could see. Most looked merry, cheerful, not a care in the world. There were one or two sour faces; but no one whose features screamed 'Murderer!' Not that he'd really expected that, of course!

All of a sudden, he froze. He could hear footsteps! They were coming straight for this room! He didn't hesitate. He pushed the album into the box, and shoved it back under the shelf. He hid amongst the clothes at the darkest end of the dressing-room, for he had no time to close the door, as at that moment, Klondike came into the room. He was with someone – someone whose voice Toby recognised at once. Marie Laroche!

He nearly died of fright when Klondike came to the dressing-room door. But it was only to close it. Toby waited an instant, heart skipping wildly, then crept to the door and pressed his ear against it.

Unfortunately, the door was good quality, and quite solid. He could only hear one word in three, however much he tried. The voices kept dipping and fading in the most frustrating way.

'. . . not bring them back . . .' he heard Marie Laroche say. Then the rumble of Klondike's voice, saying something of which he caught only, 'owe it to her'. He sounded much less precise and pedantic than he had when he spoke to Toby; in fact, he sounded rather deferential. But then of course, the old witch was his aunt. He must still have respect for her, despite everything.

Marie Laroche's voice rose sharply, in a question that Toby didn't catch. He heard Klondike's footsteps, and the voice, coming closer. The man must be pacing around, he thought.

He pressed himself closer to the door. 'I promised,' he heard Klondike say, suddenly sharp and clear. 'Aunt, you must see. I promised.'

Marie Laroche laughed. It was an oddly frightening sound, cold and unamused. She said something, sharply, of which Toby heard only one word, 'death'. He could feel the cold sweat breaking out again. Something was in that room, again, he thought; something brought in by Marie Laroche, something whose ghostly fingers, even now, might be probing under the door, reaching for his heart, freezing his brain . . .

He gave a little gasp, instantly suppressed. Shaking all over, he waited for the door to be opened and for himself to be hauled out into the room. But nothing happened. After a moment, his heartbeat slowed. It had sounded loud to him, but the door was thick. They hadn't heard.

Taking a grip on himself, he tried to listen again. This time, he caught only a fraction of what Klondike had said; he must have moved away from the door. But what he did hear wasn't reassuring. 'Isabelle . . . tombstone . . . actors . . .'

What the hell is going on? thought Toby, panicking. He felt helpless, trapped here. He had to find Isabelle. Hell, he would even have welcomed Gabriel's company and advice! Then he heard their footsteps moving away. He heard the bedroom door open, then shut. He waited a moment, heart racing, wanting only to be gone but not daring to do so till he was certain the coast was clear.

Slowly, carefully, he opened the dressing-room door. It creaked. His hair rose on his head; but nothing happened. He looked cautiously out into the room. Silence. Darkness. They had gone. Swiftly, he stepped out, closed the door behind him, and crept to the French window. He opened it, carefully, and stepped on to the balcony. He looked down. The room was on the back of the house, facing on to a quiet garden. He remembered what Louis had said about the dogs, but he'd have to risk it.

He climbed over the balcony, down to the balcony under it, which fortunately was empty. Then he shinned down a post, and landed on to the soft grass below. He picked himself up quickly. The wall was just a short distance away. All he had to do was climb up it and drop down into the street below. He looked right and left. He couldn't see or hear any dogs. Perhaps they had been allowed into the house, where the party was still going strong; he could see the lights and hear the music, amongst which he thought he recognised Bunk Johnson's trumpet solos. He took a deep breath, and ran for the wall. Fortunately it was one of those that had niches for pots and flowers at various spots, and he was able to get halfway up it before realising that the top of the wall represented a formidable obstacle – it was covered in sharp bits of broken glass, embedded in concrete. Toby hesitated a moment; then, taking off his shirt, he ripped it in two and tied the bits around his hands. The glass had been unevenly distributed. Here and there were bits that hadn't quite been covered. Very carefully, he felt for a handhold there, and pushed himself up. His boots were strong. If he just leaped up then down, he might just be able to do it . . .

At that moment, he heard a great barking, coming from the back of the house. He didn't hesitate. Swinging himself up, he landed on top of the wall, and jumped down the other side, as quickly as he could. But it was not quick enough to altogether avoid the broken glass. Bits of it had pierced his boots. Soon they'd be full of blood. But he had no time to wait. He must get away!

He ran like the wind down the road, not looking behind him to see if some big monstrous dog was tearing after him. Round one corner, round the next; breath coming faster and faster, hurting his side, feet slimy with blood, but still he kept running. At last, he reached the back of the hotel, and raced for the stables. There was a trough there he could wash his feet in. He felt dizzy and sick. He pulled off his boots and saw it was just as he'd thought. His soles were covered in blood. At least, though, no glass had actually got into the boots. It wasn't as bad as he'd feared – just superficial cuts which would soon close up. He was just drying his feet on some straw when he heard the groom coming. Quickly, he picked up his boots and crept round to the back door, hoping it hadn't been bolted for the night. He pushed open the door and went in. He half expected to see Gabriel come tearing out to challenge him, but there was nothing, and no one. He could hear someone moving about in the kitchen, and the clatter of pots and pans.

He crept down the corridor, hoping to pass the kitchen unobserved. Then he stopped; for through the half-open door, he saw someone he certainly hadn't expected to see. Isabelle! She was sitting at the table, writing something, while the cook bustled around her. He stared in at her. She looked perfectly calm and composed, not as if she'd been out on some desperate errand at all.

He must have made some noise, because she raised her head and looked up. A shadow crossed her face. 'Toby!'

He motioned to her. She came to the door, looked curiously at him. 'What's up? Why are you in your undershirt? What's happened to your shirt? And your shoes? You look as though you've seen a ghost,' she whispered.

'And so I have, in a manner of speaking,' he said quietly, thinking of the photos. 'Listen – we must talk.'

'Now?' she said, glancing in at the cook.

'Now,' he echoed.

'Right. Wait a minute.' She went back in, picked up the paper she'd been writing on, folded it, and put it into her pocket. She said, 'Goodnight, Cook,' to the oblivious woman, who was still rearranging her pots and pans, and went out.

In the corridor, he said, 'I went to Klondike's house, looking for you.'

She started. 'You did what? Oh, Toby, that's crazy! What did he do to you?'

'Nothing. He doesn't know I was there. I climbed in.'

'You did?' She sounded amazed. 'But I wasn't there,' she added, after a short silence.

'I know that now.' He looked straight at her. 'Isabelle, I don't think you've told me everything. Where were you, tonight?'

She looked away from him. 'Visiting someone.'

'Who?' Toby had had enough of this sort of evasion. His feet stung abominably, and his head was spinning.

'Tombstone,' she said, reluctantly.

'What?'

'Tombstone,' she repeated. 'Klondike's younger brother.'

He stared at her. So that was what Klondike had meant! 'What kind of name is that?'

'It's a nickname. Sort of a joke. Tombstone's a town in Klondike. It depends on the miners. Tombstone depended on Klondike when they were young, you see. And he looks . . . well, like he'd be a good undertaker. Anyway, never mind.'

'But why did you go and see him? I thought it was Klondike who . . .'

'And so it is,' she said, smoothly. 'I was just hedging my bets, as they say. That's all. Look, Toby, it's not important. Tell me – what did you see at Klondike's?'

'Some old photographs,' he said. He looked sideways at her. 'He has one of your mother on his shelf.'

He heard her quick intake of breath. She bit down on her lip. 'Yes,' she said.

'Isabelle, I must know — what was he to your mother?'

'Maminou's nephew. That's all,' she said, defiantly.

'Why then does he have her photo on the shelf? Did she give it to him?'

'Of course not!' she said, sharply. 'He . . . he must have stolen it.'

'But why . . . I don't understand. You said your father was his friend, didn't you?'

'So he was.'

'Was he in love with her, Isabelle?'

'Don't be ridiculous!' she flared. 'How could that be? He was much younger than her; she was the wife of a Baron, and she was white . . .'

'I never heard of any of those things making it impossible for someone to be in love,' he said.

She made an impatient gesture. 'Don't be a fool. Klondike didn't love her. Well, maybe he thought of her as an ideal, unreachable as the stars. Is that impossible for you to understand?'

'No,' he said, sadly. After a moment, he said, 'I see now why he wanted to help you.'

She shrugged. 'I don't care about his motives, as long as he does help.' After a pause, she went on, more gently, 'Did you see or hear anything else?'

'Your nurse was there,' he said, slowly.

'Maminou? You must be mistaken! She hasn't seen Klondike in over fifteen years! She thinks he's a very bad lot. I don't even think she knows where he lives.'

'Well, she does. And she might not have seen him for years, but she was talking to him all right.'

'Damn!' she said, surprisingly. Toby looked at her. 'It's just that she'll probably try and stop him helping me,' she explained. 'What did she say?'

'I only heard a little,' said Toby. He told her what he'd heard. Isabelle frowned. 'Just as I thought. She's trying to put the fear of God – or of my parents' ghosts – into him.'

'I doubt he'll be impressed.'

'You don't know Maminou. She can be very . . . persuasive. She can . . . make you feel very frightened indeed, when she wants to.'

Toby shivered. 'I know.'

She looked quickly at him. 'Look, Toby, I'm . . . I'm sorry about tonight. It was just an idea that popped into my head, an impulse, to see Tombstone. I thought he might be more . . . more forthcoming than his brother.'

'And was he?'

'Eh? Oh, no. He wasn't even there,' she said, a little too quickly.

Toby said, 'Please, Isabelle, if I'm to help you, we must do things together from now on. You must *really* trust me.'

'Very well,' she said, and suddenly gave that dancing, warm smile of hers. 'I'm sorry, Toby. I act before I think, sometimes. Will you forgive me?'

'Of course,' he said, gruffly. 'Of course.'

'Best go to bed now,' she said. 'Tomorrow's the big night, isn't it?'

Oh God, he'd completely forgotten the play. It seemed very small and silly compared with the adventures he'd had. He could write his own play now, he thought as, farewelling Isabelle, he hurried back to the room he shared with Gabriel, dreading what the actor would say to him, but determined to stand up to him too. Tonight had shown him he could be as brave as anyone else; he'd not let himself be browbeaten again!

Sixteen

Gabriel was in the room, lying on his bed, smoking, eyes on the ceiling. He didn't even look up when Toby came in. He said, 'So you're back.'

'Yes,' said Toby, sitting on his own bed. He suddenly felt rather embarrassed. 'Gabe, I . . .'

'Don't say anything,' said Gabriel, quietly. 'I want to tell you something, Toby. Something I should have told you long ago.'

Toby stared at him. 'What?'

'Toby, Madame Laroche was not altogether wrong about me.'

'What do you mean?' Toby's heart began thumping very loudly, so loudly he thought it must be heard, just like a drum.

'I . . . I can . . . see things others can't. Things I'd prefer not to.' He stopped, took a drag on his cigarette, and said, still not looking at Toby, 'Sometimes I can see death.'

Toby gripped his bed. His palms prickled. He whispered, 'What do you mean?'

'Sometimes, I see a kind of darkness – a thick shadow – it's hard to describe it, exactly – at people's shoulders,' said Gabriel, tightly. 'It always presages violent death – maybe their own, maybe someone else's – depending on whether they're to be murderer or victim. I can't tell which, Toby. I can never tell. And it doesn't happen all the time. It's not infallible. I don't see it with everyone who's coming close to violent death, just a few.' Finally, he turned his head, and Toby saw that his eyes were full of some fathomless dread, a darkness that seemed to have no end. 'But when it does happen, it's horrible, I can tell you. The worst of it is not knowing what to do.'

A cold hand gripped at Toby's heart. 'So what *do* you do?' he whispered.

'Mostly, I keep quiet. I learned my lesson about that long ago, and bitterly. If that person is going to die, there's no point in making their last few days or weeks fearful and miserable, is there?' His eyes darkened, as if in remembered pain. 'And if it's not their death, but someone else's . . . well, it can be very dangerous to say anything at all. They may not even know they're going to kill someone . . . and if they do, if they're planning it – why, they might not want to be stopped.' He paused. 'Besides, how do I know who the victim is going to be? How can I warn them?'

'But have you seen anyone recently who . . .?'

'There are other things, too,' went on Gabriel dreamily, his head turned away from Toby. 'Our world is full of unseen presences, Toby. They press in on us from everywhere. Ghosts, yes, but others, too, spirits that are not human, and never were. Sometimes they are in great crowds in deserted and empty places; sometimes there's just one of them, in a busy place. Most people never see them, though they're aware of what they call atmosphere, in certain places. But people like me, we see them well; and can tell them apart from humans, though they have a human shape, because they have still faces, and unmoving eyes; their faces are bleached of colour. Some of them are good, others bad, still others neutral. But all of them want to be near us, because we are warm, and they are cold. Some places are more haunted than others. Here in New Orleans, there are many such presences.'

Toby shivered. 'Stop it. You're making me feel frightened.'

'Forgive me. I've held this inside me for so long. It's such a relief to speak of it. It's something I've lived with my whole life. See, this gift – or curse, really – of mine is natural, inborn, and not something I asked for, or ever wanted. For a few others, such things can be learned. There are formulae you can memorise, tricks and spells you can master, ways of seeing you can teach yourself to do. Some people use drugs, too. I can never understand it, that desire to have mastery over the invisible world; I would rather surrender all knowledge of it, for sometimes it torments me to the very bone.' His eyes darkened, and Toby thought of his moodiness, the black rages and sorrows he was prone to. 'But there are other temperaments besides mine; some people are happy with it. They go singing into the shadow lands, and never see their peril.' He paused. 'Like Tom Nashe, for instance. He talks blithely of deals with the Devil, and I'm sure he's tried a few spells; I can smell it on people. So far, he hasn't run into big trouble with the invisible world; but it's not to be taken lightly. One day, he's going to learn that.'

The hair rose on the back of Toby's neck. 'What? He's one of your sort, too?'

'Yes,' said Gabriel, flatly. 'He's one of my *sort*, as you call it. But not in the same way. He acts as if it were a game, and that's dangerous. That's why I don't like him. Why I don't *trust* him, more to the point.'

'And Marie Laroche, she . . .'

'Why, yes, of course. She's one of *our sort*, too. But I trust her. She knows it's not a game.' His smile didn't have much amusement in it. He paused, and went on, rather more lightly, 'It's all right, lad, you needn't stare at me so, I'm still just the same old Gabe you've known for — how long is it now? — three years this summer. I'm just an actor. Acting's been my salvation, Toby, you know; without it, I might be a drunk madman, wandering the highways, head full of shrieking shadows; or worse still, some seedy charlatan fleecing honest people of their hard-earned cash in a fortune-teller's booth, pretending I could call up my gift at will and help people to control uncontrollable fate . . . When I'm acting I can be someone else. And somehow, you know, acting's domesticated and sweetened the pain of the gift, so that I can be fully a part of the human world, as well as slip into other skins, and cast other shadows on the stage.'

'Good lord,' said Toby, struck by the image. 'That's beautiful, Gabe; it's like poetry!'

Gabriel's smile was very sweet. 'You're a good friend, Toby,' he said, gently. 'Thank you for that.'

'Er . . .' Toby looked down at his hands. 'Gabriel, I just wanted to say . . . look, I'm sorry for earlier, I really am. You didn't have to tell me all those things. But I really appreciate it. I really do.'

Gabriel searched his face. 'So you don't think I'm mad? A freak?'

Toby looked at him, and saw the hurt, the suffering, the pain he'd always missed. He'd always thought the trouble with Gabriel was bad temper. He thought with a shiver of how horrible it must be, to be tormented by things you could do nothing about, to see things that for other people would be thankfully hidden. He thought of just how much Gabriel could have used this thing of his, to manipulate and dominate other people, and yet had chosen not to. A great pity, and a great admiration, seized him. But he would not embarrass Gabriel by saying any such thing. Instead, he said lightly, 'But you *are* a freak, mate. You're a freak of nature, you're such a damn good actor. It's spooky.'

Gabriel stared at him, then laughed, his eyes lightening with relief. 'You're a freak yourself, Toby, then; you'll never cease to surprise me.'

'Well . . .' Toby took a deep breath, and went on, in a rush, 'And look, this is what happened, tonight . . .' He told Gabriel what he had seen and heard in Klondike's house, and what Isabelle had said. When he had finished, Gabriel nodded. He looked up at a ring of smoke curling above his head, and said, very quietly, 'Toby, you asked me before if I had seen anyone recently with . . . with the shadow at their shoulder. Yes, I did. I saw it that first night, in Illyria.'

Toby's mind flashed back. He could see the look on Gabriel's face, as he stared past Marie Laroche's shoulder, into the darkness of the hall. He whispered, 'You saw it . . . on Madame Laroche!'

'Oh no,' said Gabriel, shaking his head. 'That was only my reflection, just as I told you. No, Toby. I saw it, right beside Isabelle. I saw it, as soon as I came into the dining-room.'

Toby's blood ran cold. He remembered Gabriel's reaction, or lack of it, faced with Isabelle's beauty. He remembered the young man's little gasp, followed by his casualness, and even lack of courtesy. He thought of how badly he'd behaved, that night; the stiffness of his acting, the bitterness of his bearing. But all he said was, 'Are you sure? Are you quite sure?'

'Yes, Toby, I am.' He looked at Toby, and smiled, sadly. 'I'm sorry.'

'But what . . . what does that mean?'

Gabriel said nothing. He didn't need to. Toby began to shake. 'We've got to do something, Gabriel!'

'There is nothing we can do,' said Gabriel, stubbing out his cigarette and running a hand through his hair. 'We had better just pray.'

'Surely there's more . . .' stammered Toby. 'We should at least warn Isabelle . . .'

'No!' said Gabriel, fiercely. 'That would make it worse.'

'But Madame Laroche – you said you trusted her – and she said you should help. She said you should help us. She said we . . . we needed you. Please, Gabriel. You can't turn your back on us. You can't turn your back on Isabelle! I know you don't like her much, but she's brave, and bright, and . . . oh, Gabriel! I want more than anything in the world to keep her safe.'

Gabriel turned his head and looked into Toby's face. There was a long silence. Then, slowly, the actor said, 'Very well, then, Toby. Here's what we'll do: we'll make sure Isabelle will go nowhere tomorrow except for the hotel and the theatre. We'll just have to escort her, unobtrusively, everywhere; and keep her busy. And the day after tomorrow, I'll go and see Klondike myself. I'll make him tell me what happened to Armand de Castelon, and who killed him.'

'You don't know him,' said Toby, anxiously. 'I doubt anyone could make Klondike do what he didn't want to do.'

Gabriel gave an unamused smile. 'He's just a gangster, Toby; I've come across people like that before. And like all those kinds of people, he'll be superstitious. My curse is useful in some ways; I can put the fear of God into people, if I choose to.'

There was a strangeness about him, a kind of leashed power, as he said this, which made Toby shiver a little, in spite of himself. He had to remember that this was Gabriel Harvey, the actor he'd known for years, and not, indeed, some avenging angel of God . . .

'So you do believe Isabelle's story now,' he said, trying to keep his voice steady.

'I never said I didn't, just that Madame Laroche hadn't said anything about it. Thinking about it, though, I came to the conclusion it was more than likely. It explained quite a few things . . .'

'But Isabelle said Klondike doesn't know who . . .'

'I doubt that,' said Gabriel, curtly. 'I think he has a good idea, anyway. I think that Isabelle may suspect, herself. I think she is in very great danger, and that she is a rash little fool who should have listened to her nurse.'

'But she—' began Toby, hotly.

Gabriel cut him off. 'But all that's irrelevant, right now. Are we agreed, then, on our course of action?'

'Very well,' said Toby, rather uneasily. He wasn't at all sure that Isabelle would allow herself to be kept within the bounds Gabriel wanted. Still, they could try. They must try, if what Gabriel had told him was in any way true. Now the first shock of it all had receded, though, he wasn't at all sure what he believed. Was Gabriel really telling him the truth, or was it another of his weird and wonderful stories?

Yet since coming to Illyria, things had changed for him. He had seen and felt things that once he'd only imagined occurred in stories. Something uncanny threatened the girl he loved; something dark sat at her shoulder, just as Gabriel had said. He couldn't see the shadow, literally, like Gabriel could; but he knew in his heart, his very fibres, that it was *there*. And that Isabelle must be protected from it, at all costs. She had brains, and spirit, and courage for ten; but she couldn't fight this alone.

Seventeen

In the morning, Toby woke with a brilliant idea. He jumped up and shook Gabriel awake.

'Something had been nagging at me,' he told the sleepy actor, 'and it suddenly came to me. We've only heard about what happened to the Castelons from people who knew them, and who were close to them. But we don't know the *facts*, do we? The police facts, I mean.'

Gabriel rubbed at his gritty eyes. 'Heavens, Toby, what are you on about?'

'I mean, we need the unbiased information,' said Toby, eagerly. 'The police case. We need to look at their files!'

'Oh, yes, sure,' said Gabriel, getting up reluctantly. 'How do you propose we do that? Just go along to the police station and say, sir, we need to look at the police files on a long-dead case, open and shut case of suicide, sir. No, we're not family, friends, or officials; we're just rubber-neckers, curious individuals, that's all. No, we have no authorisation, sir; and by the way, sir, we hope to prove you all wrong and utterly foolish, because we believe the Baron de Castelon was murdered by person or persons unknown, and you didn't do your job properly.'

'Oh,' said Toby, rather dashed. 'I see what you mean.'

'Not your fault,' said Gabriel, with a darting smile. 'It's what a penny dreadful hero would do, eh, Tobe? Police are never a match for amateur detectives there. But it's not a bad idea,' he went on, lightly, seeing Toby's crestfallen look. 'I agree, we do need some unbiased information. We need to consult someone who had no vested interest in all this; someone, however, who recorded it all . . .'

'I know!' said Toby, eagerly. 'What about the newspapers? They keep archives, don't they? I could go and see Mr Horn at the *Bugle*, and ask him if I could look them up. I can tell him I'm doing a bit of background research for Uncle Theo – that I've learned there was a local plantation with the name of Illyria, like the setting of Uncle Theo's play, and that he's asked me to find out as much as I can about it . . .'

'It might work as a cover story,' said Gabriel judiciously, 'if Mr Horn isn't of too suspicious a turn of mind.'

'Oh, he's very, very busy,' said Toby, 'he's always running hither and thither. I doubt he'll trouble himself too much as to my motives.'

'Very well, it's a good idea. You'd better go straight away, then. Newspapers generally start early. I'll cover for you with your uncle. And I'll keep an eye on Isabelle, too, don't worry.'

Toby reached the *Bugle* office in record time. The streets were still dark, but Gabriel was right: the newspaper office was already a hive of activity. And there was Joe Horn in the midst of it all. He did not seem to be surprised to see Toby so early.

'Big day today, eh, son? You looking for that pile of playbills you missed the other day?'

'Yes, sir,' said Toby, gratefully. 'Oh . . . and sir, Uncle Theo asked me to look up something, in your archives. Apparently there was a plantation near here called Illyria . . . and they used to put on a production of *Twelfth Night* every year. Madame Blanche told him about it.'

'Bless my soul, that's right,' said Joe Horn. 'I'd forgotten about that! Yes, yes . . . one of those proud and charming Creole families . . . but with a rather shady reputation, I believe, especially at the end. There was some big scandal, wasn't there? I was not in New Orleans then, so I'm not clear on the details. So your uncle is interested in that family, is he?'

'I think in the productions they put on, sir,' said Toby, hastily. 'He thought maybe there might be some local interest he could draw on – with ideas for costumes, or props, or music, you understand.' He was improvising feverishly, hoping Joe Horn wouldn't ask too many questions. But the old newspaperman seemed convinced.

'I see. Of course. Well, you're welcome to have a look in the archives, Toby. I'd help you, only as you can see I am most fiendishly busy! I think they are fairly well arranged, in order of years and months. If I were you, I'd start searching back at least twenty years. I think that the whole thing ended in disaster at least fifteen years ago.' He motioned to the stairs at the back of the office. 'They're in the basement. Now, you'll be all right?'

'Thank you, sir,' said Toby, escaping.

The basement room, though absolutely crammed with bound files rowed up on shelves, was surprisingly neat and tidy. As Joe Horn had said, the files were well arranged, with the dates printed in black on the spine of each binding. Each year was contained in two or three files; the furthest the files went back was 1887. Toby was about to take down the files for 1895 – the year Isabelle's parents had died – when he had a sudden thought. It would probably be quite useful to look at a happier, earlier year as well, just as a matter of contrast. Maybe 1894?

Twelfth Night was on January 6, of course, so if there was a report of the production at Illyria, it would be in the first volume. He took down the file and sat cross-legged on the floor, turning the pages, looking at long-dead news stories.

January 1 . . . fireworks . . . a murder in Bourbon Street . . . an affray in Rampart Street . . . January 2, no issue; January 3, police assaulted while making an arrest . . . January 4 . . . new theatre planned for French Quarter . . . goodness, it was the Terpsichore, by the description . . . January 5, no issue . . . January 6, long piece about New Orleans Twelfth Night traditions, the baking and giving of king-cakes, the parades and balls, the opening of Carnival season . . . ah yes, look, there, a mention of Illyria: 'the tradition of productions of *Twelfth Night* at the Castelons' seat of Illyria as popular as ever in high society,' he read . . .

He looked through the issue, trying to find an actual report of such a production. Of course! What a fool he was! It'd be in a later issue . . . January 7 . . . no issue. January 8 . . . Ah, here it was! But what the hell . . . He stared down at the article, which was really just a long caption underneath what would have been a photograph.

> *Judged one of the best productions of recent years, this year's* Twelfth Night *at Illyria featured an especially radiant Madame Violette de Castelon in a gorgeous costume as the Lady Olivia, a magnificently dashing Monsieur Armand de Castelon as Sebastian, and many other good parts, played by family and staff. Splendid sets and glorious costumes made this no-expenses-spared show the most glittering social occasion of the Christmas*

calendar, and made a fittingly magnificent opening for
the Carnival season.

Toby rocked back on his heels, staring. It was not the breathless prose that amazed him. For the caption explained empty air: the photograph, which should have illustrated it, had been razored neatly out of the paper, leaving a blank space.

Somebody had been at the archives before him! Someone who did not want that photograph to be easily available. A little tremor ran through him. Could that someone be . . . the murderer? Or Klondike? Toby thought of the photo he had found in the box in Klondike's dressing-room. That had been from 1893, not 1894, though. Feverishly, he pulled down the volume for the first part of 1893, and looked for a story on *Twelfth Night*. But there was none, and no photograph, either. He sat back on his heels, and tried to picture in his mind the photo he'd seen in Klondike's house. He remembered the Castelons' faces, and the baby, and Marie . . . and a couple of other faces, vaguely, but that was all. He'd need to look at the photo again; maybe to extract it from Klondike's house, and show it to Isabelle. Maybe she'd be able to see some clue in it, something he couldn't.

A sudden thought struck him. How long ago had the photo been razored out? It could have been any time, maybe years and years ago. The volume was neatly packed in, and rather dusty; it was obvious it had not been looked at very often.

Joe Horn's voice floated down the stairs, startling him. 'Are you all right down there, Toby?'

'Yes, yes, sir, nearly finished,' Toby stammered, pushing the 1893 and 1894 volumes back on to the shelf. He could learn nothing more from those. He'd come to look at the description of the Castelon family tragedy, and he hadn't even begun to look at the volumes for 1895. He'd better hurry up before Joe Horn came down to help him! Damn. He didn't even know when it had happened. He leafed rapidly through the first volume, January–June. A story like that would be bound to have a big headline, he thought, and the name of Castelon would be sure to leap out at him. Nothing that he could see. He took down the second volume.

It was in September that he found it. It was, indeed, a shrieking headline. '**THE BARON DE CASTELON FOUND SHOT DEAD IN GRISLY TRAGEDY**', it read, in big, bold capitals. Under it was a cameo picture of Armand de Castelon, in profile, showing a handsome man with a Roman nose and determined eyes. The article went on:

> *Baron Armand de Castelon, only son of one of the richest plantation owners in the New Orleans district, the late Baron Thibault de Castelon, was found dead at his home, Illyria, early yesterday. The Baron de Castelon, who with*

his wife the Baroness Violette de Castelon, was a leader of New Orleans high society, famous for the many glittering parties and balls which he threw at Illyria, had been shot. A gun was found beside him. The Baron had for some time been suffering a number of reverses in business, and the estate of Illyria itself had been mortgaged heavily. Police are investigating his death, and would not speak to Bugle reporters.

It is reported that his wife, the Baroness Violette de Castelon, is prostrated with grief, and grave fears are held for her state of mind. Their small daughter, Isabelle, is being cared for by the family's staff. The Castelons have little immediate family in the district, apart from the Biche twins, who own the Terpsichore Theatre, and it is believed that they are with the Baroness in her time of grief.

In happier times, the Castelons were well-known for the glittering social occasions which they patronised and funded, including one of the most sought-after events in the calendar, the annual production of Shakespeare's Twelfth Night, held at Illyria itself, in which the Castelons themselves, their friends and family and staff, played major roles. But cracks had appeared long ago in the shining façade of this once-proud Creole noble family. It remains to be seen whether the tragic, violent death of the Baron de Castelon will be the final blow to the fortunes

of a family that was once tantamount to royalty in this
district. How are the mighty fallen!

What a pompous fool, whoever wrote that, thought Toby, indignantly. Obviously the Castelons had no longer held that 'glittering' position in 'high society' by the time of the Baron's death, or the gutter journalists of the *Bugle* would not have dared to write such insinuating trash! They had obviously decided it was suicide, anyway. He leafed through the next issue. The death of the Baron dominated the paper for a couple of issues more, but he did not learn a great deal, the police obviously being close-mouthed about the progress of their investigations. The *Bugle* had to resort to reporting scandalous gossip, and interviewing random folks, supposed friends of the Castelons, who were obviously desperate to dissociate themselves from them now. It was sickening.

In an issue a week later, he found an item related to the Baroness's death. No shrieking headline this time, and a rather embarrassed tone about it: 'Violette de Castelon dies at the age of 25,' he read.

> *The Baroness Violette de Castelon died at her home,*
> *suddenly, on Tuesday evening last. Madame de Castelon,*
> *who had been ailing for some time, had never recovered*
> *from the shock of her husband's violent death, and had*
> *not been seen in public since the tragedy. She had refused*

to give any interviews. It is believed she suffered from a
weak heart.

Bastards, thought Toby, fiercely. Did they wonder whether their hounding had anything to do with the poor woman's death? That, and the bile and treachery of those who had happily counted themselves as friends in the good times, till disaster struck? Rats, deserting the sinking ship! Mongrels! Villains!

Furiously, he leafed rapidly through the rest of the volume. There was only one further reference to the Castelons, in an article towards the end of December. 'Inquest delivers an open verdict,' he read.

The inquest into the death of the Baron Armand de Castelon has concluded with an open verdict, that death occurred through a gunshot wound. But whether the death was self-inflicted, or the result of a tragic accident, was not revealed. Questions are being asked in New Orleans about why a more conclusive verdict was not reached. The Bugle *understands that the police will not comment further on the issue, and that the matter is now closed. But many are asking whether any other family would have received such kid-glove treatment, and whether our notions of democracy are as advanced as many would wish them to be.*

Toby took a deep breath. His eyes swam with angry tears. Couldn't they let the dead rest in peace? What kind of hypocrites were those 'many' who were 'asking questions'? Could they not imagine what it might be like? And did they have no thought for the poor unfortunate child left orphaned, penniless and friendless, except for her loyal nurse? No, of course not. The Castelon tragedy had been a three-day sensation, quickly forgotten, quickly passed over, quickly moralised over. *How are the mighty fallen!* How much humanity loved to say such things! How easily spite and jealousy is transformed into righteous indignation!

He got to his feet and shoved the volume back into its place. He had learned enough. No one had even thought of the possibility that Armand de Castelon might have been murdered; they were all too focused on their own images of what the Castelons were like. In that world-view, such people deserved to fall spectacularly from their perch, in as public and shameful a way as possible. That made a good public moral, of decadence punished, and pride deservedly destroyed.

He marched up the stairs, still fuming. Joe Horn saw him, and waved. 'Got what you wanted, son?'

'Yes,' said Toby tightly, in such a hostile way that the old newspaperman looked at him in some surprise. 'What's up, son? You look angry enough to kill someone.'

It was just what Tom Nashe had said, the other day. Toby

took a grip on himself, remembering that Joe Horn hadn't even been in New Orleans, much less written in the *Bugle*, when the events had happened. He said, rather lamely, 'It's just a little odd, looking at the past . . . All those people, dead and gone.'

'Not all of them, son,' said Joe Horn, smiling faintly. 'But I know what you mean, it can be a melancholy business. By the way, I just remembered: did you know the Biches at the Terpsichore were distant relatives of those Castelons? They could have told you about those productions.'

'Er . . . they were never involved,' lied Toby, quickly. 'They couldn't tell us much, anyway. I don't believe they were ever very close to the Illyria people.'

'Oh. Well, I hope the *Bugle* filled in the gaps, then. Did you find any descriptions of those productions? Did they sound interesting?'

'They were interesting enough,' said Toby. He thought of the razored photograph. Should he ask Joe Horn about it? On balance, he decided not to. It might lead to a whole lot of awkward questions. 'But I'm not sure they would be useful for my uncle. I think that in those productions at Illyria, money was no object.'

'Yes, well, those old families, they had plenty of money, once,' said Joe Horn, nodding wisely. 'Things are different now; land isn't as important as it once was. Take our new proprietor, Mr Wilson. He started out with nothing, out in

California. But look at him now! Ah, Toby . . . here's those missing playbills. And give my regards to your uncle and the Biches. Tell them I'll be there tonight, most definitely!'

'Excellent,' said Toby, escaping with the playbills, into the grey light of the newly dawned day.

Eighteen

Nobody, it seemed, had missed him. They were trickling in to breakfast; only Gabriel was not at the table. Toby was glad to see Isabelle's sleepy face as he went into the kitchen to get a basket of sweet rolls. She was yawning over a cup of coffee, while the cook, the maids and Marie kept up a light chatter. Toby was fully aware of the old nurse's scrutiny as he came in, but he took no notice.

'Are you ready for tonight, Miss Chiquita?' he said, lightly. The girl started and looked up at him. 'Why, yes, sir,' she said, demurely.

'There is a great deal of backstage work to be done today, and Mr Harvey and I will need your help all day,' Toby went on, boldly. Isabelle shot him a puzzled look, but nodded. Out of the corner of his eye, Toby could see the expression on Marie Laroche's face changing – from wariness to relief. He thought, she knows I've spoken to Gabriel; she knows we're going to try to protect Isabelle from the nameless malevolence that hangs over her. She approves. He gave her a smile, and she responded, the smile sweetening and lighting her face, so that he suddenly thought, why, she must have been quite a pretty girl herself, once, long ago . . .

He'd never really thought of Marie as herself, only as Isabelle's faithful nurse. All at once, he wondered; what was it like, to live your whole life for someone else's child? Before she'd been nurse to Isabelle, she'd nursed Isabelle's mother. Yet she had never married herself, never had children; her only relatives being the surely unsatisfactory Klondike and Tombstone. Poor woman, he thought, as he went in to breakfast. Poor brave soul. How lucky Isabelle was that someone at least had taken care of her! Not family, not even the Biches; but an old coloured woman, a faithful servant. Without Marie, she might well have ended up in the orphanage . . .

A little later, he went to look for Gabriel, and found him in the stable, talking to Slender and Shallow. He'd once told Toby that when he felt nervous or baffled, he liked talking to the horses — they listened to everything you said, and never tried to second-guess you. He looked up as Toby came in. Without preamble, he said, 'I found out about Nashe — he's from Pinkerton's.'

Whatever Toby had expected, it wasn't this. He goggled at

Gabriel. Everyone had heard of Pinkerton's Detective Agency, of course; it was a famous American institution, investigating everything from theft and fraud to murder and even attempted coups against governments. There were often agents from Pinkerton's, or from organisations very like it, in the detective stories he liked to read in magazines.

'That's right, he's a Pink,' went on Gabriel. 'I should have thought of that – it's a good way for one of *our sort* to find respectable employment.'

'But Gabe . . . how did you know . . . ?'

'He went out this morning, very early. I took the opportunity to go snooping in his room,' said Gabriel, shrugging. 'I found a letter from them in his violin case, introducing him as one of their agents. I think it's genuine.'

'But Gabe . . . why would someone from Pinkerton's . . . ?'

'You tell me. I have no idea,' snapped Gabriel. Toby saw his face wore a puzzling expression, a kind of mixture of shame and anger and something else, something indefinable. 'Pinkerton's agents don't come cheap. Whoever's hired his services will not be poor.'

Toby's heart beat fast. He said, 'I wondered . . . the other day, he almost seemed to be following Isabelle and me, when we'd gone to see Klondike.' Rapidly, he explained. 'Isabelle thought it was unlikely he was a spy or informer for her father's murderer,' he finished, 'but what if he's been paid to keep an eye on her?'

'Why now, though?' said Gabriel, absent-mindedly stroking a responsive Shallow. 'Why not before?'

'I don't know,' said Toby, slowly. 'But how do we know when he appeared at Illyria?'

'We don't,' said Gabriel. 'But I don't think he would have got there much before us. It's quite possible he was there, waiting for us, so he could get in more naturally, as it were. But I don't think he can be a spy for the murderer, whoever he may be. If my feelings are right, the murderer's likely to have been a gambler, someone associated with that world. I doubt such a person would employ a Pink, if he felt threatened. He'd be more likely to employ a paid assassin. And if he felt at all threatened, he'd have acted before now. No, Toby, I don't think he has any idea that he is being pursued. Therefore I doubt Nashe has anything to do with him.'

'But if that's not it . . .' A mischievous expression came into Toby's face. 'Perhaps he's investigating one of us! Perhaps he thinks one of us is really a master criminal in disguise!'

'You and your penny dreadfuls,' said Gabriel, sharply.

'That would be funny, though, wouldn't it?' insisted Toby. 'Imagine if it's Henry, who's really a safe-breaker, or cat-burglar! Or Old Fate!'

'The one most likely to be those things,' said Gabriel, very crossly, 'is Tom Nashe himself. Or me.'

Toby stared at him.

'After all, what do you really know about me?' Gabriel snapped. 'You know nothing of what I was doing before. Perhaps I'm on the run! Perhaps I have stolen diamonds hidden in my carpetbag!'

'I hope you deal me in on them, then,' said Toby, laughing. After a little silence, he went on, 'Perhaps it's Isabelle herself who's hired him?'

Gabriel snorted. 'I doubt very much that our young Mademoiselle has the money to pay for a Pinkerton's agent. After all, if she did, why would she also be looking for answers herself?'

'We could just ask him who he's working for!'

'You think he'd tell you the truth, Toby?'

'Maybe he would if he had no choice,' said Toby, winking. Gabriel smiled grimly.

'Maybe he would,' he said, almost happily, flexing his hands. 'Maybe he will, one dark night, in an alley . . . For the moment, we'll just keep it to ourselves, all right?'

Toby nodded. 'If he doesn't know we know, we might steal a march on him.'

'Yes. Now, Toby . . . you haven't told me yet. What did you find out, at the *Bugle*?'

So Toby told him. When he'd finished, Gabriel said, 'Wait, Toby. You said the caption under it spoke of how well the Baron and Baroness had performed. Did it mention anyone else?'

Toby said, 'Wait – no – that's right. It just said there were many other good parts, played by family and staff.'

'Did it say at all who had played who?'

'No . . . there was no one mentioned by name except the Baron and Baroness.'

'Probably because they were the only ones of interest to the gossip columnists of the *Bugle*,' said Gabriel. 'But somebody cared enough to take to the paper with a razor. Why? That's what I'm trying to think through. It seems to me that it must have something to do with the cast of that particular production.'

'Yes. I guess we could find out who the cast was,' said Toby. 'Madame Laroche – she might remember.'

'Yes,' said Gabriel. 'She might.'

'It's drawing a long bow, though,' said Toby. 'The whole thing could have nothing to do with the cast of the play, but with someone else altogether. An audience member, maybe.'

'I know,' said Gabriel, 'but it's something to go on.' He looked thoughtfully at Toby. 'I think you're right – perhaps we should speak to Madame Laroche. We could also try to get that photo from Klondike – all right, so it's not the same year, but maybe the cast was the same.'

'I could go, again,' Toby offered.

Gabriel shook his head. 'No. I'll go. I was intending to go and speak to Klondike anyway. Not today, of course; your uncle won't let anyone out of his sight today. Maybe tomorrow.'

'But you can't just ask Klondike for the photograph!' said Toby, anxiously. 'He'll wonder how you got to know about it.'

'Trust me,' said Gabriel, smiling faintly. 'I'll think of something.'

'Maybe we can ask Isabelle to—'

'I don't think you should say any of this to her,' interrupted Gabriel, sharply. 'It's better to be . . . safe. To keep her safe, I mean,' he added, hastily.

'Very well,' said Toby, a little puzzled by Gabriel's evasiveness. The actor saw this, and smiled. 'Let it be our secret for the moment, Toby. Let us surprise her with the results of our own deductions. Don't you think that's a good idea?'

'I suppose so,' said Toby carefully, thinking that Isabelle might just as well be angry with them for doing things behind her back. Still, Gabriel was right. She must be kept safe from the faceless, nameless threatening presence that could well send her the way of her parents. Besides, hadn't she gone off to see Tombstone on her own, without telling him? He thought a little shamefacedly of what he'd said to her then, about trusting him, and doing things with him, but she'd understand, once she knew everything – once it was all over. Once she was safe from the danger that literally hung over her like the dark shadow at her shoulder Gabriel had seen . . .

'Right, let's agree to this, then,' said Gabriel, briskly. 'We do nothing about it today. But tomorrow, I will go to Klondike's house, and somehow, I will find a way of getting that photograph. Then we'll speak about it to Madame Laroche – we'll say nothing to her today, either, just in case – and we'll go from there. Agreed?'

'Agreed,' said Toby, slowly. Well, he had no better ideas, did he?

Nineteen

The theatre had the strange, suspended atmosphere of the last hours before a play really begins. It was quite different from yesterday. There was no panic today, no hysterics, but an odd kind of breath-holding calm. Tonight would show if the play really could do a Lazarus, and rise from its death-bed to walk again. There was nothing more anyone could do about that; the die was cast, the stars in their courses. Happen what would happen, now.

Everywhere, there was a subdued flurry of activity. Isabelle, Matilda, Olivia and Madame Laroche were doing last-minute checks on the costumes; Uncle Theo and the Biches were counting out tickets and change for the box-office; Henry and Gabriel and Old Fate were closeted together, going over lines; Will was hanging around, pestering whomever he could. And Toby? Well, Toby was sweeping around the seats for the umpteenth time, shining the wooden tops of each seat to a bright glow, making sure all the backcloths were as perfectly hung as they had been yesterday, and doing all the jobs Uncle Theo had considered necessary yesterday, and considered necessary again today. He didn't mind, much. His head was too full of thoughts, his heart of feelings, to actually want to be sitting still, doing nothing.

It was when he'd finished shining the last row of seats that Tom Nashe came in and sat beside him. 'You're a hard worker, Toby,' he said. 'I've been watching you.'

'Have you?' said Toby, startled. Nashe smiled, showing sharp white teeth.

'You and the Irishman, you work the hardest of all.'

'Oh.' Toby kept his rag moving, shining the wood much more than it needed.

'I've been wondering,' said Nashe, nonchalantly throwing a leg over the seat. 'Has the Trentham Troupe always been made up of these same players?'

'Of course not,' said Toby. *What did the man want?*

'Who's been with you the longest?'

'Madame Leonard. She was in the original troupe my uncle had put together, actually.'

'Who's been with you the shortest time?'

'Henry – he only came into the troupe early on our Stateside tour. Our previous leading man, Max Walsh, he took very ill in Boston and we had to look for someone else.'

'I see. What about the others? When did Old Fate join, for instance?'

'Oh, he was in the troupe in Britain. He's from Quebec originally, though.' He didn't look at Nashe, but kept working, steadily. Maybe if Nashe kept asking questions, Toby would get to understand their direction, and thus maybe why he was interested in the troupe.

'What about Gabriel Harvey?'

'He joined about three years ago, back when Uncle Theo was reforming the troupe.'

'He's really very good. Good enough to be in a big company.'

'We know that,' said Toby, crossly. 'We're lucky to have him.'

'Yes.' Nashe tapped his fingers along the row of seats. 'What about you, Toby – haven't you ever felt an urge to tread the boards?'

Toby hadn't expected this. He looked quickly at the fiddler. 'No.'

'Really? Are you sure? I think you could be quite good.'

'With respect, Mr Nashe, I don't think you know much about acting.' He could have bitten off his tongue then. Of course Nashe knew about acting – wasn't he playing at being an itinerant, penniless fiddler when in reality he was a detective with a nice fat expense account? He saw Nashe smile, faintly.

'No, really, Toby – I think you have talent.'

'Not for acting,' snapped Toby, who only wanted the inquisition to be over now. It seemed to him that Nashe had won that, game, set and match. And he'd learned nothing at all.

'Maybe not acting,' said Nashe, casually. 'But you're a keen observer; and you have a nice turn of phrase, and a bright look; and an interest in people. I notice you read quite a lot too.'

'Oh, those,' said Toby, flushing. 'I'm always being told I shouldn't read so many sensational magazines.'

'On the contrary,' said Nashe, equably. 'They tell good stories that hold the attention. Stories of adventure, romance, mystery, tragedy and comedy: the universal human things. Have you ever thought of writing one of those stories yourself, Toby?'

This time, Toby did stare at him. 'Me, Mr Nashe?'

Tom Nashe laughed. 'You indeed, Mr Trentham. One day, I expect to see your name in print. I expect you to become a famous writer.'

Toby laughed. 'You're joking! Anyway,' he went on, casting a sideways glance at Nashe, 'I might prefer to do something else. I could be a detective, for instance. Don't you think so, Mr Nashe?'

'You could,' said Nashe, tolerantly. 'But I should think being a writer would suit you much better. Being a detective is not all it's cracked up to be. And I'm sure you have some great stories in you.'

With a nod, and a wink, he was off, leaving a flabbergasted Toby staring after him.

Nashe's tone showed he knew *Toby* knew about him being a Pinkerton agent, but didn't care. He'd shown no sign of surprise or embarrassment at being rumbled, anyway. A dismaying thought struck him, then. Of course, a good detective would never just let his identification trail around where anyone could find it. Nashe must have *wanted* it to be found; and so left it in the violin case, where it would easily be spotted. Why would he do that, though? And what was he after? His questions hadn't seemed to lead anywhere very far. He had an interest in the company; or had he? Were they just a blind, a red herring designed to throw Toby – and Gabriel – off the scent?

And what about that business, about Toby becoming a writer? Had the fiddler just been soft-soaping him? The idea had never really entered Toby's head before, but now it nagged at him. It was true that he did like to read, and dream, and watch people, and Uncle Theo often said that his imagination ran away with him. But was that what you really needed to be a writer? Didn't you need to be really smart, and really well-educated, and well-off? The only writers whose lives he'd read about were famous ones, like J.M. Barrie, and Sir Arthur Conan Doyle, and Jules Verne, and people like that. They seemed like unreachable stars. But they'd have had to start somewhere, he thought. Once, they'd been seventeen, too. Maybe they hadn't known they were going to be writers, back then.

He shook himself, and went resolutely back to work. He, Toby Trentham, company dogsbody, a writer, with his name in print? The idea was ridiculous, surely. And yet, and yet . . . He couldn't help vivid pictures jumping into his mind, pictures of a glowing future: himself with his name in print, not just in penny dreadfuls, but in respectable magazines like the *Strand*, or the *Spectator* . . . Perhaps he might even write a novel, or a play! And he might earn a lot of money. Enough money to ask the girl he loved to marry him. Because in his present state of pennilessness, with no prospects, he couldn't even dream of asking her. Yes! he thought, enthralled by the pictures in his own imagination, he'd have enough money to make her quite forget the sorrow of the past, and to live happily, surrounded by love and honour and comfort all the days of her life . . .

He started. The girl herself was there, beside him, smiling at him in such a way that he wondered for a mad instant if she'd read his mind and shared his thoughts. But all she said was, 'Toby, your uncle is calling for you.'

'Oh, is he?' Toby's mind was still full of those pictures. Before he could think what he was saying, he burst out with, 'I hoped it was *you*, Isabelle, calling for me. At last.'

She looked at him. Her face was unreadable. He hurried on, knowing he must finish, no matter what it cost, 'Oh, Isabelle, do you think . . . do you think you might care for me . . . just a little bit . . . one day . . . perhaps?' Choked by his own emotion, he fell silent, not daring to look at her.

There was a long silence. Then Isabelle said, very gently, 'Why, Toby, I do care for you. I like you a very great deal. You have been a good friend.'

He felt sick. He didn't want to look up and see the pity written on her face. 'I don't . . . I don't just want to be your friend, Isabelle.'

'Oh, Toby!' She laid a light touch on his arm, quickly withdrawn. 'Friendship is all I can give, Toby. I cannot give more; not now.'

'No, not now,' he said, looking up quickly, hope suddenly flaring in his heart. 'I mean, later. I know right now I have no prospects, nothing, but I'm going to make myself worthy of you. I'm going to earn a good living, Isabelle. I'm going to be a writer; I'm going to write stories, books. I'm going to be rich and famous. I promise you that, Isabelle. I'll be able to offer you so much, if you'll just . . . if you'll just wait for me, Isabelle. If you'll wait for me to get there.'

'Oh, Toby!' she said, again. He saw with a pang that she had tears in her eyes. 'I wish I . . . I wish I . . .'

'Don't wish anything,' he said, catching up her hand, fervently. 'You don't need to promise me anything, to vow anything. I would do anything for you, I would go to the ends of the earth for you. Just tell me if I have any chance at all.'

'I don't . . . I don't know,' she said, confused, biting her lip. It came to him then that he had never seen her so uncertain, and that gave him absurd hope. She hadn't said she loved him as he loved her. That was to be expected. But she hadn't completely rejected him, had she? And she had said she cared for him. As a friend, maybe; but Toby had read enough romances to know that feelings like that could easily turn into passion, given time, patience, luck.

'That will be enough for me, for the moment,' he said, and bringing her hand to his lips, kissed it, in a courtly fashion. 'That will be enough. Thank you, Mademoiselle Isabelle de Castelon. Thank you from the bottom of my heart.'

'Oh,' she said, weakly, and fled, Toby following her, but slowly, his whole being flooded with a most beautiful light.

Twenty

The day sped by after that. Toby's mind was so full of dreams and plans – and ideas for stories he might begin to write, to start off his grand money-making plan – that he hardly noticed the passing of the time, or the conversations that went on around him. He worked happily, not even trying to catch Isabelle's eye, content just to dwell on the images in his head, and the sweetness of the words she had uttered to him. He had awakened something in her, he thought, something that might grow and blossom, given time. He had done it; he had nailed his colours to the mast, and now she knew. Everything had changed.

He spoke once or twice with Gabriel, but only briefly, and only about matters concerning the performance. The Irishman appeared to be concentrating solely on his part, and to have put all other concerns out of his mind. How he could do that,

Toby didn't know. But then, he wasn't an actor, nor could he ever be. Gabriel had never felt as he did about Isabelle, anyway; in all the years he'd known him, in fact, Toby had never known the actor to fall in love with anyone at all, or even to express any interest in such things. Henry Smallwood had said he was too bitter and sardonic to attract any woman, but now that Toby knew Gabriel's secret, he thought it was likely the actor, with his terrible gift, was simply not a part of the normal world, the world where people met, fell in love, and were married. Gabriel's world was a world of shadows and haunting presences; a world where Death might seem more real than Life. Poor Gabriel! It was indeed a curse rather than a gift.

Four o'clock arrived, and with it a delightful little surprise. The Biches had hired extra staff for the night: a couple of dressers, a lighting man, a couple of cleaners, and three very grand ushers, who looked rather like a trio of very sleek and solemn penguins, in their neat black and white. The extra staff would help to free Toby up from a lot of work, and instead he was to be put on a job he always enjoyed: selling tickets in the box-office. It would give him a good view of the atmosphere in the foyer and of the people who came in. And it would give him time to dream, free of Uncle Theo's booming voice issuing last-minute instructions!

Five o'clock. Uncle Theo, the Biches and Madame La Praline were pacing around in the foyer, talking in low voices.

They were dressed to the nines, all except Uncle Theo, who was, of course, dressed in his costume. The Biches' clothes were so splendid yet so outdated that they might have been worn at a ball in the palace of Versailles, but Madame La Praline looked more than ever like a French doll. A very fashionable French doll, dressed in an exotic evening dress of embroidered muslin and satin crepe de Chine that looked as if it might be at home on a Paris catwalk right now. She wore a long string of pearls to go with it, and her spun-sugar hair was neatly piled up under a satin turban, set off by a pearl pin and a nodding blue feather. Toby grinned to himself, remembering Matilda Leonard's reaction when she'd seen this turban – 'Oh, I must have one just like it, Madame La Praline, or die! – while Olivia, open-mouthed at this illustration of a fashion plate, had wondered aloud if her father might be persuaded to let her buy the pattern of that gorgeous dress . . .

Isabelle had said nothing, though. She was not the sort to be mooning over silly fashions when important things were on hand, he thought proudly. His beloved was not the usual sort of girl, no, sir! She was spirited, bright and incredibly brave. She was a girl in a million, in a billion . . . And she had not rejected him! She had given him hope!

Happily, he stacked the tickets again in their boxes, dusted the little desk, and the chair, at which he'd sit, flourished the pages of the accounts book, and got the jars ready for change.

Uncle Theo poked his head in at the door, wanting to know if he had everything in hand, and was he sure of all ticket prices – all unnecessary but pleasant queries which Toby answered so cheerfully that his uncle looked at him in faint surprise, a surprise dispelled instantly when Toby said, 'Oh, Uncle, I'm so excited!'

'And so are we all,' said his uncle, cheerfully. 'Let us hope the theatre gods smile on us tonight, and our luck holds.' Then he was off, smiling vaguely, back to his whispered, excited conversations with the others.

Five-thirty. The curtain would rise at seven. The audience should start arriving in the next half-hour. Toby tapped with his pen on the accounts book, thinking up ideas. For his first piece, he thought, he'd write a detective story. Better still – he'd create a detective series, just like Sherlock Holmes! Better still – it would be a series set within the theatre; within a travelling company just like this one! Yes, yes! Now who would his detective be? He smiled. Perhaps he could be the company dogsbody, just like Toby himself!

He started. Madame Blanche was at the door. 'Toby,' she said, 'we've decided that when Mrs Wilson comes, we'll offer her a complimentary ticket. On account of its being her birthday soon. But we don't want it generally known, in case there's jealousies. Just slip it to her and say, "This is the ticket you ordered, ma'am." Do you understand?'

'Right. But how will I know her?'

Madame Blanche smiled broadly. 'You haven't been reading the papers, Toby! She's been in the social pages these past few days. Very fashionable, very glamorous; lots of auburn hair, one of Madame La Praline's creations perched on it no doubt, and a New York accent you could cut with a knife. You can't miss her.' So saying, she left him to it.

Toby, looking after her, hoped the millionaire's wife would not disappoint them by not turning up. He'd read somewhere that rich people were notoriously unreliable, that they made promises they didn't keep, and vows that were meant to be broken. Well, he wouldn't be like that, when he was rich. He'd never deviate from his course; and he wouldn't ever change his mind about Isabelle. He'd be her rock, on which she could always, always rely . . .

'Excuse me, can I buy three tickets for tonight's performance of *Malvolio's Revenge*?' The elderly man behind the glass smiled anxiously in at him. 'I promised my wife and my sister-in-law that I'd get good seats in the gallery. You haven't sold out yet, have you?'

'Not yet, sir,' said Toby stoutly, gathering up the man's money. 'But we soon will be – you were wise to get them now.'

'Thank heavens for that,' said the man with relief, taking the tickets. 'I will be back directly with my party.'

'Very well, sir,' said Toby, without expression. Hell! He

hoped that he hadn't spoken too soon, in vain, angered the theatre gods with his rash lie . . .

But he needn't have worried. Driven by some mysterious quality that turns a queue into a crowd very quickly, the audience had begun lining up. Toby was soon very busy indeed, handing out tickets, taking money, giving change. The glass jars started to change colour to silver as coins filled them; while the tin was full of green notes. Out of the corner of his eye, Toby could see the Biches and Madame La Praline welcoming people, shaking hands, chatting, smiling, introducing Uncle Theo to this person, then that. Things were going well, he thought. Things looked set – touch wood – to be at least a reasonable success. The theatre should be quite well filled. Uncle Theo must be thrilled with the success of his playbills and the pension keeper's word of mouth; for most of the audience seemed to be people known to Madame La Praline, or the Biches . . .

'Young man, I should like two tickets for the show.' Toby looked up, into the firm, fleshy face of a man well into middle age. He wore smart evening dress, tails, top hat and cloak, and diamond cuff links on his sleeves. But his thinning blond hair had coarse strands of grey in it, and his face and hands had a rather weather-beaten look that suggested he might have once earned his living outdoors. There was one more thing about him that was out of keeping with his conventionally elegant dress: he wore a black satin patch over one eye, just like a pirate in a story; just like Captain Hook. Toby took all this in at a glance; then, in another glance, took in something else. There was a woman hovering at his shoulder; a tall woman with bright red hair, a pretty, discontented face, and more diamonds than Toby had ever seen in his life, pinned against her rather imposing satin-clad chest. He said, in a rush, 'Mrs Wilson? Mr Wilson?'

'That's right,' said the man, a little surprised, but pleased. 'I decided to come with Susanna tonight – she persuaded me most prettily! Now how much is it for seats, son?'

'Oh, sir, we have two tickets, compliments of the house,' said Toby, quickly, but Wilson shook his head. 'No, no, son. We pay our way, just like anyone else. Isn't that right, sweetie?' he went on, turning to his wife. She smiled, rather petulantly. 'Anything you say, Clarence dear,' she said, in a fluting voice.

Toby could see Madame La Praline bearing down on them, smiling and fluttering her hands in greeting, the Biches in dignified tow. 'But sir, it would give us great pleasure—' he began, but the millionaire shook his head. 'Don't be silly, boy. This is a democratic country, and we're people like everyone else in this audience.'

'Oh, Monsieur Wilson! Madame Wilson!' said Madame La Praline, coming towards them, hands outstretched. 'It is such a great pleasure to see you here – both! Goodness me, Mr Wilson, we are most glad you were able to tear yourself away from your business for this night!'

'Well, well, all work and no play makes Jack a dull boy, eh?' The millionaire shouted with laughter. 'Susanna tells me I'm a grumpy old Philistine. I'm determined to prove her wrong! Now then, Madame La Praline, what is this nonsense about free tickets?'

He had a booming voice, just like Uncle Theo, and he pronounced the French name abominably, with a terrific Yankee accent. People had already turned around at his arrival, and now they were listening in. Toby flushed as Madame La Praline looked at him in dismay. 'I'm sorry . . . I didn't mean . . .' he began, miserably, but it was Mrs Wilson who interrupted him.

'Oh, come, Clarrie,' she said, raising her eyebrows, 'he thought he was doing the right thing. Stop making such a fuss. Besides, can't you see he's a Limey?'

'Now look here, kid,' said the millionaire, indulgently, turning to Toby, 'you gotta realise you're not in England here – there's no earls and lords and things, no false jumped-up class with nothing to recommend them but some mouldy old name and arrogant manners – so you can forget about giving special treatment to the likes of me, right? Now, those two tickets, son.'

Toby looked helplessly over at the poker-faced Madame Biche, who nodded, imperceptibly. 'Right away, sir,' said Toby, flushing brick-red as he took the man's money and handed over some tickets. Ha! he thought, angrily. No class-consciousness, eh? Just because Wilson insisted on being so ostentatious about paying for his ticket – and humiliating Toby into the bargain – didn't mean he *didn't* get special treatment! Look at them all now, hovering around him and his blowsy wife as if they were some kind of royalty! Look at the others, simpering, waiting for their turn to be talked to! Yet he couldn't help admiring the gall of the man. Wilson strode around the foyer like a colossus, greeting people here, introducing himself there, quite as if this was *his* theatre, and *his* first night!

Soon, they moved out of the foyer and were ushered into the theatre itself, the Biches and Madame La Praline eagerly following. Toby sold a great many more tickets after that; every person making some casual comment about 'did we hear the Wilsons were coming tonight?' and pretending not to be interested in the reply. Ha, he thought sourly, as the money jingled and clinked and tickets changed hands, I wonder if anyone will be actually looking at the action on stage tonight, or at that taking place in the best seats in the house, where the Wilsons would undoubtedly be sitting, if he knew anything at all about the world!

Bang, bang, bang! The great hollow triple knock resounded through the building. The play would start in five minutes. No one was left in the foyer. Toby glanced down at the pile of tickets. There were only ten or so left – a most respectable showing. He locked the money away in a strongbox. *Knock,*

knock, knock! Second call. He'd better hurry to the wings, and the prompt-book.

He was just locking the box-office when the street door banged open and a man strode in. Dressed all in funereal black, including gloves, buttoned-up coat and dark glasses, he was tall and very thin, and his neatly cut hair was pure white, the face under it almost as white as the hair. Yet it was not an old face, but quite young, unwrinkled, and hard. The man made a gesture to someone outside, and Toby saw two men take up positions on either side of the street door.

The man gestured at Toby. 'Come here, boy.'

Toby obeyed. Something puzzled him: the man was a perfect stranger, yet there was an uncanny familiarity about him, something he half recognised.

'I'm afraid the play will start in a minute or so, sir. I have to . . .'

The man took off his dark glasses and looked at Toby, who couldn't help taking a step back. He'd never seen eyes like those before: the irises were a deep pink, almost red, set off by stubby white eyelashes, and red-rimmed lids. The man was an albino!

The stranger put his glasses back on, and smiled, not very pleasantly. Something flashed in his mouth. Toby stared. The man's two front teeth were set with diamonds!

Recognition leaped into Toby's brain.

'You're Mister Klondike's brother!' he stammered. 'You're Mister Tombstone.'

'Sure I am, boy.' Tombstone's voice was husky, deep. 'And I've not come to see the play, but to deliver a message. To Chiquita.'

'Oh,' said Toby, anxiously. 'She's . . . she'll be on stage any moment now, sir, you see. She's in the first scene, and—'

'Tell her I'm here.'

'I can't, sir. She's about to go on stage!' Toby saw that Tombstone was looking at the theatre door, and thought, Oh my God, he intends to go in there and haul her off, disrupt the play, oh my God, I've got to stop him! But how? He doesn't look like the type to be stopped by the likes of me . . . And he has his henchmen outside. No, Toby thought, I'll have to dream up something else!

'Mr Tombstone, sir,' he said, earnestly, 'could I give you a complimentary ticket to the play? On the house, you see. Then afterwards you'll be able to go backstage and . . . and meet Chiquita, and deliver the message.' I'll warn her, though, he thought; once he's safely there in the dark, I'll go backstage and warn her he's here. Oh Isabelle, Isabelle, what was she doing, getting tangled up with such unprepossessing creatures!

Tombstone frowned. Then his face relaxed. He said, with a faint smile, 'Very well. It will be amusing.'

Relieved, Toby unlocked the office and retrieved a ticket.

As Tombstone took it, the flaps of his coat fell open, revealing a very businesslike-looking gun, nestled in a holster just under his shoulder. Toby gulped. He hoped that he'd done the right thing. What if the man should just start taking out his gun and shooting people? He tried to take a grip on himself. That was ridiculous. Why should Tombstone do such a thing? Everyone carried guns in this country, especially gangsters. And Isabelle must have been friendly enough with Tombstone to go to his place last night and attempt to see him – no, she must have seen him, or he wouldn't be here tonight. Dear God, he thought, I hope I'm doing the right thing . . .

Suddenly, he thought of the henchmen. If they continued to stand there like two big gorillas, what on earth would the patrons think, in the intermission, if they saw them?

'Er . . . sir . . .' he said, carefully, 'perhaps you'd be as good as to ask your men to . . . to . . . not be so conspicuous, sir?'

The dark glasses looked in Toby's direction, the diamond smile flashed. 'Scare off the audience, would they, eh, son?' he said, and he sounded like the prospect pleased him. But to Toby's intense relief, he went swiftly to the door and spoke a few whispered words to the two goons, who retreated to a flashy car Toby could just see through the door.

Tombstone strode back to Toby. 'Now, then . . .'

'Come this way, sir,' said Toby meekly, and went to the theatre door. The ushers would be just inside; Toby slipped open the door, very quietly. It was very dark, but he could just about see the ushers. He motioned one of them over. 'One more patron,' he whispered. The usher nodded, Tombstone went in. 'This way, sir.' As the door closed, Toby took a deep breath. He could hear the beginning strains of Tom Nashe's violin solo. He must be ready to catch Isabelle as soon as she came off-stage, and before Uncle Theo came off.

She would come off in the opposite direction to where Toby was meant to be waiting with his prompt-book. Too bad. He'd have to risk it. He waited tensely as the speech trailed to a halt. He'd have at most a second between the gypsy girl skipping off-stage and Count Sebastian exiting in his turn.

There she was! He grabbed her, and whispered in her ear, 'Tombstone's here. At the back. If you want to get away, go now, I'll cover with Uncle Theo.'

'Don't be silly, I'm glad he's turned up,' was all she said, and then she rustled past him, leaving him feeling like a complete fool. Would he ever understand her? Would he ever—

'Toby! What the hell!' came Uncle Theo's fierce whisper. 'You're meant to be in the right wings, not the left, you idiot! How can you forget, tonight of all nights!'

'Sorry,' said Toby, and raced around the back to the other side. As he passed the open door of one of the dressing-rooms, he saw Madame Laroche, standing very straight and absolutely still, staring into the mirror. On her face was the same look he'd seen a couple of days previously, when she had her ghost-ridden fit: a look of utter terror, and horror.

She saw him in the mirror. Her face changed. She attempted a smile, and croaked, 'It's going well, Toby, is it not?'

'Madame,' he said with quick concern, 'are you all right?'

'I'm fine. Fine. Just had a bit of a . . . a dizzy spell,' she replied. 'Don't you worry about me. I'm sure you're needed.'

'If you're sure . . .' Toby flashed her a grateful smile and a nod and fled to the wings and the prompt-book, just in time to catch Olivia's first stumble.

Twenty-one

'It was excellent, sir, most excellent!' Clarence Wilson's booming voice would carry easily right into the street, thought Toby, smiling to himself. The big millionaire went on, 'I'm a plain man, sir, and I like things to be plainly done, easily understood, full of fight and fire! And that, sir, was your play! A romance, a melodrama – no basis in reality, of course, but a rattling good yarn!'

Uncle Theo was basking in the compliments. His smile was so huge it looked as though it might swallow his whole face. 'Oh, Mr Wilson, sir, you are too kind!'

'Ha! Never too kind!' said the press mogul. He strode around the theatre foyer, a small crowd following him. The play had ended to a great ovation more than an hour ago, but still people milled around excitedly, watching every move the Californian and his wife made. Mrs Wilson was herself at the centre of an admiring circle – Madame La Praline, and Madame Leonard, and Olivia, as well as several privileged members of the audience. Toby watched the antics with a mingled mixture of dismay and hilarity; it was dismaying to see everyone kowtowing, and yet funny, and thrilling too, because it meant the millionaire's enthusiasm might very well launch *Malvolio's Revenge* like a rocket, into Carnival festivities.

Everyone in the cast had been introduced to the Wilsons, but not all of them were in the foyer right now. Isabelle had pleaded a headache and asked to go back to the hotel, Madame Laroche in tow. Gabriel had also excused himself; he was tired, he said, but Toby knew it was because he was going to keep an eye on Isabelle, especially after he'd heard about Tombstone's visit to the theatre. He would have gone himself, but Uncle Theo wouldn't let him. And he'd looked for Tombstone, when the curtain fell, but the man must have slipped out just before or just as the play ended, for he was nowhere to be seen. Had he delivered his message to Isabelle? Toby was not sure, but would have been prepared to bet that he had. What kind of message had it been? He remembered, with a little tremor, what Isabelle had said about the albino: that he looked like an undertaker. If that was the case, what was he . . . ?

He came back to reality with a start. Mr Wilson had stopped in front of Violette de Castelon's painting of Malvolio in cross-garters. He pointed imperiously at it. 'What is this, Madame Blanche?'

The Terpsichore director looked puzzled. 'It's a scene from Shakespeare's *Twelfth Night*, Mr Wilson, and it—'

'No, no!' boomed Mr Wilson. 'You do not understand. I mean, do you own this painting, Madame Blanche?'

'Why, yes, I—'

'I wish to buy it, Madame Blanche.'

'Buy it, sir?' The talk had hushed, and everyone was staring at the little scene.

'Yes – I wish to buy it for my wife's birthday. As you know, *Twelfth Night* is her favourite play. I'll give you two hundred dollars for this painting, ma'am.'

'*Two hundred dollars?*' Madame Blanche gave a little gasp, as well she might; it was the price of a new car. She looked quickly at her brother, whose face was alight with cupidity. Then slowly, regretfully, she shook her head. 'I am sorry, sir. It is not for sale.'

'Not for sale?' The millionaire's laughter filled the room. 'Come, come, ma'am! Is there nothing I can say to persuade you?'

'It was painted by a dear friend of ours, Violette de Castelon, who is now dead,' said Madame Blanche, quietly. 'And we cannot sell it.'

Something flashed across the millionaire's face at that moment – annoyance? Admiration? Pity? Regret? Toby wasn't sure. Mr Wilson shook his head. 'I am sorry, then, Madame Blanche, for it would have had pride of place in our home back in California, ma'am. But I respect your decision; and because of it, I should like to put another proposition to you.' He looked proudly over at his wife. 'It was really Susanna's idea. You know we are to give a masked ball for Twelfth Night? You will not sell us your painting; but what do you say to us buying the entire theatre – and yes, your company too, Mr Trentham – for the next few days, till Twelfth Night?'

There was a dead silence for a few seconds. Then Monsieur Bruno said, in a voice made hoarse by emotion, 'Good God . . .'

'Now, now, Mr Bruno, no taking of the Lord's name in vain!' The millionaire wagged a playful finger. 'You all look stunned, my friends – but indulge me. Listen. I propose to commandeer the Terpsichore for the next few days because I want you to host my Twelfth Night ball. Now, Twelfth Night, my wife tells me, is a big occasion here in New Orleans. There are parades, parties, balls, shows. It's always the same. Now I, my friends, am a plain man – but I love a party. My dear wife loves a party even more. I want to shake this city up; I want to give a party like no other. Not in the usual stuffed-shirt places, but right here, in the Terpsichore.'

'But sir,' began Madame Blanche, 'did you not already have a venue . . . ?'

'Oh, pshaw! The New World theatre, in the Garden District

– a distinctly snobbish place. I refuse to kowtow to Creole pretensions. I'll give them a good pay-off, anyway. No. I'm quite determined. It shall be here.'

Anyone try and stop him, thought Toby, vastly amused and excited. What true gall the man had! No wonder he was so rich, with all that energy and crash-through style! I bet he can be a bully, though, too, he thought, sobered. I bet his staff live in fear of him, as well as in admiration . . .

'But, Mr Wilson,' said Uncle Theo, looking distinctly pale, 'we have a season of our play . . . we have playbills up . . . we have advertised. You cannot just close the theatre, sir! We will be out of business . . .'

'Oh, no, no, no, Mr Trentham!' Susanna Wilson gave a tinkling laugh. 'My husband has not explained properly. You are very much a part of this, dear Mr Trentham. What we propose is that your next performance be on Twelfth Night. We propose you give a command performance for us and all our guests, Mr Trentham. And in the meantime we will publicise your play in all our newspapers, won't we, Clarrie?'

'Indeed we will, my poppet,' said Wilson, fondly. 'I promise you, Mr Trentham, it will be well worth your trouble. Now here's the deal: we take over the theatre for the preparations; we will pay for the hire of the hall and for the fact you'll be standing idle – well, not idle, but without those extra performances, Mr Trentham. We'll have the play first, I think, then supper . . . Now, we'll have a good, solid menu: oysters and crab and shrimp and crawfish, followed by Westphalia ham, mutton, venison, chicken Marengo . . .'

The petulance had completely vanished from Susanna Wilson's vapidly pretty face. It was alight with a childish delight. 'Oh, and king-cakes, Clarrie!' she breathed, clasping her hands. 'We must have lots of them, with prizes inside, instead of beans.' King-cakes were a tradition of New Orleans Twelfth Night festivities – brightly iced yeast pastries, they contained within them a bean that, when found, bestowed the title of King or Queen of the day on the lucky finder.

'Why of course, yes, that as well.' The millionaire looked at Madame La Praline. 'I've been told you have a famous kitchen, ma'am, and make wonderful king-cakes.'

'Well, yes,' stammered the pension keeper, quite red under her powder, 'but we—'

'Don't worry, I'll send over hired staff to help yours,' said Mr Wilson. 'Now then, will it be agreeable for you to stage the play before supper, and the dancing, Mr Trentham?'

'Why, certainly,' said Uncle Theo, his words tripping over themselves. He looked dazed, and no wonder. 'Most agreeable indeed, Mr Wilson.'

'Good! And then after the supper, we will have the ball itself – a masked ball. We'll have a good orchestra – a decent full-piece one, nothing tainted with that awful black row they call jazz.'

Toby, remembering the music in the Rising Sun Saloon, felt sorry about that. It could've been fun, dancing to such pulsing music. Not that he'd likely get a chance to dance, anyway!

'Mr Wilson,' said Madame Blanche, very low. 'I . . . this is all wonderful, sir, but the idea to stage a supper and ball, sir! It . . .' Words seemed to fail her. She gestured around. 'There is no space, sir, much as we'd like . . .'

'Oh, Blanche!' Monsieur Bruno shook his head. 'There is the dance-hall next door. I am sure Mr Leroy – who owns the concern, Mr Wilson – would be more than agreeable to hiring out the space for the occasion.'

'Excellent idea!' Mr Wilson rubbed his hands. 'You are a man after my own heart, Mr Biche. Is there a communicating door between this theatre and the dance-hall, sir?'

'Yes, there is,' said Monsieur Bruno, happily.

'Excellent. Then all problems are solved!' He beamed at them, like a benevolent king showering bounty. 'You are very quiet, friends. What do you say?'

There was a chorus of voices, all speaking at once, all expressing immense pleasure, surprise, amazement. Toby met Tom Nashe's eye. The fiddler winked.

'What's the betting, this'll be in the *Bugle* and all the other organs of the press Mr Wilson owns,' he whispered to Toby, as they stood on the fringes of the excited crowd. 'And in every mansion as well as every hovel. A canny man, Mr Wilson –

he's earned himself the enduring attention of New Orleans society, in one stroke of dazzling genius.'

'He's earned us amazing publicity, too,' said Toby. 'Uncle Theo won't be able to sleep for days, he'll be jumping out of his skin with excitement.' He looked over at the millionaire. 'I suppose that's how you get to be so rich – you just do whatever you please.'

'I'm not sure it was always like that,' said Nashe, slowly. 'I'd say he denied himself a lot, at first. But now he's making up for lost time. There's one thing that puzzles me, though: why does he like your uncle's play so much? Don't look so cross, Toby, I don't mean to say it's bad; in fact, it's rather good. *Really*. I just mean – it's rather old-fashioned, and it has an old-fashioned moral. Malvolio's a steward made good, and cruel with it; and he's destroyed by his own wicked revenge, ground back to dust where he belongs. Hardly the sort of thing a self-made man could be expected to approve of.'

'I think it's his wife,' said Toby, thoughtfully. 'I think he's potty about her; he wants to please her; and it's her that likes the play. I think he probably doesn't give a hoot about our play, one way or the other. I saw him nodding off once or twice, in fact; he was actually snoring a little in Malvolio's death scene.'

Tom Nashe laughed. 'Why, that's priceless! Priceless indeed!' He looked at Toby, amused. 'Perhaps you would make a great detective after all, not just a writer.' Without waiting for an answer, he went on, 'I wonder how our reclusive friend Mr Harvey's going to react to this.'

'Gabriel will be pleased, of course, like—' began Toby, irritated, but before he could finish, Olivia came running over to him, face aglow. 'Toby! Mr Wilson wants to have a word with you!'

'Well, well,' said Nashe, smiling, 'looks like your fortune's made, my son. Just remember – ask him for an editorship, at least!'

'Don't be silly,' stammered Toby, but he couldn't help a little thrill of pleasure. Perhaps this was indeed the beginning of something big? Perhaps – you never knew – it might even launch him on a brilliant writing career? All thought of darkness, danger and Tombstone had quite left his head as he sauntered over – it didn't do to show too much eagerness – to see what Mr Wilson had in store for him.

Alas, it was just to give him instructions on how to get to the rented mansion occupied by the Wilsons, the very next day. It seemed he was going to play his good old role of dogsbody and errand-boy once again. Oh dear. Perhaps Wilson's first impression of Toby – of the meek little class-ridden dogsbody who automatically pulls at the forelock – was still dominating his thoughts. Toby was not a person after his own heart, he might think. Still, you never knew . . . maybe he'd be able to catch the millionaire's ear at some stage, and show him he really was different – really. Ambition had entered Toby's soul now, and he wasn't about to let any opportunity go by, especially an undreamed-of one such as this. But then, burning ambition had entered the soul of every member of the Trentham Troupe present. It would be a most pleasant sleep-fellow in all their dreams tonight.

ACT THREE

Twelfth Night

And so the whirligig of time brings in his revenges . . .

Twenty-two

The Wilsons' rented mansion came with a full complement of servants, from butler down to scullery staff, head groom down to stableboy. They would normally be a grand source of gossip for any visitor such as Toby, but because they were not the personal staff of the Wilsons, they knew precious little about their employers, only what they'd been able to observe for themselves. Mrs Wilson travelled with a personal maid, but Mr Wilson had not brought any personal servants with him, only a secretary, a colourless man named Guy Follett, who always wore white gloves, considered himself well above Toby's station and showed it quite plainly. The egalitarian Mr Wilson would not approve, thought Toby, spitefully, as the Follett creature rejected his overture of friendship once more; he acts as though his employer was only slightly lower in status than the President of the United States.

Since that first night at the Terpsichore, Toby had not seen the Wilsons to speak to, though he'd caught glimpses of them once or twice as they arrived at the theatre in their expensive saloon to discuss preparations for the Twelfth Night extravaganza. Two days had gone by since then, and there had been a great deal of activity at the Terpsichore, and the dance-hall next door. Wilson had been as good as his word; a variety of hired staff had been sent over to do all the work, and all that the excited owners of the Terpsichore and of the Famous Dance-Hall and the director of the Trentham Troupe had to do was sit closeted in endless discussions and plans about the night. Many curious sightseers had come cruising by, as Wilson's papers had all covered the exciting story of this unusual 'glittering occasion' – Joe Horn himself had even interviewed Theo Trentham for the *Bugle*. Invitations for 'Mr Trentham and family' kept arriving, and though these did not include the rest of the cast – or, indeed, Toby – it was felt that they gave a certain social cachet to people who might otherwise have simply been dismissed as 'just these theatrical folk'. Mind you, thought Toby, it was quite clear they had come from only certain sections of society – the old Creole families kept well away, and it was only the 'uptown crowd', as Madame La Praline called them with a wry lift of the eyebrow, and even then only those of a certain broadminded cast of thought, who took an interest in Mr Wilson's pet project. But there were more than enough of them – with more than enough money – to make up for any snubbing on the part of the rest. Besides, Wilson was clearly a hero to a great many humbler people – a living exemplar of the American Dream, perhaps – and it would do the theatre, and the play, no harm at all to be associated with such as he. Even the snobs couldn't quite dismiss a fascination with money, and money's whims.

It had been a strange couple of days, Toby reflected as he made his slow way back to the theatre in the click-clacking streetcar. Not only had he and the rest of the troupe been whirled into a fairytale, but it had quite overshadowed everything else. Despite the activity at the theatre, it seemed to Toby as if there had been a kind of pause in all other action. Nothing at all had happened on the murder mystery front; Gabriel had showed up at Klondike's house the day after first night only to be told that the gambler had gone away to the country for a few days. His house was shut up tight as an oyster, with flunkies watching every entrance and exit. Gabriel had said he had not thought it prudent to try his luck.

Meanwhile, Isabelle had shown no sign of being in a hurry to learn more, or of being dismayed at Klondike's absence; indeed, she seemed rather detached, and avoided conversation, for the most part. Yet she did not seem unhappy, only a little remote. When Toby had challenged her about the purpose of Tombstone's visit, she had simply raised her eyebrows and said, 'Why, he just came to tell me his brother would be away for a few days.'

Toby wasn't convinced. 'Why come in person to tell you that?'

'That's Tombstone,' she shrugged. 'He can be . . . er, rather dramatic. He likes the effect he has on people. Besides, because he's an albino, he can play tricks with those Jim Crow segregation laws. Coloured people aren't meant to sit in the same theatres as white folks. It rather tickled him, to sit in the theatre with an unknowing all-white audience. He has a strange sense of humour.'

Toby thought of that now. Strange indeed, he thought. If Tombstone had a sense of humour, it would be a macabre one, to go with his name and appearance, not a playfully rebellious kind. No, he wasn't altogether convinced about Isabelle's explanation, but as she made no attempt to go off on more unheralded excursions of her own, but stayed within the confines of hotel and theatre, and as Klondike did really seem to be away, there was nothing much more that could be done till the gangster got back. Madame Laroche kept to the servants' quarters in the hotel, and seemed content helping the cook to prepare the king-cakes that had been ordered; though her eyes appeared to swim more than ever behind the disfiguring glasses, and she seemed a little stiff and weakened, she did not have a recurrence of the uncanny fit she had suffered from. As to Gabriel, he was quite preoccupied, not disposed to talk; Toby had heard him pacing about in the dressing-room at the theatre, going over his speeches quite obsessively, in a way that made Toby think that ambition had even – at last – burned into the actor's soul too.

Later, he would think of those couple of days of lull as the calm before the storm hit with blinding force; but at the time, they were pleasant enough. And they, and the long streetcar rides he had to take between the theatre and the Wilson mansion, gave him the opportunity to look more at the city, and the people who lived in it. It gave him a sense of freedom he'd never had before. He purchased himself a little notebook, and jotted down observations, and ideas, and even little sketches of places he found interesting and picturesque. His first story should be set in New Orleans, he thought, and it would feature millionaires and paupers, theatre folk and society beauties. There would be a murder mystery . . . the killing of an odd, murderous villain with a macabre name, like Tombstone – except he'd call him something else, like, like . . . the Reaper, or something like that. He would have to disguise all the names. Perhaps he should even give the city another name, too, one that was close enough to it – like, like New Paris. Yes! That would be excellent! His pencil flew busily across the paper.

The streetcar lurched to a stop. Some people got on. From his seat in a middle row, Toby saw a familiar face – the child Louis, behind an imposing old black lady who looked like she might be his grandmother. He looked rather different to the street urchin Toby was accustomed to – he was dressed very neatly, his hair slicked back, his face solemn and well scrubbed. He was probably on his way to church.

As they went past, Toby said, brightly, 'How are you, Satchelmouth?'

A delighted grin spread over the boy's face. 'You remembered . . .' he began, when the old lady turned around and gave him a clip on the ear. 'I've told you before, Louis, not to talk to strangers,' she said, very clearly, and sending Toby a glare, dragged the child off down the back, to the coloured people's seating. Toby blushed a little at the curious glances of his fellow-passengers, and bent to his notebook. But the back of his neck prickled with feelings he had never really had before. He hadn't thought; he had acted just as he wanted to. He had forgotten about the colour bar – forgotten, because *he* never really had to worry about it, and Louis was young and merry enough to forget it too, sometimes. But not his grandmother – a lifetime of Jim Crow must have made her wary and protective in public.

He got off at the next stop, though it was still a certain distance away from the theatre. The little encounter had thrown discomfort into a mild, sunny day that had started off most pleasantly. New Orleans was a beautiful city, he thought, but that was a horrible thing about it, the Jim Crow stuff. Now he thought about it, he could see all the signs so boldly:

all the signs that said, 'Coloureds Only'; or 'Whites Only'; or 'No Coloureds Allowed Here'; or 'Exclusively for Coloureds', and so on. How stupid and shameful it was! What had been the point of abolishing slavery, then, if people were still not free?

His steps had taken him towards the Mississippi. And there it was, the river that was so big it almost looked like the sea. It stretched in front of him, the river that was the stuff of legend; the river that had carried Indian tribes and French adventurers and Spanish grandees and American carpetbaggers . . . the river whose voice sang in the melancholy music of the plantation slaves, whose roar rang in the echoing cemeteries where every tomb had to be above ground; the river that had brought immense riches and slavery and deathly sickness; that had ferried souls of all kinds, from the angelic to the diabolical, and every shade in between. It was a shape-shifter, an elemental actor: it could look sinister, grand, blank, frightening or magnificent. Today, it looked benign and sparkling, blue and gaudy, almost tinselly, as if preparing itself for the beginning of Carnival on Twelfth Night. The river-boats that plied up and down its shining length looked touched with that same gaudy magic today, as if they were mere festive ornaments themselves.

What a strange place New Orleans is, thought Toby, as his steps took him downriver, back towards the French Quarter and the Terpsichore. Wicked and beautiful, sad and charming, it's put a spell on me, I do believe; I'd never have thought those kinds of things before, I'm sure. I'd have looked at the river and seen just a sheet of water . . .

'Toby.' He started violently; it was Isabelle.

'Toby, what are you doing here?'

'Taking a walk,' he said, recovering from his surprise. 'Coming home the long way.'

She nodded. 'It's a beautiful river, isn't it?'

'Yes. I'd love to sail on it, to take one of those river-boats, right to the delta . . .'

'Would you? So would I. But I'd like to sail right out, into the ocean, sail far away from here . . .'

'What?' He looked at her. 'You'd really want to leave Louisiana? But I thought . . . Illyria . . .'

A shadow darkened her face. 'Yes. I know. It's a dream, that's all.'

He could have kicked himself. 'Oh, no! There's no reason for it to be a dream. Isabelle, we could—'

'Don't, Toby,' she said, very distinctly. 'You promised.'

'Did I?' What a fool he was! 'Sorry. I didn't mean—'

'Sshh, Toby.' She put a finger to his lips and smiled at him, very sadly. 'I am so glad for you; for you, and your kind uncle, and all the cast, everyone. So glad.' She looked away, at the river. 'It's wonderful when dreams come true. I think Maminou was wrong when she said your coming to our door was a good thing for us; hush, Toby, let me finish. It was a good thing for you – we were the instruments of your good fortune. Don't look so sad, Toby, I am really glad for that. But I do not think the dream was meant for us.'

'What do you mean?' said Toby, frightened.

'I mean, that we should part company. You do not need us any longer; we should go back to Illyria.'

'What?' Toby's skin felt cold all over, his throat choked with tears. 'You can't do that!'

'Don't worry, I'll play my part on Twelfth Night,' she said, misunderstanding him deliberately. 'I'll not let you down. But after that, Maminou and I will go back to Illyria, where we belong.'

He stared at her set face. What had the old witch said, to make her take such a decision?

He said, coldly, 'What about your father's murder?'

'What about it?' she said, softly. 'He is dead; so is my mother; nothing will bring them back. Klondike knows no more than anyone else. It was just a dream, Toby; a dream, to try and give some meaning to the wretched past.'

'Has she spellbound you or something?' said Toby, angrily. 'She's made you as frightened of shadows as she is.'

She looked back at him. 'You don't understand, do you, Toby? It's not Maminou who has persuaded me; it is myself. And . . . and Gabriel,' she added, after a short silence, looking away at the river again.

Toby felt as if his heart would stop. He stammered, 'What . . . do you mean?'

'I had a long talk with Gabriel,' she said, still without looking at him. 'The other night, when you . . . when you stayed at the theatre.' Into her eyes came something very like terror, and Toby remembered what Gabriel had said: that he could 'put the fear of God' into people if he chose to. His hands shook. He said, 'What did he say to you?'

'I can't really tell you, Toby. I'm sorry.'

Fury filled him. 'Why can't you tell me? Did he make you promise?' There was no answer, so he took that as assent. He said, sharply, 'I bet I know, anyway.' So this was how Gabriel thought he could protect Isabelle, by 'putting the fear of God' into her! 'You don't want to believe everything Gabriel says; half the time, I don't know if he's making things up or not.'

She looked at him. 'Don't you?'

He tried to calm down. 'No. You have to take it with a grain of salt. Gabriel's a strange one . . .'

'I've never met anyone like him before,' she said, simply. He stared at her. The terror in her eyes had been replaced by . . . what? He didn't really want to know. But he could not stop himself from asking, 'Isabelle . . . Isabelle . . . you don't . . . you don't *care* for Gabriel, do you?'

'Care for him?' she said. 'Care for him? Tell me, Toby: is there any woman alive who could *care* for Gabriel – so that he'd notice?' Her eyes were glowing, feverish, disturbing.

He said, through a lump in his throat, 'No, I don't suppose there could be. Not really. He doesn't really live in the same world as most of us, Isabelle. He doesn't have the same feelings as most human beings, not really.'

'I think you are right,' she said, and fell silent for a little while, gazing out at the river. Then she said, without turning her head, 'Yes, I think you're right. And you've brought me to my senses, Toby. I had let him persuade me. I had let him . . . let him almost frighten me into doing so. But now I've changed my mind.' She turned to him now, and he saw there was a faint smile on her face. 'Toby, I'll not go back to Illyria; I'll stay here, in New Orleans, in the Trentham Troupe. I'm not too bad at acting, am I, Toby?'

'You're very good,' he said eagerly, grasping her hand. She slipped it out again, gently. 'You're a natural actress, Isabelle.'

'Am I?' she smiled. 'That's good to know. Gabriel said I was very bad.'

'Gabriel doesn't know anything,' said Toby hotly. 'He's away somewhere else in his mind, Gabriel is. Forget what he said.' He'd have it out with the Irishman as soon as he got back to the theatre, he thought, angrily. What the Devil did he think he was playing at? This was no way to protect Isabelle. He went on, fervently, 'And I don't think you should just forget about your father's murder, either. I think the truth must come out, and justice has to be done.'

'Do you, Toby?' This time, it was she who grasped his

hand. 'It is good to hear you say that. Everyone else has been against it — even Klondike. I've been feeling so discouraged . . .' She trailed off as she saw Toby's baffled expression.

'I thought you said he was determined to help you track the killer!'

'Well, I thought that's what he *would* want,' she said uneasily. 'But that's the message he sent via Tombstone, you see — that he thought we should let sleeping dogs lie, and not disturb them. He said sometimes it was better to let the dead rest in peace, even the violently despatched dead.'

'Maybe the old lady — your nurse — maybe she did persuade him after all.'

Isabelle stared. 'Maminou? Oh, maybe. But I think that it's because he is a businessman. Even gangster businessmen have the same impulses as the law-abiding sort; they don't want unnecessary disturbances to their business. I think that he's afraid that stirring all these things up will cause problems for him.'

'And is that his final word?'

She nodded.

'What about Tombstone?'

'He wouldn't go against Klondike. Not openly, anyway.'

'And secretly?'

'I don't know, Toby.'

Toby made a decision. 'Listen, Isabelle, the other day I

went to the newspaper office, and this is what I found . . .' Swiftly, he told her about the razored photograph, and the gist of the articles. He finished by telling her what Gabriel had said. She nodded, slowly. The shadow had lifted from her face. 'I see.'

'I think he thought you had to be stopped in your tracks, that that was the only way to protect you from whatever it is he thinks is threatening you,' he said, fairly.

'I don't need protection!' she said fiercely. 'I can take care of myself. Haven't I, for years?'

He didn't say, no, your nurse did that. How could he say it to this wonderful girl, this girl he loved? Instead, he said, 'We're not ghost-ridden like him and your nurse, are we, Isabelle? And if he thinks you've really had the fear of God put into you, and that no one will help us, and as he's preoccupied with his role at the moment, we might just have an opportunity.'

'Oh, yes, Toby!' Her face was alight. 'You could say that Mr Wilson has requested my presence at their mansion. I could go with you . . . but slip away, find Tombstone, and ask him for his help. He might, while Klondike's away. Oh, Toby! You can't know what this means to me.'

'Oh, I think I do,' he said, heartened by her warm tone.

'Tomorrow morning, first thing, then?'

'Tomorrow morning, first thing,' he agreed. He was a little uneasy about Gabriel – and about Madame Laroche – but it couldn't be helped. Isabelle and Toby might not have the supernatural skills of those other two, but they had a very human capacity for lying and dissimulation. Gabriel would think that Toby was still just keeping watch over Isabelle, as they'd agreed; he'd have no idea Isabelle would tell him everything, because he doesn't realise how much we understand each other, thought Toby. And what we both understand is that there are some sleeping dogs you can't just let lie, but must creep up on when they aren't looking, and trap once and for all. Because you can't be a coward all your life, and run from danger and hidden shadows, but must confront them full on, and stare the truth in the face, or else you couldn't live, not really, not properly, not like a proper human being. Who wanted to creep about the world like Gabriel and Madame Laroche, scared of and resigned to evil and injustice?

Twenty-three

She was waiting for him bright and early the next morning. When he came out of his room, still tousled from sleep, she said, eagerly, 'Well? Did you arrange it?'

'Sure. I told Uncle Theo that Mrs Wilson had taken a fancy to you, as a charity case, and wanted you to pick through some of her cast-offs. The servants told me Mrs Wilson has a thing about orphans – apparently she was one herself – and so I thought that'd be a convincing explanation. Uncle Theo was delighted by the thought. He had tears in his eyes!'

'Oh, Toby!' Isabelle said, laughing, linking an arm with one of his, to his secret thrill. She seemed full of high spirits. 'You're just as good an actor as the rest of them!'

'Hardly,' he said, laughing in his turn.

* * *

As they hurried along, Toby said to Isabelle, 'Will you let me come with you to Tombstone's? Please?'

'Of course,' she said, and smiled, a meltingly warm smile that had Toby's knees turning to jelly. 'We're partners in crime detection now, Toby, aren't we?'

'Oh, yes!' he said fervently, quickly revising his story idea in his mind. His detective character – Roger the Dodger would be his name – would be accompanied by a beautiful, brave female detective, who always carried a pearl-handled revolver in her bag. Her name would be—

'This is the street!' said Isabelle gaily, motioning to him to hurry. Toby followed in a great clumsy rush, still pondering on his idea. Her name would be Mirabel, he thought happily. Mirabel the Marvel, perhaps?

Then the story vanished like smoke from his mind as they turned the corner and there they were – in Tombstone's street. He could see the same goon standing at the entrance to the archway: the flat-faced man with little piggy eyes. He whispered to Isabelle as they approached, 'Why do gangsters always have to employ such ugly men?'

She snorted with laughter. 'Do you think that handsome ones would have the same effect? Besides, a truly ugly man, who knows he's ugly and suffered from it, hates the world; he's mean to his own reflection in the mirror, let alone those who get in his way. There's nothing like humiliation to make a man full of hatred.'

'That's true,' said Toby. 'That's probably why they make good henchmen: if their boss treats them well, they'll be full of fanatical loyalty to him if no one else.'

'That's the general theory, I think,' said Isabelle. 'Of course, it doesn't always work. You can't always judge a book by its cover, Toby. Oh, good morning, Oliver,' she said, very sweetly, to the big thug. 'I've come to see Mister Tombstone again.'

The flat-faced man she'd called Oliver swung his head in Toby's direction. 'Who he?'

'He's my friend Toby,' she said, pertly. 'Mister Tombstone knows him – Toby gave him a ticket to the play the other day.'

'Oh, right,' said the goon. The unreadable eyes stared unblinking at Toby. 'Mister Tombstone enjoyed that play, so he told me,' he said, at last. He shot out a hand and grabbed Toby, who gave a yell.

'Don't worry,' said Isabelle, smiling faintly. 'He's just going to frisk you, as they say. Can't let you go in without checking you're not carrying a gun, can you, Oliver?'

The big man nodded, without speaking or smiling. Carrying a gun? Me? thought Toby, both outraged and delighted.

'Lift your arms,' grunted Oliver, and Toby did as he was told. He looked over at Isabelle, and thought how beautiful she looked, even under the gypsy girl disguise; how alive and bright, her eyes glittering and dancing. She was in her element, he thought with a little, pleasurable shock; she likes danger and gangsters and excitement. Maybe that's what her father was like . . .

'Right,' said Oliver, finishing. 'Follow me.' He turned and went in under the archway, Isabelle and Toby at his heels. Beyond was a pleasant courtyard, with a little fountain in the centre, and a few bougainvillea shrubs. Oliver took them straight through the courtyard, through a door at the far end. Up a flight of stairs, and then another, and then down a long corridor to a closed door. Oliver knocked; once, twice, in two short raps, then one longer one. A voice called out, 'Yes?'

'Monsieur, it's the girl. And a friend of hers. The boy from the theatre.'

A silence, then Tombstone's voice came again. 'Very well. Show them in.'

Oliver opened the door and ushered them inside. He closed the door and took up a position beside it.

Toby stared. Tombstone, in his usual all-black clothes, but without his dark glasses, was sitting at a desk in an amazing room. Everything was white, pure white: painted floorboards, rugs, desk, white cane chairs and couch scattered with white velvet cushions, and white-on-white wallpaper. A fringed and beaded white table lamp gave the room light, and on one wall was a single picture, quite the strangest picture he had ever seen. It was a blown-up photograph of Tombstone himself, standing straight and tall, top hat on head, cane in one hand, staring into the camera. But the photo was in negative, so that his face and hands were that strange, smoky-blue photographic-negative black, and his funereal clothes and hat and cane were transformed into ghostly white.

'You like me as Baron Samedi, son?' Tombstone said.

Toby started. 'Sorry, sir, I don't know who . . .'

'The voodoo Lord of Death, Toby,' Isabelle explained, a little impatiently. She didn't seem in the least bit overawed by the room, or Tombstone's presence.

The albino smiled at her. 'You are in a hurry, Mademoiselle de Castelon?' He laid ironic stress on the title, but in so subtle a way that Toby couldn't decide if it was good-humoured or warning. It didn't faze Isabelle in the least, anyway.

'You know I am, Tombstone,' she said.

'While the cat's away, the mice play, eh?'

'You're as much cat as your brother, Mister Tombstone,' she said, brightly. Toby winced. He wondered how much it took to offend the gangster. But he didn't seem at all offended, only amused. He got up from the desk and came towards them.

'And you're the darnedest mouse I ever met, Miss la Creole,' he said softly, looking into her eyes, 'but you know I do not like to go against my brother.'

'Creditable family feeling,' said Isabelle, looking back fearlessly into those strange pink eyes, 'but I know you and me, Mister Tombstone, we share something else.'

'Oh?' he said, and put a gloved hand under her chin, tipping up her face to his. Toby felt a wave of anger and revulsion flow over him, but he knew he must not move, must not say anything, must not betray by a flicker of emotion what he was feeling. Isabelle was playing a dangerous game, but one she had to play. He fought down his feelings and managed to present a blank expression as the gangster searched the girl's face with his unearthly gaze.

'You and I share the conviction that betrayal and dishonour must be punished with death,' Isabelle said, in a voice that only had a slight tremor in it.

'Yes,' said Tombstone, softly. 'And so?'

'And so, Mister Tombstone, I have come to ask of you – as a man of honour – what you would give any petitioner who came to you. I ask only that you do your business in the usual way. I ask only that you treat me as you would treat any other customer, regardless of what you know about me, or what your brother has told you.'

Toby's blood ran cold. What was she saying? What was she asking? He did not dare to move, or look around, especially when Tombstone jerked his head towards him. 'And what of him?' said the gangster, mildly.

'He is the only one who understands – apart from you, Mister Tombstone.'

'I see,' said Tombstone, and dropping his hand from Isabelle's chin, he looked at Toby. The red eyes raked into

234

him. 'I see,' he said again, and smiled, faintly. Toby was sure he could see the depths of Toby's love for Isabelle, written in his eyes. He wanted to tear away from that gaze, afraid that somehow it would turn his love to stone, but could not. His throat felt tight and sore, but he managed to croak out, 'Sir, I would do anything to help Isabelle. Anything. I believe in her quest, absolutely.'

Tombstone nodded, smiling broadly. 'Well, well. The old things are not yet dead, eh? The knight in shining armour lives again in a shabby theatre boy.' All at once, he clapped Toby on the shoulder. 'I like you, son. My brother's right. You've got guts, and heart. Take care, though. Take care.' He motioned to the silent Oliver. 'Fetch it, will you, Ollie?'

The goon went out of the room. Tombstone returned to his desk. He took out a silver cigarette case and, opening it, held it out to Toby, who shook his head, as politely as he could. 'Thank you, sir, I don't smoke.'

'Very wise,' said Tombstone, lighting up. 'They'll be the slow death of you, given time.' He laughed, and blew a puff of smoke. 'Me, I'm in no hurry.'

Isabelle said, 'Tombstone, what will you . . . what will you tell your brother, when he comes back?'

Tombstone looked at her. 'The truth,' he said, negligently. 'I never lie to my brother. He was practically like my father, Toby, did you know that? Did she tell you? I wasn't brought up like him in the bosom of Tante Marie, sharing escapades and books with the Baron de Castelon . . . no, by the time I was old enough to be abandoned by our mother in my turn, my wild brother had been given his marching orders by my aunt. Yet it was he who made me learn to read, taught me history, philosophy, and how to survive in this wicked world. He worked a protection racket for old Dr Hook in the days, and in the nights he was my tutor, in our shabby room above the Rising Sun . . .' He saw Toby's rapt expression, and laughed. 'Like the picture, kid? Matter of fact, it'd make a good romance, don't you think?'

Toby nodded, not sure whether the gangster meant he'd actually been romancing, or telling the truth.

'Matter of fact,' said Tombstone, 'I think I—' But whatever he'd been about to say never got finished, for at that moment, Oliver came back into the room with a black box in his hands. He handed it to Tombstone, who gave it to Isabelle.

'I think this is what you were after,' he said lightly. Isabelle's eyes widened. Without speaking, she unclipped the clasp of the case – and there, nestled in dark red velvet, was a revolver. Not the tiny pearl-handled one of Toby's imagination, but fairly small, still, with a shining, dark wooden grip that looked like it might be walnut, and delicate floral engraving on the frame, cylinder and barrel.

'Oh, Tombstone!' said Isabelle quietly.

'It's French,' said the gangster. 'Lefaucheux, 1880s or so – I guessed it would be the closest thing to the one your mother had. Besides, I thought the gunsmith's name was appropriate – "the reaper", who comes for us all.' He paused, and went on, 'You have to be careful, with these babies, as with all revolvers – they have a high rate of fire, but reloading's slow. This one's not too bad, but you have to be sure you know what you're doing. Do you?'

'Of course.' She stroked the metal of the gun. 'Tombstone, how can I ever—'

'Don't thank me,' he said sharply. 'Not till it's proven itself.'

'The money—' she began, but he cut her short. 'We'll discuss that later. Afterwards. You understand?'

'Oh, Tombstone!' she said, and leaning towards him, she kissed him on the cheek. He stiffened, then relaxed. 'Now get out of here, girl, before I change my mind. You too, son.'

Toby had been silent through all this, struck dumb by the sight of the revolver, and by what the others had said. Now, motioning at the revolver, he burst out with, 'But I don't understand! What is *this* for, Isabelle?'

Tombstone and Isabelle exchanged a glance. Isabelle said gently, 'Why, it's for my protection, Toby. Because you see, I think I know who the killer of my father is . . . and I mean to lay a trap for him.'

Toby felt all the blood drain from his face. 'Who . . . who is it? Do you mean to say you've seen him here, in New Orleans?'

Tombstone said smoothly, 'It would seem so, wouldn't it,

son? Now, get out of here, both of you, and conduct your discussions elsewhere. And remember what I said, Mam'zelle dear. Oliver, escort them out.'

Out in the street, and out of Oliver's earshot, Toby rounded on Isabelle. 'Why didn't you tell me before? Don't you trust me?'

'Of course I do,' she said, vaguely. She had the case with its deadly cargo in her hand, and a pleased smile on her face; Toby could see her mind was far away.

'But you can't, if you haven't told me something as important as that!' he wailed.

She sighed. 'Look, Toby, I don't think you quite understand. My life – my experience – has been nothing like yours. I'm sorry if I've not been able to tell you everything, but I've learned not to betray my confidences. Not even to Maminou, these days.'

'But I love you! I'd do anything for you . . .'

'So would she,' said Isabelle quietly. 'But she thinks she knows what's best for me. And so do you, I suppose. And others, too . . .' She broke off, then went on, sharply, 'What none of you realise is that I might know what's best for me. I might actually know what I'm doing!'

'I never said you didn't—' Toby began.

She interrupted him. 'You never said, but you imply it, with all these questions, these recriminations. Look, Toby. I said I think I know who the killer of my father is; but I'm not sure. Not quite yet. I need to know. I need to lay a trap for him; but I know he's likely to be dangerous, if his secret is discovered, after all these years. And so I need something to protect myself . . .'

'But why this one? Why this one in particular? From what Tombstone said . . .'

'Tombstone likes symbols and images. You saw his room. He should have been a film star, not a gangster. Perhaps he would be, if it wasn't for Jim Crow. Forget what Tombstone said. This revolver will do what I want it to: it will put the fear of God into the killer, and be insurance for me.'

'But if this man — are you going to tell me who it is? — has killed once, why should he hesitate to kill again? What chance do you have against him?'

'You want to see?' said Isabelle, smiling strangely. 'You want to see if I can use a gun or not?' She made as if to take the revolver from out of its case, but Toby stopped her.

'Are you crazy? You can't fire a gun in broad daylight in the street!'

'You don't know New Orleans, then,' she said lightly, but she tucked the case under her arm. 'Don't worry, Toby — I know how to shoot, it's one of the accomplishments of my kind.'

'For God's sake!' Toby was furious, frightened and elated,

all at the same time. 'You should hide that thing away. Someone might see.'

'Sure thing,' said Isabelle, grinning at him. 'Are you scared, Toby?'

'Course I'm not!' he yelped indignantly. After a pause, he went on, 'But you said we were partners in crime detection. You've got to tell me who you suspect, at least, if we're really partners, or I might found a new agency.'

'Very well,' she said, seriously. 'I'll tell you . . . but you must promise to keep it a secret.'

'Of course I promise!'

'I think it was the head groom at Illyria, a man named Malpence,' she said. Toby stared at her. Whatever he'd been expecting, it wasn't this . . . this *ordinary* revelation.

'Are you sure?' he said.

'I told you I wasn't sure! That's what I've got to be sure of!'

'But . . . I don't understand. Why would a groom kill your father?'

'He was a jealous and wicked man; a man who pretended to be good but whose heart was black as night. He fancied himself in love with my mother, and he pressed himself on her, most unpleasantly. My . . . my father found out, beat him half to death, and threw him off the plantation. He returned months later . . . and killed my father, making it look like suicide. He was a clever man, Malpence.'

'Oh, my God,' gasped Toby. 'But . . . but you say *was* . . . Is he dead? He can't be – you said you saw him in New Orleans . . .'

'I didn't say I saw him. It was you who said so.'

'But you have, haven't you?'

'Yes.'

'Where?'

'I prefer not to say,' said Isabelle. 'Just . . . just in case I'm wrong about the man I saw, and Malpence is really dead . . . as we thought, because after my parents' deaths, he vanished without a trace.'

'Oh, my God,' said Toby again, heavily. 'It was probably him, then, who razored out that photograph in the newspaper.'

'Possibly,' said Isabelle.

'What do you mean, possibly? Of course it was him! Look, Isabelle . . . I wish you'd tell me who—'

'No,' she said, shaking her head, firmly. 'I might be quite wrong, and target an innocent man. I have to be quite, quite sure before I—' She broke off, but Toby thought he knew what she was going to say.

'You can't really be thinking of shooting him!' he whispered. 'Oh, Isabelle! You can't do that! It would be murder, and you'd go to gaol, no matter who he was, and what he'd done!'

'Who said I was going to shoot him?' she said, rather

evasively. 'You're romancing, Toby. No, I want to make him confess – to confess fully to the truth, to write it down, so the world will know. After that – well, it's up to the world. I only got the gun so I can frighten him with it. Why would I want to go to gaol for that worthless piece of rubbish?'

Toby swallowed. 'But Isabelle . . . a man like that is bound to be desperate. He will certainly be dangerous.' He paused, and went on in a rush, 'Gabriel told you what he saw, didn't he? I mean . . . the . . . the . . .'

'The ghost at my shoulder?' She shrugged. 'Yes, he told me. It . . . it impressed me when he told me, but now I can see it was just his way of keeping control of me, of stopping me from doing what I wanted. Him . . . and Maminou, they're in it together.'

'I don't think it was just that,' said Toby desperately. 'I think . . . I think he really saw something, Isabelle.'

'You said it was just a story, yesterday,' said Isabelle, rather haughtily. 'Now you want to control me too, don't you, Toby? You're scared. It's all too real now, isn't it?'

'Stop it,' he said miserably. 'I only want to make sure you're safe. I think if this man – this killer you want to trap – if he gets wind of what you know, of what you want to do . . . well, I think you're going to be in very great danger.'

'I told you, I can take care of myself,' she said. 'It's true, Toby, not just something I say. Life hasn't always been safe at

Illyria. There are cut-throats and bandits roaming the roads who think two women alone in a big house are fine and easy prey. Maminou taught me to defend myself from a very early age; you do not need to worry about me.' She paused. 'I shot a burglar in the leg, once; he bled to death before we could do anything to save him.'

Toby took a step back. She smiled rather sadly. 'It doesn't fit your picture of me, does it, Toby? I didn't intend to kill that man, but he would have killed us, cheerfully, without compunction. He was armed to the teeth. It was just sheer luck I got him first. And sheer luck I got him in a vital artery, so that there was nothing to be done. I shed no tears over him; would you have done?'

'No,' stammered Toby, 'but . . .'

'But nothing. I would have preferred to have the police deal with him, but that was not what happened.' She smiled. 'Word must have got around the outlaw fraternity after that. We were never bothered again.'

'Lord,' said Toby weakly. It sounded just like the Wild West stories in the magazines, he thought. What a one Isabelle was! A woman in a million, taking on burglars and killers and outlaws without turning a hair!

'Don't goggle at me like that,' said Isabelle lightly. 'It makes me feel uncomfortable.'

Toby flushed. 'Sorry.'

'Maybe we should go to the Wilsons' mansion now and see

if we can find a cast-off or two to back up our story,' said Isabelle pertly.

Toby stared at her an instant, totally at sea. Then he remembered. 'Oh, dear, that's right! But you can't just walk in and get cast-offs, just like that . . . No, don't let's worry about it. No one will notice, they're all too excited. Uncle Theo won't even remember, I'll wager.'

'You should know him best,' she said, and linked her free arm in his, gently. 'Oh, Toby! You've been so wonderful, I can't thank you enough!'

'No need for thanks,' he said gruffly, trying to still the drumbeat of his heart.

Twenty-four

Toby was right: Uncle Theo didn't notice. And no wonder; the theatre was in uproar, the last touches being made to the décor for the following day. When Toby and Isabelle scuttled in, the communicating door between theatre and dance-hall was off its hinges, the doorway decorated with gaudy floral motifs and tinsel of various shades. You could see right into the dance-hall's cavernous interior. It had been transformed, for the ordinary walls had vanished behind screens of painted backcloths depicting fanciful classical scenes: nymphs in gardens, fauns poking their heads up from fringes of leaves, and so on. The stage for the orchestra had been decorated in lengths of bunting and tinsel, with some plaster pillars at either end. A long table decked in purple and gold – apparently the colours Mr Wilson's racehorses competed under, back home in California – was ready to be set for the supper, with fanciful plates and goblets that looked like they'd come out of a masquerade shop. It all looked most vulgar, but most cheerful, and Toby thoroughly approved of it.

He was peering in at this scene when a hand fell on his shoulder. He turned. It was Gabriel.

'Oh, it's you,' he said, trying to sound casual. He looked around for Isabelle, but she had vanished. Good, he thought. 'Doesn't it look grand in here, Gabe?'

'Toby,' said Gabriel, ignoring the delights of the ballroom, 'where were you, just now? I've been looking for you.'

'I had to go to the Wilsons',' said Toby, quickly. 'I took Isabelle too – don't worry, I kept an eye on her.'

Gabriel looked a bit evasive. 'Did you? Good.' He doesn't know I know, thought Toby. He doesn't know I know he tried to scare Isabelle off her quest. He thinks I think we're just doing what we said before. Well, at least his gift doesn't extend to mind-reading. That'd be a curse, all right – for everyone else!

'You should see the Wilsons' mansion,' chattered Toby, trying to sound quite normal. 'It's just vast, and they have all these—'

'Toby,' broke in Gabriel, unceremoniously, 'there's something I've got to tell you. Or rather, that Madame Laroche told me, and which I think you should know.' He motioned into the dance-hall. 'Let's go in here. It's quieter.'

Once in there, he pulled Toby aside and said, 'She's very ill, you know, Toby; she's got a very bad fever; they've had the doctor in this morning, and she may well have to be taken to hospital.'

'Oh,' said Toby. 'Poor thing . . .'

'She told me last night . . . She knows who Isabelle is after; it's a man who was once employed at Illyria.'

Toby stared at Gabriel, trying to will shock and surprise into his face. 'What?'

'Yes. And you know how we thought the clue might have been in the razored-out photograph? Well, she says this man, like all staff, usually took part in the production. She said she thought he was Malvolio that year.'

This time, Toby didn't have to fake surprise. 'Malvolio!'

Gabriel's smile was rather wintry. 'The very same. Nicely ironic, isn't it? She said she thought it was the first time he'd played that part.'

'So he wouldn't have been in Klondike's picture . . .'

'Maybe he would have been. She said she couldn't be sure . . . though I'm not sure, Toby, if she's telling me the absolute truth.'

Are any of us doing that to each other? thought Toby, confusedly. Aloud, he said,

'Blimey, Gabe . . . did she say where he was, this man?'

Gabriel fixed Toby with a dark stare. 'She said he was here, in New Orleans. And she said she felt sure he'd be amongst the crowd at the Twelfth Night Ball, tomorrow night. She said she knew that because she could feel the presence of the Baron de Castelon very strongly; that he was rising up from the grave to accuse his killer . . .'

Toby gave an involuntary shiver. He stammered, 'Why doesn't she tell us who he is?'

'Because I don't think she *knows*, Toby. You can't, necessarily, not with this kind of . . . gift. You only see incomplete things. She said she's tried everything to stop the spirit of the Baron from breaking the bonds of death, but she cannot; it's too strong, and dark, and determined. She said it's followed us to New Orleans . . . and that it will not rest until it has had its revenge.'

'Good Lord,' breathed Toby. In a flash, he had a picture of Isabelle, standing at the tomb . . . and then, with the revolver under her arm, eyes alive with anticipation, with glee, even. He'd thought then, that's what her father might have been like . . . He whispered, 'But a ghost . . . a ghost can't kill anyone . . .'

Gabriel looked at him strangely. 'Of course it can,' he said. He leaned up against the door. 'It's nearly killed poor Madame Laroche . . . And a living man can certainly kill a young girl, if he feels himself cornered.' His eyes searched Toby's face. 'Did she say anything to you, when you were out?'

'Not really,' said Toby, frowning as if he were trying to remember. 'Oh — she did say that she thought she was on to something, but she wouldn't tell me what it was. She shut up like a clam, actually.'

'Oh, damn,' said Gabriel, low. 'I thought I'd frightened her enough . . . Toby, you must promise me that tomorrow you will watch Isabelle like a hawk, you understand? Meanwhile I will try and keep watch over all the people who come in. I've got to see if I can feel anything . . . see anything . . .'

Toby thought of what Gabriel had told him, of how he could see violent death standing at someone's shoulder. 'Do you really think . . . something will happen?'

'I'm sure it will,' said Gabriel, gravely. 'I think—' He broke off suddenly. Toby, looking behind him, saw that Tom Nashe had entered the room, and was standing looking at them, a little smile on his lips.

'You're wanted, Mr Harvey,' he said. 'And you too, Mr Trentham. Mrs Wilson has just arrived, with a gaggle of stage-struck ladies who want to meet just everyone.'

As they went back into the theatre, Toby wondered uneasily if the detective had heard anything of what they'd said. If he had, would it matter? Doubt struck him. What if the agent was really acting for the killer, the mysterious Malpence who might, if Madame Laroche's psychic feelings had any basis to them, be haunting the Twelfth Night Ball like Death at a party? Surely not . . . or else, wouldn't he already have moved against them? No, no, Nashe must be working for someone else, on quite some other matter. It must be about Henry, he thought. It must be. He's the one that arrived last, after all. But Henry Smallwood – vain, silly Henry Smallwood – as a master crook was hard to picture. Unless he was really the best actor of all time!

How odd to think that Malpence had played Malvolio! The names were even close, he thought. Perhaps that's why they'd chosen him for the part. But what a horrible irony, that it should be the head groom in love with his mistress, playing the steward in love with his mistress! Fate could be a real joker. Then another thought struck him, a worse thought by far: perhaps the trap Isabelle had spoken of concerned just that – concerned the fact of Malvolio's revenge. She was hoping to trick Malpence into revealing who he really was, through the play! She must have some trick up her sleeve – something she would insert into the play, so that she'd make him betray his identity, somehow. Oh, my God . . . she intended to use poor Uncle Theo's play as a mantrap to catch a murderer!

Twenty-five

All that day, he thought about it, without coming to a conclusion. He'd promised Isabelle he'd tell no one about what had happened that morning, and he intended to keep that promise. He wasn't sure he altogether believed in the dramatic warning from the old lady; but he had no opportunity to ask her, she was far too ill for that. In a lucid moment, she had begged not to be taken to hospital, an understandable enough feeling, given that hospitals for the poor were hardly places you wanted to be in if you were healthy, let alone sick. One of the maids at the hotel was acting as nurse, sponging her forehead, giving her drinks, with Isabelle looking in on her from time to time as well. But not much time could be spared for her, as she did not seem to be in imminent danger of death. As the day wore on, the old lady fell into an exhausted sleep, the fever slowly leaving her, taking the glitter from her eyes and the heat from her cheeks.

Toby had no chance to speak much to Isabelle, either, beyond a whispered, 'Are you all right?' once or twice, receiving a quick nod and a smile in reply. The girl was preoccupied, as well she might be, not only with her nurse's illness, but everything else. Toby thought he'd have to wait till the evening to speak to her, try to beg her not to do anything as foolish as thinking she could do a Hamlet as in Shakespeare's play, and trap the wicked killer into betraying himself in public. After all, to do that would show Malpence quite clearly she was on to him – and then there'd be no stopping him. Whatever Isabelle thought, however brave she was, no matter how many burglars she'd seen off in her time, Toby thought she couldn't really imagine just how dangerous a murderer – whose murder has lain hidden for fifteen years – might be if he thought he was discovered. He could imagine it well enough, because he'd read about it in lots of stories. She'd say that was just romancing, but those things were based on fact, and on a knowledge of the human soul. The sleeping murder is always the worst one, he thought, because the killer thinks he's got away with it; he's got everything to lose, if he's unveiled . . .

He wished he could speak to Gabriel. He felt bad about not being able to. Despite his shortcomings, the actor was intelligent and resourceful; and he'd trusted Toby with his own terrible secret. He *should* tell Gabriel! But every time he'd nearly decided to do so, he'd think of Isabelle's bright, beautiful face, making him promise not to tell. And so he couldn't. He had to be a man of honour, even when it hurt. He had to take it right to the end, for the girl he loved.

He wondered where she'd hidden the revolver. He wished he knew. He felt very nervous with the thought of that thing around; try as he might, it wasn't easy to get used to the idea of it. This was America, of course, not England, and he had to remember that Isabelle's life had indeed been different to his. Still, it wasn't easy. The thought of that elegant little engine of death sleeping peacefully in its red velvet bed, ready to shoot down the man who had destroyed the Castelon family – for he was increasingly sure Isabelle didn't intend to stop at confession – was almost more than he could bear. Where did she intend to do it? In the theatre itself, like John Wilkes Booth assassinating the American president, Abraham Lincoln? Or at the ball, into the crowd? Surely not. Surely not. Perhaps, he thought finally, perhaps what she's going to do is find out for sure who he is, through something strategically inserted into the play, and then arrange to meet him somewhere isolated, where she can kill him. That had been the plot denouement of one of the stories he'd read a little while back – well, not the play, but the trap, and the luring to a deserted spot. Oh God . . . oh God . . . he'd have to convince her not to do it!

He finally got his chance that evening. The Wilsons had

invited them all to their mansion for dinner, but Isabelle had asked to be left behind, to look after Madame Laroche. Toby, after a glance from Gabriel, said casually that if Uncle Theo thought the Wilsons did not mind, it might be better if he stayed behind too to double-check everything. Uncle Theo was delighted with his conscientiousness, and anyway opined that the Wilsons had not necessarily included crew in the invitation, no matter how hail-fellow-well-met they might seem to be. So he waved them all off in the cabs, and tinkered around with the sets for a little while, till he thought the coast would be sufficiently clear, when he raced back to the hotel.

Isabelle met him at the door of her nurse's room. She had a finger to her lips. 'Sssh. She's sleeping peacefully now, my poor Maminou.'

Toby peered in. The old lady was lying against her pillows with her eyes closed, her withered face quite grey with exhaustion, her breath coming fast and shallow. Without the startling green light of her eyes, she looked like any old body who was not long for this world. As Isabelle closed the door, he whispered, 'Do you think she'll be all right?'

Isabelle crossed herself. She bit her lip, so the blood came. 'I hope and pray she will.' She paused. 'But it's better this way. She won't worry about me. She can just recover, without thinking of me.'

Toby doubted the old lady would do that, but all he said was, 'Isabelle, Gabriel spoke to me, earlier.'

'You didn't tell him, did you?' she flashed, at once.

'I told you I wouldn't. And I didn't. And he didn't seem suspicious, anyway. He just told me something your nurse had told him, last night, something about Malpence . . .'

'She told *him*!' Isabelle's eyes glittered. 'Go on.'

'She said that Malpence had played Malvolio, in that last production of *Twelfth Night*, and that it was the first time he'd played it. She also said that he'd be there at the Twelfth Night Ball, that . . . that the ghost of your father had . . . told her so, in a manner of speaking . . . and that it would be very dangerous to—'

'Oh, hang it!' said Isabelle fiercely. 'She's just trying to frighten me again; and so is Gabriel. Can't you see, Toby – if there is any ghost of my father, it's in here . . .' and she jabbed at her chest with a finger, 'and if it's going to kill anyone, it'll be through me. I am not my father, but I can avenge him, and my poor mother. Has she forgotten about them? Has she forgotten how much she loved my mother? Or doesn't it matter to her any more?'

'I don't know,' said Toby, taken aback by her vehemence. 'I'm only telling you what Gabriel said . . .'

'Don't let's ever get old!' said Isabelle fervently. 'Don't let's get old and tired and cautious and resigned, Toby!'

'Er . . . the alternative to getting old isn't really that attractive,' said Toby nervously.

'Bah! If you mean staying alive just for the sake of it – I spit on it!' said Isabelle fiercely. 'Isn't there anything you'd risk everything for, Toby? Isn't there something you'd die for? Or would you prefer to creep along the years, to old age and a dull death in your bed?'

'Isabelle!' cried Toby. 'Don't say such things! When your poor nurse lies ill in her bed, sick with worry about you! Don't talk like that, you make me feel sick with fear – not for myself, but for you! Do you have any idea what you've got yourself into?'

Isabelle stared at him, her colour high. Then, in a markedly calmer tone, she said, 'Do *you*, Toby? Do *you*?'

'I know that a cornered tiger is more dangerous than one roaming loose,' he said, crossly. 'And you should think of that. Think too that there are other people besides you, and me. There's the whole troupe – there's poor Uncle Theo, who is dreaming of success and fame and fortune . . .'

'Oh, that!' she said with scorn.

'Don't mock it,' he said, furiously. 'It might mean nothing to you . . . but that doesn't mean it's worth nothing. Uncle Theo is very brave, in his own way; he's never given up, never surrendered, always thought there'd be a better day around the corner. Well, now it's here – and no one's going to spoil that for him, you understand? Not even you!'

He hadn't known he felt like that. He hadn't meant for the words to come pouring out of his mouth. He looked at her still face and thought, Well, I've done it. Any chance I had with her is gone, now. But all she said was, 'So, Toby, you thought I was going to do a Hamlet, didn't you, and show the black heart of the killer through the medium of your play? Is that it?'

He said nothing. She went on, 'I can see why you might think so. But I assure you, I would never do that. I know what this play means to you all. I can't deny that when I heard what the plot of your play was, something like that did enter my head. But I decided that was wrong, dishonourable. And besides, it's stupid. And so it is not what I intend to do.'

'But I thought . . . Malvolio – you know – the similarities . . . it would be the obvious thing to make him betray himself . . .'

'Oh, Toby! That's what it would be like in one of those stories you're so fond of. But even if Malpence was struck dumb with awe at the similarities between the play and his miserable rotten life . . . why would it make any difference to him? It's just a play, after all; and his life, and his secret, are real enough. He is a hardened criminal, a wolf in sheep's clothing. Toby . . . not only did he kill my father, but I am almost certain he was blackmailing him.'

'Blackmail? But over what?'

'I don't know, exactly. But I fear it was over a woman –

some unsuitable association of my father's. So you see, this man is a hardened criminal indeed.' Her voice changed. She said, a wryly amused expression on her face, 'Don't look so bleak, Toby. I will not interrupt the play in any way. I promise to act my part, and my part only.'

'But . . .' Toby began, but she was walking off to her room, throwing a goodnight over her shoulder. She went in, and closed the door firmly, and he heard the key in the lock. She was making it quite clear she did not want to be disturbed.

There was no way Toby could go to sleep, not yet. Slowly, thoughtfully, he made his way back to the Terpsichore, and a bit more tinkering with the sets.

Twenty-six

At breakfast the next morning, Madame La Praline served
them a king-cake. The golden-glazed cake, jewelled with pieces
of glacé cherries and angelica, was made in the shape of a king's
circlet, as a reminder of the visit made by the Three Kings to
the baby Jesus, that first Twelfth Night, centuries ago.
Somewhere inside the cake, the pension keeper said with a
twinkle in her eye, was hidden a broad bean. The person who
found it would be King or Queen for the day, and might choose
their consort to reign with them. And the others would have to
obey their orders! There was much mirth as the cake was cut
and distributed amongst the company; but Toby was holding
his breath and wishing with all his might that he might get the
broad bean, and then he'd rush out to the kitchen, haul Isabelle
out and proclaim her as his Queen, and then they'd all know
what he felt, and then . . .

But of course, he didn't find it. It fell to Henry Smallwood, who took it smilingly as his due . . . and then chose Madame La Praline as his Queen.

'Well, well,' whispered Gabriel to Toby, under cover of the general merriment. 'Old Harry's got his head screwed on tightly, I'd say – with an eye to a good investment. Mind you, he's been stepping out with her once or twice, the last few days. Almost as assiduous as your uncle with Madame Blanche. Especially as Monsieur Bruno's been so attentive to our Matilda.'

Toby nodded, vaguely. He'd been so preoccupied with his own concerns that he'd really taken no interest in what the others were doing. Gabriel went on, 'What's the odds on New Orleans being the last posting for the Trentham Troupe, do you think, Toby?'

This time, Toby took more notice. Staring at Gabriel, he said, 'What have you heard? What's my uncle been saying?'

'Nothing. But it's my strong feeling an announcement for a permanent home here for the troupe will be made; if not tonight, then soon after.'

'Oh,' said Toby. He thought for a moment, then said cautiously, 'I don't think I want to just stay here. I want to see a bit more of the world.'

'Really?' said Gabriel, smiling.

'Yes, I thought – a river-boat, then out to sea, I don't know, maybe head for South America?'

'A pleasant prospect of adventure, then. Alone, Toby?'

Toby coloured a little, then, gazing defiantly at Gabriel, he said, 'I hope not.'

After an instant, he added, 'And you? Are you going to stay here, once the season's over?'

Something flickered in Gabriel's eyes. 'I have no idea,' he said, curtly. 'Now, hadn't you best go out the back and check on Isabelle?'

She had finished her own breakfast, and appeared in very good spirits. When he enquired after Madame Laroche, she said that the old lady was much better, and had passed a peaceful night. 'But she's still weak, Toby, and though she's determined to get to the performance tonight, and watch from the wings, I doubt she'll be strong enough. Oh . . . and she's been asking for you. Do you mind calling in on her?'

'Of course I don't mind. But Isabelle . . . you'll wait for me before you go anywhere else, won't you?'

'Of course I will, pardner,' she said, with a smile that made him dizzy.

He knocked on Madame Laroche's door, and received a faint, 'Come in,' in reply. He entered cautiously, and closed the door. She was propped up against her pillows, her pinched face still without its normal colour, her eyelids drooping a little over that brilliant green. 'Come close to me, Toby. Please.'

He sat by her bed. She looked at him. He thought her eyes looked dulled and filmed over, and on the coverlet, her thin hands shook a little. But her voice was steady enough as she said, 'Toby, I'm dying.'

Toby started up. 'Oh, no, Madame! You're getting better!'

She smiled, sadly. 'You're a kind boy, Toby. Will you do something for me?'

He stammered, 'Anything, dear Madame . . . anything.'

'You've always called me that as if you really meant it.' She paused, and bit down on her lip. 'But I think you're a little afraid of me, aren't you?' When he did not answer, she went on, with a sigh, 'After my death, Toby, I want you to go and see my nephew Charles – you know him as Klondike,' she added, seeing Toby's puzzled expression. 'Just say to him that I sent you.'

'But, Madame . . .'

'Please, Toby. Will you promise?'

A lump came into his throat. 'I promise, Madame. But won't you tell me . . .'

'No, Toby.' She closed her eyes, an instant, then they flew open again. She said, 'Forgive me, Toby.'

'Forgive you? But for what?'

A tear trickled down her thin cheek. 'For this,' she whispered. 'For all this . . .'

'Madame . . .'

'Please . . . you and Gabriel, you will take care of her, won't you? So much has already been destroyed. No more must be.' Her voice was surprisingly strong.

He nodded, unable to speak.

'Don't say anything to her,' she said. 'I don't want her to know. But will you . . . will you ask Gabriel to come and visit me?'

'Yes, Madame.' He paused, then went on, quickly, 'But I think you'll get better, Madame. I am sure you will! You look much better than yesterday . . .'

'Yes, Toby,' she said, smiling faintly; then she closed her eyes. Toby knew he was dismissed. He left, quietly closing the door behind him.

Isabelle came out of her room. 'What did she want to talk to you about?'

Toby shook his head, lying fluently, the first thing that came into his head. 'She's very keen to see you perform.'

'Hmm,' said Isabelle, wryly. 'I think she's just scared of what I might do; she thinks I'm going to do something rash and silly.'

'And are you?' Toby dared to say.

She glared at him. 'I told you, Toby, I wasn't going to disrupt your precious play. I promise: it'll go off without a hitch, at least as far as I'm concerned.' She paused, then added, 'And Maminou shouldn't think she has to be there. I know her. She's stubborn, but she must see sense. She needs complete rest. Don't think you have to fulfil any promise you might have given her, Toby – her mind's still feverish, she's not thinking clearly.'

'Yes,' he said, miserably.

Isabelle looked sharply at him. 'Look, I'll ask Madame La Praline if perhaps some decoction could be made for her – something that will make her sleep, say, for twenty-four hours, so she'll be at rest, completely, and be refreshed by tomorrow . . .'

'You mean a sleeping draught?'

'Yes. I think that would be the best thing, don't you?'

Unease nagged at Toby. Yet perhaps a sleeping draught would help the old lady; she was very weak, and full of morbid imaginings. A complete uninterrupted sleep for a day and a night might do the world of good. So he said, 'If you think that's the best idea . . .'

'I do,' she said, briskly. 'I'll see to it right away.' She smiled at his expression. 'And I'll stay with you all day, Toby. You can keep as close an eye on me as you like. I'm sure Maminou told you to.'

She laughed as he blushed scarlet.

True to her promise, she stayed close by him, or where he could glimpse her, all the rest of that long and packed day, through all the final rehearsal, the arrival of the orchestra –

who would also provide music for the ball scene of the play – the toings and froings of a small army of caterers, ushers, dressers, waiters, decorators, and so on. Toby gave Gabriel Madame Laroche's message, but wasn't sure if he did go back to the hotel or not; too much was happening.

Mrs Wilson was a frequent visitor to the theatre during those last frantic hours, but Wilson himself made no appearance. In the late afternoon, Wilson's secretary Guy Follett arrived with a message saying his boss regretted not being there, but that he'd had an urgent communication from one of his newspapers in San Francisco, and was busy solving a major crisis by telephone, but would be along shortly to discuss the final shape of the protocol for the evening. The dour secretary, who had not troubled, thus far, to examine the theatrical investment of his employer – and who had given distinct signs that he thoroughly disapproved of such frivolities – was even persuaded by the general excitement to stay on for a little while and watch the rehearsal.

'He was even heard to say that we were not as bad as he'd thought,' Toby overheard Madame La Praline say to Uncle Theo, late that afternoon. 'How most typical of a killjoy like him, to look down his nose and think himself a judge of other people's characters!'

'Oh, never mind that sour-faced old thing, Madame,' said Uncle Theo, roguishly. 'What do we care of the sensibilities of the man, if the master likes us? Ah, Toby,' he said, catching sight of his hovering nephew, 'can you go and tell Mr Nashe that I need to have a word with him? I think he's backstage somewhere . . .'

Toby caught Isabelle's eye. She was helping to set out some chairs, and gave him a barely perceptible nod, and a resigned little smile, as if to say, 'Where do you think I'm going to go?'

Nashe wasn't in any of the dressing-rooms, or in the prop room, or in the wardrobe room. Toby was about to go looking for him in the dance-hall, when he heard voices coming from behind the closed back door of the theatre. One of them was Nashe's; the other, Gabriel's. He was about to bang on the door and call out to Nashe to come and see Uncle Theo, when he caught what Gabriel was saying, and paused, one hand poised to knock.

'Not till after tonight – I beg of you, Nashe – say nothing till after tonight.' In content and tone, it sounded so unlike anything Gabriel would ever say that Toby was rooted to the spot.

'It's got to be told, sometime,' said Nashe's voice – calm, benign, light. 'You know you couldn't get away with it for ever.'

'And why not? Why couldn't you all leave me alone?' Gabriel's voice was harsh, almost desperate.

'You know we couldn't do that,' said Nashe. 'We've been looking for you for a long time. And you're good at hiding,

I'll grant you – you've not got talent for nothing. But now it's over. Come, come, man, don't look like that . . . it'll be much better to make a clean breast of it.'

'After tonight,' said Gabriel, tightly. 'Give me at least that, Nashe. Wait till tomorrow, before you tell them.'

'Very well,' said Nashe, after a short silence. 'I'll give you till tomorrow. But no longer.'

Toby fled. He had heard quite enough. Heart pounding, palms clammy, he raced to the wardrobe room and began shuffling costumes around, to the annoyance of one of the dressers, who had popped in to check a hem. He heard the back door slam, and then Nashe's footsteps. As he was about to go by, Toby called out, trying to sound as casual as he could, 'Mr Nashe!'

The fiddler turned. 'What? Oh, it's you, Toby. What do you want?'

'It's Uncle Theo,' said Toby, shoving his shaking hands into silk and velvet. 'He wants to have a word.'

'Oh, very well.' The fiddler's usual friendly composure seemed to have deserted him for a moment, for he did not hang back to banter with Toby, as he would normally have done, but left without another word.

'I don't know what you think you're doing, mister,' began the dresser, a disapproving eye cocked on Toby's rustlings, 'but you'd better . . .'

But Toby didn't wait to hear the rest of her lecture.

He stood in the street, pacing around, trying to think. Oh God, what did it mean? Obviously, that Thomas Nashe and Pinkerton's Detective Agency had been on *Gabriel's* trail all along. But why? What had he done? For an instant, a horrible thought flashed through his mind – that Gabriel was none other than Malpence – before he dismissed it. Gabriel was far too young; he would have been only five or six when the Castelons had died. Even if he'd lied about his age, it was inconceivable. To be head groom, Malpence must have been at least thirty-five, fifteen years ago. That would make him at least fifty today. And though Gabriel might have second sight, he most certainly didn't have the elixir of eternal youth – no fifty-year-old, no matter how well preserved, could pass as a man in his twenties.

No, it must be something quite unrelated. It must be something pretty major, judging from what he'd heard, and yet not something violent, or else Nashe would not have allowed him that grace of time. Perhaps it was some robbery – non-violent, of course – some spectacular jewel heist of some kind? He could imagine Gabriel using his brains to pull off a daring robbery, but could not imagine him mixed up in something ugly. He remembered that comment Gabriel had made the other day, when he'd discovered Nashe was a Pink's, and Toby was speculating on who he might be after. He'd said, half bitterly, 'What do you know about me? Perhaps I'm on the run . . . perhaps I've got stolen diamonds hidden in my carpetbag . . .' Had it been, then, so close to the truth? Stolen diamonds or no stolen diamonds, it was obviously something that had happened some while ago, given that Nashe had said they'd been looking for him for a long time. And he was obviously meaning to give himself up, once tonight had passed. Tonight! It must mean a great deal to him, the play, the performance, the possibility of fame and fortune for the troupe . . .

Toby's heart lurched. Perhaps it wasn't that which meant so much to him – but *Isabelle*, and Isabelle's fate. He was afraid for her; he had been convinced by that old lady that she really was in mortal danger. He, too, was intending to do something . . . something that would keep her safe. Something, perhaps, that Madame Laroche had asked him to do. It must mean a great deal to him. A great deal. Toby swallowed. It must mean he . . . he *felt* for Isabelle, that he cared for her. Hell and damnation, it must mean he *loved* her! A scalding heat rose in him. Gabriel had seemed almost to dislike the girl, to flinch from her, or at the very least, to be detached, to avoid her company. Toby had thought of his odd reaction to her first as Gabriel being Gabriel, then, when he knew about Gabriel's secret, he'd thought of it as showing how Gabriel could never feel normally; now, with a great bottoming-out of his stomach, he thought, no, it's because he feels *too much*, because he loves her. Because he loves her so much he can't trust himself around her; because he loves her so much he'd do anything to keep her safe – but would never importune her with *talk* of love.

And she . . . what did she think of him? With an inward groan of pain, Toby saw, with sudden clarity, all the things that showed Isabelle was not immune to Gabriel's presence. He remembered her sideways looks at Gabriel, back in Illyria; her sudden performance, to impress Gabriel, at the theatre, after which she'd been cast in the play; the strange way she'd recounted how he'd tried to frighten her off doing anything about Malpence; and her first reaction to Toby's own admissions of passion. She'd been embarrassed by them, he thought, bleakly; she's just been humouring me, her thoughts were all for someone else . . .

Damn Gabriel! Damn his complicated soul, his outrageous talent and his romantic air of suffering! How could Toby begin to compete with him? It wasn't fair . . . it just wasn't fair . . . Then an ignoble thought entered his mind. Well, nothing could come of it, anyhow. Tomorrow, Gabriel would be unmasked by Thomas Nashe for whatever crime it was he had committed . . . and that'd be the end of it. He'd be out of the story . . .

Toby pushed the thought away. It was a horrible thing to think, even of a potential rival. Doubly horrible, when that rival had been his best friend who had never treated him with anything but friendship. And triply horrible, when it meant that he not only wished jail and disgrace on that best friend, but pain and sadness on Isabelle – if she did love Gabriel, or at least felt for him . . .

'Toby!' Isabelle's voice made him jump out of his skin. She waved a little packet in the air. 'Mrs Wilson asked if you could deliver this to Mr Follett, back at the mansion. Their driver will take you.'

He could feel his freckles flaming as she looked at him. But he managed to say, 'Sure, I'll do that.' Well, it's me she asks to do things with her, he thought. With her. Or *for* her . . . Good old Toby, reliable crutch, errand-boy, gofer . . .

'Toby? Can I come with you? I'd love to see that place, after what you said.' She had her head on one side, rather coyly, he thought crossly. She thinks she's got me twined around her little finger, and I'll do whatever she wants, when she wants me to. 'Sure,' he said, miserably.

She raised her eyebrows. 'What's up, Toby? You really look out of sorts.'

'Nothing. I'm tired,' he growled, making her eyebrows raise still more. I could easily wipe that smugness off your lovely face, he thought, with a surge of pain, if I told you the man you're in love with will be arrested tomorrow! 'All right, let's go,' he added, and strode off towards the Wilsons' car, where the uniformed driver, who'd been snoozing cheerfully in the front seat, nodded bemusedly to yet another Wilson request for to-and-fro.

They rode in silence to the Wilsons' mansion. Toby didn't have the heart to speak, and Isabelle seemed content to look out of the window at the passing parade. The streets were full of people; there was an air of feverish anticipation which told of the partying season ahead. *Beignet* and hot chestnut sellers were doing a brisk trade, and masked revellers had already begun to appear, some of them blowing paper cornets. Around one corner, Toby caught a glimpse of Karnofsky's wagon, piled high with scrap and old junk, and Louis Satchelmouth, sitting happily on top of the pile, swinging his legs, tin horn in hand. For an instant, he wished he could be there with him, uncomplicated, happy, looking forward to Twelfth Night – the noise, the colour, the music and merriment – without any thought for anything else. Then he looked across at Isabelle, and thought, with a gripping of the heart, that despite everything, he still felt the same way about her, and always would . . .

'Toby, you're mighty solemn,' she said, gently, just as they turned into the Wilsons' street. 'Don't worry – everything will be fine. You'll see.'

'Will it?' he said, quietly. For the first time that he could remember, she blushed under her walnut-juice tan, and looked away.

They were not long at the Wilson mansion. They delivered the packet to Guy Follett, who made it quite clear, with a contemptuous lift of the eyebrow towards the delivery boy and the gypsy girl, that they had performed their commission and could now go. Isabelle was not to be daunted by this, and looked as if she were ready to make a dash inside and explore, but Toby, flushing under the secretary's icy glare, dragged her away. He could feel the man's eyes burning into the backs of their heads as they made their way back to the car, and saw him standing on the doorstep, watching them drive away. Damn Follett! What did he think they were going to do — make off with the silver?

But Isabelle was in high good spirits. All the way back, she chattered about traditions of Twelfth Night in Louisiana, and about some old-time pageant holders, the Twelfth Night Revellers, who were famous for their big parades and masked balls, and the extravagant prizes they awarded to their reigning monarchs of Twelfth Night, the Lord of Misrule and his Lady. 'Fancy,' she babbled on, 'one year they even put tiny gold watches instead of beans in their king-cakes and they gave out prizes of diamonds and rubies and emeralds to their lady revellers . . . My grandfather was one of them, you know. Those people really knew how to enjoy themselves! Today, everyone is so stuffy and timid!'

'I don't think what the Wilsons are planning is stuffy and timid,' said Toby.

She shrugged. 'Bah, a mere bagatelle beside what used to be done!'

He found himself annoyed by her high spirits. She had no right to be so bright and merry, when all those affected by her – her nurse, Gabriel and himself – drooped like wilted plants. But he said nothing; after all, there was nothing to be said. And he couldn't help thinking of Gabriel, sitting in his dressing-room, making up as Malvolio, and all the time the knowledge in his heart that *tomorrow* . . . tomorrow would be the end.

And damn that bloody fiddler too, he thought in an excess of temper and sorrow. What right did he have, destroying a man's life in this way! Who cared what Gabriel had done, in some past life – he was a good friend, a good actor, a good man. He had never done any of them any harm, ever. Yes, damn and blast Tom Nashe to Hell; why didn't the Devil he was so fond of joking about take that light and hollow soul of his and make him leave them all in peace!

Twenty-seven

Toby peered cautiously out from between the curtains. The theatre swirled with tulle and muslin and velvet and satin; buzzed with conversation, with rows of powdered, shining, expectant faces. The Wilsons were there in the front row, she in an amazing gown of lilac and gold, he in elegant black and white, with a lilac and gold stock above a white brocade waistcoat. They were surrounded by their friends and guests, most of whom were just like themselves, rich self-made men and their vivacious wives. There was a smell of perfume and money in the air, a smell that the troupe must find intoxicating, for backstage, they were chattering like magpies, light-headed with excitement, with relief, with pleasure and sharp fear. Would that well-heeled audience out there like the play? Madame Blanche had assured them that they would, of course they would, but it was easier said than really thought or felt . . .

Knock, knock, knock! The audience rustled, shifted; the buzz of conversation rose then began to die down. Toby's heart leaped. He'd better get to the wings with his prompt-book. Hurrying there, he went past the men's dressing-room, and saw Gabriel sitting before the mirror, checking his eye make-up. He saw Toby in the mirror, and looked at him, but said nothing. Toby would have liked to say something, but just then the second lot of knocks sounded. He whispered, 'Break a leg, Gabriel!' The actor's green eyes, outlined with black, gazed into his bleakly for an instant, then he turned back to his job, with an apparently steady hand.

Knock, knock, knock! Now there was silence, out there in the audience, a complete, hushed, waiting silence. Now was the moment of truth. In the wings, Toby sat with the prompt-book on his lap, hands clenched, fingernails digging into his palms. Please, God, he thought, please, God, let it all go smoothly. Let it all go well, let everything be for the best . . . let all the fear and confusion vanish like mist . . . Let it be, God. Please, let it be . . .

The orchestra began to play, quietly; then Tom Nashe's violin rose above them all, and Count Sebastian entered, slowly, shuffling, head down.

> *'In vivid strips, the skin of evening*
> *Peels off into the dark of night . . .'*

began Uncle Theo. The music began to die away, only the violin insistent, melancholy under the words, a thin, despairing thread of sound. What was that tune again? Yes — that's right — Marie Laroche said it was about an old-time king, Renaud, who was dying far away, but who must drag himself home to his family, for love's sake . . .

The hairs rose on the back of Toby's neck. The scene was working wonderfully well, there was no doubt about it. Isabelle entered as the gypsy girl, and the light fell on her oddly, making it seem as if she glided rather than walked, turning round and round the disconsolate Count as if she were a haunting spirit from the past. Still the violin played underneath, quietly. Toby could hear the quality of silence out there in the audience. They were gripped. They were hooked! He wished he could look out there, see how the Wilsons were reacting, and whether the millionaire was gripped too, or simply indulgently bored as he'd been last time.

The scene ended, and so did the melancholy music. Olivia, radiant as Lydia, came on, followed by her faithful, sharp-tongued nurse Dame Vera, played by Matilda. This was a scene with some comic relief, and Toby could feel the rustle of relief in the audience. And the pleasure. For the first time ever, Olivia made not a stumble, forgot not one word or gesture, and Matilda was brilliant. Ripples of laughter filled the theatre. Toby felt very proud. Yes, yes, *yes*, he was thinking, we're doing it, really doing it! How exciting the theatre is!

Now came Henry as Lysander, hiding in the woods, talking of his plans and fears with his fellow exile, the cynical jester Feste. Old Fate was always good in that role, but tonight he was even better, wisecracking away with a straight face, and as to Henry, his Lysander had a restless, anguished impetuosity that was all too rare in his usually self-satisfied performances. Blimey, it's a *good* play, Toby thought as he watched, spellbound. I've done Uncle Theo an injustice, I really have. When it takes off like this – well, it's just marvellous, everything falls into place. No wonder it had been a success in the West End!

Now came Malvolio's first scene. The entrance of the villain was usually a high point, and this was no exception. People gasped and hissed as the wronged ex-steward-turned-cruel-master signed orders for tortures and executions, and when Gabriel lifted his head to directly address the audience, Toby was thunderstruck as much as the audience. Hair slicked back, eyes ringed with darkness, a little black goatee adorning his chin and upper lip, dressed in supremely elegant black and gold, with a little black satin cloak flung over one shoulder, Gabriel looked like nothing so much as the Prince of Darkness. He didn't usually dress like this for Malvolio – he usually preferred more subtlety – but it was oddly effective. He must have gauged his audience well, for they were obviously most taken with him; when he left the stage, people stood and clapped.

Toby craned his neck. He could just about see the audience. And there were the Wilsons, enthusiastically clapping with the rest. The millionaire's face looked flushed with pleasure; he didn't look at all sleepy. In the row just behind him, Toby caught a glimpse of a dour, sour face: Guy Follett. As Toby watched, he got up, and slipped along the row. Well, there's one customer we can never hope to satisfy, thought Toby with a sigh, turning his attention back to the play.

There was to be no interval, as supper and dancing were to start straight after. Two hours was a long time to sit, but sit the audience did, and happily, apparently mesmerised by the action. Toby himself couldn't drag himself away from his post, though it was obvious now that Olivia wasn't going to forget any of her lines, and neither was anyone else.

The climax was coming; the confrontation between Malvolio and the Count, their duel, Malvolio's fatal wounding, and his death scene. The whole audience was still as a mouse. Nothing rustled, nothing stirred. Malvolio entered; the theatre erupted. He held up his arms, his dark face showing a cruel glee, then said, 'If there are ghosts to speak, let them speak now/ For my time has come, the time of final triumph/ Never will the house of Illyria rise from the ashes of the past to accuse me . . .'

Puzzled, Toby looked down at his prompt-book. As he'd

thought, it wasn't quite the speech Malvolio was supposed to say. Gabriel had altered it, slightly. It was meant to be, 'There are no ghosts to speak, now or never/ For my time has come, the time of final triumph/ Never will the house of Olivia rise from the ashes of the past to accuse me . . .'

Gabriel never forgot lines. Never. Toby looked at the prompt-book, out at the stage, and began to shake, inwardly. It was *Gabriel* who was doing what he'd thought Isabelle might: pulling the tail of the tiger, trying to make Malpence betray himself, by word or gesture. Toby could feel the cold crinkling of his scalp. He craned his neck to try to see the audience, but could see nothing out of the ordinary. They were all just sitting there in the dark, staring at the stage . . .

Count Sebastian came on. Malvolio spoke to him; and his lines, now, were just as set down in the prompt-book. Toby breathed more slowly. Nothing had happened; Malpence wasn't out there. They had been worrying over nothing. Perhaps the man was not even in New Orleans, let alone the theatre. Perhaps Isabelle had been mistaken. Perhaps everything would be just fine . . .

The scene ended. Malvolio expired on stage, with the right lines. Lydia was reunited with her father, now restored to his former honour; Lysander was reunited with *her*. Now it was time for the happy ending: the marriage scene, the concluding ball. The orchestra struck up a merry waltz, the violin's brightness hopping and skipping above them all. Everyone was on stage now, except for Gabriel; and Isabelle, no longer gypsy girl but adopted by Count Sebastian, twirled in a gorgeous pink tulle dress, one of the old Illyria Carnival costumes. How beautiful she looked! Toby would have given anything to be out there, twirling with her, leading her through the steps. But he was a clumsy dancer – and he was prompter, not actor. He could only watch, and wish, and hope, against vain hope . . .

As the last strains died away, the audience was on its feet, clapping, cheering, stamping. A well-heeled audience it might have been, but it was not a stuffy one. After a while, shouts of 'Malvolio!' went up, and Gabriel came on. He looked exhausted, drawn, his face a white mask, drained of emotion. But he bowed, deeply, and said, suddenly, in sepulchral tones, 'And so ends the revenge of Malvolio, in the place where it began. With my death the curse on Illyria will be lifted, and the sun shine once again. All is discovered of my duplicity; all is lost for me. I should have fled when I had time; but now, even my ghost will know no rest . . .'

There was a silence, then a burst of cheering and clapping, once again. The audience thought it all part of the play. Toby, struck to the heart, could see the quickly concealed bewilderment on the faces of the other actors, but professionals that they were, they pretended, too, it was part of the act, and bowed and smiled and waved as cheerfully as if they'd expected it all along. Not Gabriel . . . Toby saw how his glance flashed to Isabelle – and how she alone of the rest of them was unable to school her emotion – and then the Irishman bowed, waved, and strode off the stage.

The curtain fell. The actors milled around, excitedly discussing the performance. Uncle Theo grumbled, 'Blast that Gabriel, why'd he have to add to my play . . .'

'Oh, come, Theobald!' said Matilda, coquettishly. 'The audience loved it. You saw.'

'I'm not sure I do,' said Theo, still a little disgruntled.

Toby looked at Isabelle. She smiled, faintly. He said, 'It did work, Uncle Theo. But it shouldn't have, not really. Over-egging the pudding is always dangerous.'

'Silly boy, what do you know about it?' said Uncle Theo, magisterially. 'Now, where is that Mr Harvey?'

'I'll get him,' said Toby quickly, and slipped away. Isabelle followed him.

'I suppose you know he did it for you,' Toby said, as they hurried to the dressing-room. He didn't look at her as he spoke.

'I know,' was all she said, but in those words, Toby knew that what he feared was absolutely true. The girl he loved was in love with his best friend. Pain stabbed at him. He swallowed and said, 'He was very good.'

'He was,' she said. Stopping in front of the dressing-room door, she looked at Toby. 'And so are you, Toby.'

'Me?' said Toby, bitterly. 'Me? I'm——' But what he was

about to say never got finished, for Isabelle had opened the dressing-room door, on to a dreadful shambles. The floor was covered in upended baskets of props; costumes, ripped off their hangers, were strewn about the floor; and the mirror lay on its side, miraculously unsmashed, amongst the mess. But there was no one there at all.

Isabelle and Toby looked at each other. Then with one accord, they raced out, to the other dressing-room. It was perfectly neat and tidy. They peered in at props and wardrobe; nothing wrong there, all peaceful. And no Gabriel!

It was an incurious dresser in wardrobe who said, 'Oh, he never got undressed. He went off in a tearing hurry, just as he was, with a gentleman who called for him.'

'What gentleman?' said Toby anxiously.

'That stone-faced gentleman who's the secretary of Mr Wilson,' said the dresser, comfortably.

'Mr Follett!' said Toby and Isabelle, together. They went out into the passage. Toby whispered, 'My God, so it's Follett. I should have thought! He's the dourest, most self-satisfied prig there is – just like Malvolio. I could see his face, in the play . . . he was all twisted up, Isabelle, it was hitting home, to him . . . Good lord, I should have seen it a while ago! He's just the right age, and he's just—'

Isabelle did not appear to have heard. 'Toby, what are we going to do?'

'What do you mean? We're going to go right away and tell

Mr Wilson. Find out where Follett might have gone . . .'

'No!' Isabelle's voice was harsh. 'We have to go ourselves. I think I . . . I think I know where Follett might have gone.'

Toby stared. 'How?'

She went red, and began to speak very fast. 'I . . . you see . . . I wrote a note. I put it in the packet we delivered this afternoon, to the mansion.' She didn't look at Toby. 'It was strange; it was almost like what Malvolio said, on the stage. All is discovered, I wrote. You are lost, if you do not listen. Tonight, meet me at St Louis I, Crypt 3, if you do not want the ghosts to rise.' She paused and added, miserably, 'I signed it, One who wishes you well.'

Toby said, bleakly, 'So you knew. You knew already it was Follett.' He felt sick. 'Yet you didn't trust me enough to tell me.'

'Toby, I swear I *didn't* know! I was fishing! I told you I had my suspicions, but I wasn't sure. I had to *be* sure. And when he just turned up tonight, cool as a cucumber, and didn't seem to react, I thought I was wrong.'

'How did Gabriel know?'

'I don't know! I had no idea he knew anything. He didn't say anything to me . . .'

'Did your nurse know?'

She wailed, 'Toby, I don't know. Maminou has not spoken to me about it. She's been lost in her own haunted world. Toby, you must believe me when I—'

He spoke harshly. 'Where is this place?'

'St Louis cemetery. The Voodoo Queen's tomb,' she said quietly.

He looked at her. 'It is just a game to you, isn't it, Isabelle? All of it; even those magical beliefs you spoke of. You don't really believe any of it, it's just a masquerade to you. Your nurse was right: you're not like other people.'

She turned away. Her voice was cold as ice. 'You can say what you like. Think what you like. I'm going there. Don't come, Toby. You're not needed. I've got my gun.'

'He's my friend,' said Toby, furiously. 'I'm coming, so shut up, all right?'

'Gabriel doesn't need you,' she said, her eyes flashing. 'He's like me – he has always taken care of himself.'

'You're a little fool,' he said, and left the theatre, not looking behind him to see if she was following. He could hear music pouring out from the dance-hall; the ball would start soon. The audience would be tucking into all those goodies Mr Wilson had ordered, happy after the play, discussing how good it had all been, unaware that a real-life revenge drama was happening just under their noses . . .

He had gone round the corner before he thought, Hell, I don't even know where this place is. He was close to the Magnolia; he'd call in there, speak to Madame Laroche, ask her where it was. They could go there together; he'd order a cab. If only he'd done what she wanted! She'd seen it coming, poor woman; she wanted to stop her reckless, naïve, foolish charge from putting her head in a noose. Instead, Gabriel had done so . . .

He pounded up the steps, and through the back. All was quiet – the servants were working at the dance-hall tonight. He knocked on Madame Laroche's closed door. No answer. So he opened the door . . . and saw her lying there asleep, or dozing, her eyes closed, her face grey. He came in. 'Madame Laroche . . .' he whispered. She didn't open her eyes. She must be deeply asleep. There was a feather on her lips, a white feather that appeared to have come from—

Good God. The feather wasn't moving. There was no breath coming from those pale lips! Sick with fear, he leaned over and touched the still face. It was cold. Marie Laroche was dead!

He stepped back, heart hammering. She must have died in her sleep, he thought, in a panic. She'd said she was dying . . . Had that sleeping draught, then, finished her off? Then his gaze fell on the feather again. He stared at it, and at the pillow under the old lady's head. It was slightly askew. The feather had come from the pillow, he thought, with a shock of clarity. Madame Laroche hadn't died in her sleep – she'd been suffocated by her own pillow!

It must have been Follett. He must have slipped out during the play. Cold gripped him as he thought how he'd even *seen* the man getting up and going out. Oh, if only he'd known!

But why had he come here, though, if the note had said to come to the cemetery, after the play? Had Marie Laroche herself contacted him? He looked down at the dead face, and a sob filled his throat. Poor woman. Poor woman . . . Gently, he bent over her, crossed her cold hands, and said a soft prayer to rest her soul. 'Forgive me, Madame Laroche,' he whispered then, tears in his eyes. 'Forgive me for not listening to you.'

He was about to go out when all at once, he heard the front door banging, and rapid, sure footsteps coming towards the room. 'Follett? Are you in here, man? What the Devil's going on?'

Wilson! Toby's heart leaped with relief. He opened the door and called out, 'Mr Wilson!'

He heard a surprised silence; then Wilson's voice, calling out, 'Is that you, Limey kid? Where are you?'

'Here, sir,' said Toby, poking his head out of the door. 'Oh, come quickly, sir, something terrible's happened!'

The big millionaire came striding down the corridor. There was a baffled expression on his face. 'What's going on, kid? I was told Follett—' He went quiet as he took in the still form on the bed. In one stride, he was by the bed. He lifted the old lady's hand, and felt the pulse. He shook his head. 'She's been dead at least an hour, son.'

'Yes,' said Toby. 'She was murdered, Mr Wilson. Suffocated with her own pillow!'

Wilson looked sharply up at him. 'What?'

'The feather, sir,' said Toby, pointing. He paused. 'Sir, I'm afraid . . . I'm afraid it's your secretary, sir, who's done this.'

Wilson stared at him. 'Follett? What is this nonsense? Follett's not got enough red blood to shout at anyone, let alone kill them. Besides, he didn't know this old mulatto from Adam. Why kill her?'

'Nevertheless, I'm sure it was him, sir.'

Wilson straightened. He looked shrewdly at Toby. 'I have an idea you know why, kid.'

'My name's Toby, sir,' said Toby, steadily. 'I do have an idea why, sir. But do you have your car here?'

Wilson stared. 'Why, yes. I drove it over myself . . .'

'Mr Wilson,' cut in Toby, 'do you know where the St Louis cemetery is?'

'Why, yes. I believe it's over near Rampart Street, son.' He looked puzzled. 'Surely it's too early to think of burying this woman and—'

'Sir,' broke in Toby again, quickly, 'will you please take me there?'

'But, Toby, I don't quite understand . . .' began the millionaire.

Toby said, 'Please, sir, I'll explain on the way . . . but we must hurry. Please . . .'

'Oh, very well,' said Wilson, with a sharp glance at Toby.

'Come on then, son. We'll be there in a jiffy, in my car. And I want the full story, as we're going along.'

As they left, Toby took a last look at the still figure of Madame Laroche. Tears stung his eyes. Poor woman! Poor woman! She had paid the ultimate price for her charge's recklessness and stubbornness, and for his own wilful blindness. Pray God receive her soul in peace – and save Gabriel from a similar fate. Pray God they'd be at the cemetery in time!

Twenty-eight

Wilson was silent a moment when Toby had finished explaining. Then he said, quite calmly, 'Good God. I never would have thought it. But I should have done. You know, Toby, Follett has always been so cagey. He never spoke of his past. Now, a man's past is his own, and as long as he works well for me, I don't ask nosy questions. But my wife said he was like a ghost, Toby; someone with no family, past or present. I don't even know which part of the country he really came from, though he always claimed to be from the Midwest. Yet oftentimes I thought, hey, there's a burr of the South there, in his accent. But why should it concern me? The man worked well. And he's utterly discreet.'

'Yes,' said Toby, harshly. 'Utterly discreet. The wolf in sheep's clothing.'

'Absolutely, kid,' said Wilson, looking sharply at him.

'So you believe me, sir?'

'Of course. Why would you lie? And there's that poor dead mulatto woman . . . and all sorts of strange things that make sense to me now. Like the fact he was quite beside himself this afternoon; jumping out of his skin at the least thing. Your little Miss Thing took a very great risk, you know; if he's been hiding blackmail and murder for fifteen years, he's not someone who can be easily tricked.'

'I know,' said Toby, sadly. 'I told her that. But she does just as she wants, always, without regard for anyone else.'

'That's Creole pride for you,' said Wilson. 'Now you say she was going there too? And that she had a gun? Does she know how to use it?'

'She says she does,' said Toby. Sighing, he added, 'But I'm not sure what to believe about her any more. She's told me a lot of lies, and half-truths.'

'I see,' said Wilson, looking shrewdly at him, but making no further comment. 'And your Malvolio fellow — can he handle himself, other than on stage?'

'He might well, sir, but I know he has no gun, and Follett is sure to . . .'

'Well, Toby, open that glove box. There, take out the case. That's my trusty friend, Toby. I know how to shoot; and shoot to kill. You have to, in a mining camp.' He grinned rather ferociously. 'I must say, this little adventure's warming my blood! I must have got soft in my prosperous age. Ah. Here we are.' He stopped the car, and took the gun case from Toby. He opened it, and there was a handgun – not a pretty little thing, like Isabelle's revolver, but a big Browning. Wilson smiled, and put it away in his jacket. 'I always keep it loaded,' he said. 'You never know what can happen.'

Toby paid little attention. The gates of the cemetery rose up before him; beyond, the shapes of those white house-like mausoleums, like the one in Illyria, stood in rows, like ordinary houses on silent streets. Behind him, Wilson said, startling him, 'City of the Dead, they call it here, Toby. Ready?'

Toby swallowed. 'Yes, sir.'

'The one we're looking for – it's just inside the gates, I believe.' Wilson seemed perfectly at ease, but Toby could not restrain a tiny shiver as they went in. The night was bright, and there were no ghostly shapes or mist clinging to any of the tombs; but somehow, the sharp light made their stillness seem all the more eerie.

Wilson was striding ahead. 'It's here,' he said, sounding puzzled, 'but there's not a soul here. Except for the dead ones,' he added, with a laugh, as Toby caught up to him. Toby stared at the tomb before which they'd stopped – it was an ordinary white above-ground crypt, looking like a blank-walled house with an ornate roof, discoloured by time. 'This is it? You're sure?'

'Sure. See those chicken scratches on the wall? They're made by superstitious folk who think the old voodoo lady who's buried in there can still grant wishes beyond the tomb. Quite a one in her time, Marie Laveau.' He was looking around as he spoke. 'She'd be pleased to see she's still remembered so fondly.'

Toby had no interest in dead voodoo queens. 'Isabelle said it would be here. Where can they be?'

'Maybe she was pulling the wool, son,' suggested Wilson, quite kindly. 'I mean – you say she's stubborn and reckless, and wants to deal with things herself. Maybe she—'

'Sssh!' said Toby, suddenly, pulling Wilson behind the tomb. 'I heard something . . .'

They crouched, listening. Voices could clearly be heard now, though not what they were saying. Gabriel's; and Follett's. Toby crept to the edge and peered out. The two men were standing on the pathway some distance away; they appeared to be arguing.

Wilson elbowed him. 'We'll creep up on them,' he whispered. 'You go up this way . . .' he gestured to the backs of the tombs, 'I'll sneak round the other. We'll come on them in a pincer movement. Quiet, now . . .'

Toby nodded. Wilson bent down, and going much more swiftly and quietly than you would have imagined in a man of his height and bulk, he slipped around the front of the tomb, and across the pathway, keeping in the shadows. Toby saw him reach the tombs on the other side. Gabriel and Follett had not seen anything; they were too busy arguing. Toby set off round the back, taking care to keep out of sight. He had almost come level to the men when all at once his stomach dropped. He had heard Isabelle's voice!

'Guy Follett!' she said, and her voice rang cold and clear in that cold, dank place. 'Or should I say William Malpence?'

Follett whirled round. She was standing in the path, some distance away, revolver in her hand. It was aimed directly at the secretary. The man said, 'No! Don't shoot! Wait!'

'Don't shoot,' echoed Gabriel, and his voice was sharp. 'Don't be a fool, Isabelle. It's not what you—'

Isabelle cut in, fiercely. 'I've waited for too long,' she said, and aimed and fired. Or would have done, if the gun had worked. But there was just a click; then another. Incredulously, she pulled the trigger again; but still, nothing happened. Someone had unloaded the revolver!

Everything happened very quickly then. Gabriel moved towards her; Toby jumped out of his hiding-place. But Follett was quicker than any of them. In a flash, he was on Isabelle, knocking the gun out of her hand. Something bright flashed in his hand: a thin, sharp flick-knife. He shouted, 'Back, both of you, back! Stay right there. Or I'll cut her throat.'

Where the hell was Wilson? thought Toby. He had a gun . . . He could—

'Follett, don't be a fool . . .' Gabriel began, but the secretary broke in. 'Enough! You don't understand.' He looked around warily. '*Where is he?*'

'Where's who?'

Just then, Toby thought he saw a movement, just beyond the tomb, at Follett's back. The secretary sneered and said, 'You poor saps, you don't even seem to realise that—'

There was a loud crack. Follett screamed, and spun sideways, blood spurting from his throat, the knife flying out of his hand. There was another loud crack, and the secretary fell to the ground, jerking, gurgling blood. It was the most terrible sound Toby had ever heard.

Isabelle had flung herself down. She crouched with her hands around her head. Toby and Gabriel both dived for her in the same moment. But Gabriel reached her first.

'Hang on there! Stay down!' It was Wilson's voice. There was another crack; and Follett was finally quiet.

'Everyone all right?' Wilson was bending over them. 'Here, give me a hand, miss.'

'No!' said Gabriel, jumping up. 'Isabelle, don't . . .'

Then came something Toby would never forget, as long as he lived. Clarence Wilson, millionaire, cheerful *bon vivant*, benefactor of the Trentham Troupe, smilingly fired straight at Gabriel, the bullet hitting him directly in the chest, where the heart is. The actor fell without a sound. In a swift movement, Wilson hauled the paralysed Isabelle up by her hair, forcing her to stand upright, the gun pointing directly at her temple. He looked at Toby, who had scrambled to his feet and stood swaying, unable to believe the evidence of his senses.

'Don't even think about it, boy,' he said calmly, that faint, deadly smile still on his face. 'I like you, but I wouldn't hesitate to kill you.'

Toby knew he meant just what he said. But he could not bear the sight of Isabelle's terrified, frozen expression – the look of someone caught in a nightmare that she could not escape from. He felt numb. Gabriel's body lay behind him, and Follett's; he was staring into the face of a callous, cold-blooded murderer, but all he could think of was saving her. He stammered, 'Please, sir, please, don't hurt her. She'll leave you alone . . . and I won't tell anything of what I've seen. I promise . . .'

'Shut up, kid. That's a stunt that isn't worthy of you,' said Wilson, coolly.

'But I won't,' said Toby, desperately. 'I won't!'

Wilson raised his eyebrows, but made no comment. He merely said, 'You just stay there, kid, and nothing'll happen to you, or the girl.' He began to move backwards, dragging Isabelle with him, her face like a mask of stone. Suddenly, Isabelle gave a little sighing gasp, and went limp in Wilson's arms. She had fainted.

'Stay back,' ordered Wilson sharply, as Toby was unable to restrain a movement. 'Her life depends on you doing what you are told. Do you understand, Toby?'

'Yes, sir,' said Toby. 'Where will you take her, sir?' He must keep him talking, he thought dully, somehow he must keep the man talking, while his brain whirled, trying to think of what to do.

Wilson grinned. It was horrible; an animal's snarl. But he had halted. He said, 'I like you, Toby. You've got guts. I could have used someone like you. What a fool you are! Why did you have to listen to those damnfool stories of hers?'

'Sir, where will you take her?'

'Where? Why, with me, Toby, of course.' He looked down at the limp figure in his arms. 'Good God, but she looks so much like her mother, Toby. I was fooled at first by that fake tan and that cringing gypsy manner . . . but now I can see it, clear as day. How could I not have seen it that first time? She is just like her mother . . .' He traced the line of her face with one hand. 'I loved her, Toby. I really did. She was unhappy with that skirt-chasing degenerate, the Baron. He was a bad man; I was a good one. I could have made her happy, if she'd let me.'

Toby nodded. He had moved forward one step, without Wilson noticing. He had to do it slowly, carefully. He had to keep the man talking. He had to pretend he was defeated. He said, 'He was a jealous man, sir.'

'He was, he was! He was a wicked man; he was a gambler, a whorer; he frequented criminals and he made Violette very unhappy. But he was a Baron; and he was of an old family; and he could do no wrong. He treated me like a dog, or like a black; beat me so hard that I lost my eye. But you know what, Toby?'

'What, sir?' He had advanced two steps. Gabriel's body lay beside him. Rage and grief soared through him, chasing away the numbness. He repeated, carefully, 'What, sir?'

Wilson said, dreamily, 'I saw to him. I put him on the rack. He ended his days in torture and pain and fear, never knowing when the next blow would come. He died like a dog, Toby, like the cowardly cur he was. He shot himself, like a lamb, when I told him that was the only thing he could do, the only way I would leave his family alone. I promised I would do it. I didn't need to pull the trigger; he did it happily, himself. He did it, in the end, Toby, with gratitude, to me, that I had shown him at least that mercy. And I kept my promise, Toby; I left them alone.'

A shiver rippled over Toby's skin. There was a cold in him that was slowly gaining, freezing his blood, making his teeth chatter. It was the cold of a hatred such as he had never felt before. He forced himself to say, 'That is a true revenge, sir.'

'It is, Toby. You know what? The Baron despised me; but he is dead and buried, and I am rich and famous and respected beyond his wildest dreams. In the end, he was only a tinpot nobleman in a muddy swamp.'

'But, sir, what did you have on him to make him fear you so?'

Wilson laughed. 'If you knew, boy, you would be amazed. No, I don't think I'll tell you yet – not till I have his daughter in a safe place.' He stopped, suddenly. 'What's that?'

'What, sir?' But Toby had heard something, too. Something completely bizarre . . . the thread of a tune . . . a tune he recognised. 'Le roi Renaud', the tune that Tom Nashe played at the beginning of the play. Toby thought wildly, He's here, somewhere.

Wilson's eyes were glittering now, manic, full of a craziness that had burst into full view. 'Who's there?' He cocked the gun. The click of the hammer filled Toby with dread. 'Who's there?' Then his eyes widened. A wild look came on his face. 'Why, you!' he screamed, and fired, straight over Toby's shoulder. Toby heard the whistle of the bullet; later, he said he felt it graze his ear. In truth, he'd ducked down, instinctively, without thinking, shouting in his turn. And then he saw . . .

He saw not Nashe, as he'd expected, but *Gabriel*, walking towards them, quite sedate, and unmarked, still in his Malvolio costume, not one hair out of place. He heard Wilson shouting, and firing again; and Gabriel walked straight on, though Toby clearly saw the bullet hit him in the chest. He passed by Toby, and Toby saw, with a thrill of horror, that though he was dressed in Gabriel's clothes, the man was *not* Gabriel. He had something of his features, but only superficially, from a distance; close up, he was much paler than Gabriel, very, very pale, with eyes not green, but dark, hollow with darkness. In a sudden flash of clarity, Toby knew just where he'd seen that face: in the *Twelfth Night* photograph, back in Klondike's place. It had been laughing, then, full of life . . . but it was of a man dead these fifteen years.

Wild-eyed, Wilson fired again, but still the figure kept coming. With a little whimper of fear, the millionaire dropped Isabelle and the gun. He turned to flee out of the cemetery, but still the figure kept going after him, relentlessly, without making a sound. As they reached the gate, Toby saw the figure catch up to Wilson, and tap him lightly on the shoulder. He thought, wildly, but I can see him, he's solid, not transparent, he looks real, real . . . and yet he doesn't speak, he's a . . . a *ghost* . . . The ghost of Isabelle's father – the ghost of the Baron Armand de Castelon . . .

'Please,' came Wilson's whimpering voice, 'sir . . . please . . . leave me alone. I wasn't going to hurt her . . .'

The ghost of Baron Armand de Castelon said nothing. Its eyes looked deep into Wilson's.

He kept whimpering, 'You who have come from hell, what do you want from me? What do you want?'

The ghost turned slightly. It pointed at Toby. He could feel its hollow gaze on him, and it made the very pores in his skin dilate with fear, sweat breaking out on every part of his body. The ghost beckoned. When Toby was closer, it made a scrawling motion in the air. Toby stammered, 'I . . . I don't understand . . .' The ghost's eyes burned coldly into his, and it made that motion again. This time, Toby thought he could understand. 'You want me to write something?' He fumbled in his clothes. He still had the prompt-pencil in his pocket, and yes – the notebook he'd been carrying around for days, with ideas for stories. He said, 'What do you want me to write, sir?'

It felt odd to be addressing a ghost, but what else could he do? Then out of the corner of his eye, he could see Wilson, getting slowly up from his knees. Terror was still dribbling out of his mouth and eyes, but Toby could see that the man was going to—

'Oof!' In one quick, savage movement, he had sprung at Toby, knocked him down, and fled in the opposite direction. Not for long, though, for all at once, a leg shot out from the pathway, and Wilson, running headlong, crashed into it and fell to the ground.

'Gabriel!' Toby couldn't believe it. The actor's face was dust-streaked and dirty, the grease paint running, the false goatee askew, the slicked-back hair a wild mess. But he was alive. Smiling grimly, he sat on top of the stunned Wilson, and patting the left side of his shirt, he said, 'I never saw the death he carried with him . . . how odd that it should be this that saved my life . . .' As Toby stared, he drew out a familiar, small but fat leather-bound book from his top pocket, and Toby saw the words, 'Lamb's Tales from Shakespeare', on the front. Gabriel's lucky book had a neat bullet hole in the very centre, right between the words 'Lamb's' and 'Tales'. Stunned, Toby looked at it, then all around him. The ghost had vanished. It had completely disappeared, as if it had never been at all. Had he imagined it? But there was the prompt-pencil in his hand, and the notebook. He'd been about to take dictation from a ghost! His heart turned over at the thought. What was real, what was not? He hardly knew any more . . .

Wilson stirred. He opened his eyes. He looked fearfully into Gabriel's green ones. He said, 'Baron?'

'I'm not the Baron,' said Gabriel, grimly. 'But I'll act for him.' Yes, thought Toby, looking at the dirty black and gold clothes, and the goatee, you acted for him, *indeed*. He was sure Gabriel had seen the photo in Klondike's house. He must have gone there; he must even have spoken to the gangster. He had been one step ahead all the way. 'You will do just as I say,' went on the actor. He motioned Toby to come forward with his pencil and paper. 'You will pay back in full the money you blackmailed from the Baron.'

'I spent it long ago, but I invested it, instead of wasting it, like he would have done,' said Wilson. He was recovering some of his colour, now that he knew the ghost had gone. Or did he think that Gabriel had somehow acted that part? Well, had he? Toby wasn't absolutely sure, though on balance he thought not. That ghost had been *real*. It had not borne Gabriel's face. No – it was real.

'All the better,' said Gabriel, smiling unpleasantly. 'It should have nicely accumulated. Here, write.' Wilson scrawled a figure down. Gabriel snorted. 'Twice that, I think. Follett told me you keep a diamond in your pocket – getaway treasure, was what he called it. An old superstition of yours. He said no one but he knew about it, not even your wife. He also told me what it was worth. Give it to me.'

'That double-crossing, black-hearted traitor,' growled Wilson. He stared at Gabriel. 'If I do this, will you leave me alone?'

'No!' said Toby fiercely, but Gabriel waved a hand at him. 'If you mean, will you save your miserable skin, yes. A hired thug lies dead – you can cook up whatever story you choose about the late and unlamented Mr Follett – but you will give the Baron's daughter your diamond, you will sign this piece of paper to show you have given it to her, of your own will, and you will go away tomorrow and never come back to Louisiana. Is that clear?'

Wilson shrugged. 'As crystal.' He put a hand in his pocket. Gabriel kept the gun trained on him. With a cynical smile, Wilson pulled a velvet pouch out of his pocket. He looked at Gabriel, and opening the drawstrings, tipped the contents of the pouch. It sparkled on his flesh like a radiant bit of captured moon: a brilliant, beautiful pink diamond, big as a pigeon's egg.

Gabriel held out his hand, and the millionaire tipped the diamond into the actor's palm. He said lightly, 'You have played well, Malvolio. You have won the prize, *and* the girl. Well done. You can retire, now.'

Unable to restrain himself any longer, Toby burst out, harshly, 'And what about Madame Laroche?'

'This was her idea,' said Gabriel, without missing a beat.

'I mean, what is *her life* worth, Gabriel? Another gem, or just a few dollars?'

Gabriel stared. 'What do you mean?'

'She's dead, Gabriel. This man had her killed.' Toby stared accusingly at Wilson. 'I came here from the Magnolia; she'd been suffocated to death with her own pillow.' He gestured at Follett's body. 'He did it; I saw him leave during the performance. But it must have been Wilson who ordered it.'

'No . . . you don't understand . . .' Wilson was looking from one to the other, the ghost of a smile on his face. 'She was already dead when Follett got there. I do admit I sent him there to put the frighteners on her. I'd found out about her being at the Magnolia; she didn't hide her tracks very well, unlike your little actress friend. I thought the girl must have died years ago; and that the crazy old witch was trying to take her revenge . . . especially when the note came, to meet at the Laveau tomb. Everyone in Illyria knew the Voodoo Queen was an ancestor of hers . . .'

'I don't believe you,' said Toby. 'Her pillow was askew. There was a feather on her lip. Someone had used that pillow to suffocate her.'

'You read too many romances,' said Wilson sharply. 'She was dead already, I tell you. And she had these under her pillow . . .' He pulled out something from his pocket, something Toby recognised at once. The little voodoo dolls from the Castelon tomb, in Illyria! 'Follett found them, and brought them to me. I instructed him to leave things as he'd found them, then, and sent him to meet you, Harvey—' He broke off, abruptly. His eyes widened, the expression in them suddenly changing. 'Violette . . . Baroness . . . is that you? Oh God . . . it *is* you . . .'

They looked swiftly behind them. She was there, standing with pale, pale face and dark eyes and cloud of dark hair, beautiful as the night, the moonlight shining through her ghostly ball-gown, her translucent hand held out towards them. She opened her mouth as if to speak; but before she could make a sound, the millionaire cried out, 'I never meant for you to be hurt! I never meant you to be, my darling! It didn't matter to me, what you were; it never did, only to him, don't you see? But you let me be beaten like a dog and never lifted a finger to help me! No . . . don't look at me like that . . . forgive me . . . forgive me . . .' All at once, he gave a great despairing shriek, and he slumped, heavily, as if felled by a tremendous blow. His eyes rolled back, and spittle came from the corners of his lips. But he was quite still. Gabriel grabbed for his wrist. He said, 'He's dead. Stone dead. Heart attack.'

'Dead?' whispered Isabelle, swaying before them. The ghostliness had vanished from her presence, and she no longer looked so much like her dead mother, but more vital, more alive, than ever. She kicked a disdainful foot at the millionaire's prone body. 'Death was too good for him; especially this kind of death.'

'Stop it,' ground out Toby. 'Stop it, Isabelle.' He thought, dully, Gabriel was right about the shadow of death at her shoulder, she's a death-bringer; she killed her nurse, and she killed Wilson, without firing a shot. She's a death-bringer, without firing a shot . . . He could see the voodoo dolls where they had fallen, just near Wilson's body. He thought, they are just dolls, now, just crude little stick figures of rag and wood. They will never rise again, those spirits. And suddenly, he thought, of course they'll never rise again. They have no need to. It is all done . . . all done. And not by Isabelle, or by Toby, or by Gabriel. But by . . .

He raised his head. Could he hear that tune again? Just there, at the edge of his hearing? That haunting tune – 'Le roi Renaud' – the song of the strength of love crossing even the bitterness of death . . . Tears started in his eyes as he strained to listen. No; it was gone now, quite gone, like a last, dying breath of wind . . .

Isabelle was speaking. She said, 'Toby . . . Toby . . . is it really true? Is my darling Maminou dead?'

Toby nodded. He didn't trust himself to speak.

She cried out, 'It is my fault; my fault that she is dead, no matter what killed her.'

'No,' said Toby, quietly. 'It is not. You don't always have to bring everything back to yourself, Isabelle.' Death-bringer he'd thought her; but now the glamour and the shadow were both gone, and he saw her, clearly. He saw she was just a young girl, unformed, wilful, unable to see the suffering of others; a proud girl who had a lot to learn. Something dropped away from him then. He felt pity for her, and tenderness; but his infatuation had gone for ever.

She flushed scarlet under his scrutiny. 'You don't understand . . .'

'Oh, but I *do*. She exhausted herself for years, trying to protect you with all of her powers, earthly and not. She gave the *last* of her power for you, Isabelle, and it killed her. She did what she'd hoped never to have to do: she unbound the restless spirits of your parents, and especially your father, that vengeful and jealous man. Aren't I right, Gabriel?'

Gabriel said, heavily, 'Yes, Toby. You are quite right. She had an idea what you were planning, Isabelle; she had found your revolver, and took out the bullets. She told me I must lure the killer out. And she said . . . she said she had to do one final thing, to save you, Isabelle. She was afraid, I could see that; but she risked it for you.' He paused. 'She was a fine woman, a great soul; and you are fortunate to have had her with you for so long.'

Isabelle hung her head. 'I loved Maminou,' she said, softly. 'I know you think I don't know how to, Gabriel Harvey; but you are wrong.'

Toby looked at the pair of them, and at the body of Clarence Wilson, who had once been William Malpence, a wicked, wicked man who had nevertheless loved a woman to the very gates of hell. He thought of Maminou. He thought of the pink diamond, still in Gabriel's grasp. He said, very quietly, 'I think I will go and get help, now. Someone needs to start all the official things. I think it had better not be you; you had both better run away together with your diamond, before Tom Nashe drags you off to prison, Gabriel.' He saw Isabelle's eyes widen at that.

Gabriel said quietly, his eyes on the girl, 'I guess you could call it prison, Toby, for I do not want to go back there. But I was saved tonight by the book, my only relic of home, and so perhaps it is a sign. You see, my name is not Gabriel Harvey, but Gabriel de Burgh, and my family is quite famous, and quite wealthy, back in Ireland. They had many plans for me; but I wanted to be an actor, and they would not allow it. And so I ran away from home. They tried to find me, but failed; and finally engaged Pinkerton's. It took Nashe quite some time to find me; but now he's tracked me down. I was going to tell you all tomorrow. That's all.'

'So that's it, *that's all*,' breathed Toby. 'I thought you . . .'

'You thought I was a master thief,' said Gabriel, and he

gave the ghost of a smile. 'And why not? I've played those often enough, after all.'

Toby cried, 'I wish you had trusted me . . . I wish *both* of you had trusted me.'

'Toby,' said Gabriel, gently, 'dear friend, it wasn't that I didn't trust you . . . just that I didn't trust myself.' He looked at Isabelle, and Toby saw the joy, the hope that shone deep in the actor's eyes, reflected in Isabelle's. He knew he'd certainly never seen that expression in Gabriel's eyes before. It was all right, it was all right, Toby told himself, it doesn't hurt me any more, it doesn't hurt me. But there it was, the heart didn't let go quite so easily of its dreams, and something painful twinged at him as he said, a little roughly, 'What are we going to do, now?' He gestured at the bodies of the millionaire and his deputy. 'What are we going to say about *this*?'

'I think,' said Gabriel, 'I think we should say that we found out that Follett was embezzling Mr Wilson. He told me as much, when I was talking with him. I think then we'll say—'

Toby said, with a little surge of excitement, 'We'll say he threatened you with his gun, and Mr Wilson shot him then, but that the whole thing was too much for him, and he collapsed and died. I think that would be the best story, don't you? It will stand up to an autopsy, and to a ballistics investigation, if we're all agreed.'

'That's an excellent idea, Toby,' said Gabriel, smiling a little. 'I suppose reading detective stories isn't altogether a waste of time.'

Toby flushed. 'If you can think of a better . . .'

'No, no, Toby.' Isabelle was smiling uncertainly. 'You are quite right. It will satisfy everyone.'

Toby looked at her. He said quietly, 'We have to protect Mrs Wilson, who's been very kind, and Uncle Theo, and the Biches and everyone, who are innocent bystanders in all this mess, don't you think?' He paused. 'And nobody need know about the diamond.'

'Toby, I would like to——' Isabelle began, but Toby turned and walked away. He heard her protesting a little, and heard Gabriel's gentle, 'Let him be, Isabelle. Let him be.'

He turned, once, and saw Gabriel and Isabelle looking into each other's eyes, and a sharp dagger of pain pierced his chest, then was gone, the spot throbbing and tender. 'I don't think I want that kind of life,' he said, speaking to himself now, as he walked out of the cemetery and into Rampart Street. 'I think I want a different life to you, Isabelle, and to you, Gabriel. I do not yet know what sort of life it will be, but I will find it, one day.'

He didn't even know the tears were flowing till he tasted salt on his lips. He kept walking, down the street which even at this hour was jumping with people and activity. Some people looked curiously at him as he went by, but most of them didn't seem to even notice he was there. He was nearly out of Rampart Street when he heard a voice behind him, calling his name. He turned. It was Klondike. He was dressed in elegant evening wear, and a rather flashy platinum-blonde girl in furs was on his arm.

'What's the matter, boy?' he said, not unkindly. 'You look like you've seen a ghost.'

'And so I have,' said Toby, looking straight into the man's eyes. 'I saw a ghost at St Louis I, Crypt 3. In fact, two.'

'Oh, you've been to pay a visit to the Voodoo Queen of New Orleans!' squealed the girl in a rather Cockney accent. 'She brings you luck in love, so they say!' She looked curiously at Toby, who nodded. 'So they say, miss.'

'Ooh, Klondike, can we go there now?' said the girl, coquettishly.

He smiled, faintly. 'Why? You think you need luck in love, *chère*?'

'Ooh, really, honey, you are terrible, it's for both of us!' said the girl, bridling a little.

'Another night, perhaps. Now you carry on walking, I'll catch up,' said Klondike, and his pale eyes held an expression that made the girl flush a little, under the made-up porcelain of her skin. 'Very well,' she said crossly, flouncing up the road.

As soon as she was out of earshot, Klondike said, 'So, Toby, did the ghosts tell you what you wanted to know?'

'Oh, more than that. Much more than that,' said Toby, heavily. 'And yet not enough. One day, Mister Klondike . . . can I come and visit you, one day? Your aunt said I should.'

Klondike looked at him, thoughtfully. He nodded. 'Of course. Any time you wish.' He paused. 'Don't look so sad, Toby. There are much greater things ahead for you than our corrupted little corner of the world. You won't be trapped in the past. You belong to the future.'

Toby said stiffly, 'Sir, I confess I am bushed, and in need of a rest. Will you excuse me?'

'Of course, Toby.' The gangster hesitated, then put out a beringed hand. 'You are a man after my own heart, Toby. Goodnight.'

I'm not sure I want to be complimented by a gangster, thought Toby, bleakly, as he shook Klondike's hand. It was curiously limp, like a wet fish – a spiky wet fish, with those rings. He said, 'Goodnight, then,' and walked away. He could feel Klondike's eyes on his back, but he didn't turn around, not once.

Epilogue

There were police, and autopsies, and investigations, for quite a time after that, but it was just as Toby had said. No one thought to question the stories that he and Gabriel and Isabelle told; no one investigated Clarence Wilson's past, only Follett's; and he turned out not only to have been clearly involved in diverting money from one of Mr Wilson's newspaper accounts, but also to have a rap sheet from the Midwest, where he'd had to leave in a hurry after running afoul of the law. There was a three days' wonder about it in New Orleans, but the city was hardly a stranger to violent death, or to crime and corruption, and so after a time, it passed into obscurity, even in the *Bugle*.

Mrs Wilson wept a few tears over the death of her husband, but she hadn't married him for love, and though not heartless by any means, she was a shallow, bouncy, pleasant woman who took comfort in the fact that her bank balance remained healthy. She also developed quite an interest in, and a knack for, the newspaper business, and under her tutelage, the *Bugle* and other newspapers not only grew, but flourished.

As to the Trentham Troupe, its fortunes after the spectacular tragedy of Wilson's death showed the truth of the old saying that there's no such thing as bad publicity. In the course of the three days' wonder, the story of how Wilson had taken the company, and the play, under his wing, was carried not only in New Orleans newspapers, but in New York, and even beyond, in London. *Malvolio's Revenge* and its author had undreamed-of publicity; and after a couple of days' decent wait, the play was put on again, and the Terpsichore packed every night for weeks. New York agents soon came to see the play, and made competing offers to a delighted Uncle Theo for the right to put it on in their theatres.

But not every member of the company would be performing their old roles in New York. Faithful Slender and Shallow were to stay behind in Madame La Praline's stables, and be pampered in their retirement, for there was enough money now for everyone to travel in style, by train, to the great city. Henry Smallwood had quietly dropped his courtship of Madame La Praline – who showed no disappointment – and begun discreetly squiring the Merry Widow Wilson to social functions. It seemed likely he might want to stay on a little longer in New Orleans, his prospects having suddenly looked up, so that even the New York stage seemed small beer to him now.

Tom Nashe had left for pastures new, his investigation complete, and his report in, to the family that awaited Gabriel's return, far away across the sea in Ireland. The whole troupe had been delighted at the news of Gabriel's real identity; the women sighed and said how romantic it was, the men expressed surprising pleasure. And of course, Isabelle loved it; she understood it; it was her story, blood of her blood, bone of her bone . . .

But of course Gabriel would not stay in the troupe. He would not go to New York either, though he'd had many offers. He and Isabelle were to sail back to Ireland, where they would be reunited with his family, and get married. After that, it was anyone's guess, including the couple themselves. Would they stay in Ireland, or come back to Illyria? Would Gabriel keep acting, or give it all up to be a respectable landholder? Toby rather suspected acting was a fever in Gabriel's blood, which he'd not easily turn his back on; and on the other hand, Illyria was a fever in Isabelle's blood, which she'd not easily give up, even though she had laid her ghosts, now. Only time would tell . . .

And what of Toby himself? He had decided the Trentham Troupe was still his home, for the time being; he was still odd-job man and company carpenter, but his notebook was filling with ideas for stories. Weeks later, the wounds of the past had scarred over almost completely, so that he could watch Isabelle and Gabriel's happiness with equanimity and even pleasure, and he could look back on the terrible events of that night in the cemetery with a kind of detached wonder. Some days, he even thought things had turned out for the very best. He was happy for Uncle Theo's good fortune, and appreciated him and his cousins with a new, gentle affection. They were all the family he had, and despite their failings, despite their taking him for granted, they had always been loyal and kind, according to their lights. He was grateful for small things. He would forget many things. But what he could never forget was the memory of Marie Laroche . . .

She had been farewelled with a dignified, rather lovely funeral in the Cathedral of St Louis – which was attended by a surprisingly large number of people – and then buried next to the Castelons, back in Illyria. But it was the whole company, and Madame Blanche and Monsieur Bruno, and Madam La Praline, as well as Klondike and Tombstone, who all pitched in money for Madame Laroche's personal memorial. It was a beautiful statue of an angel with a flaming sword, twin to the other that stood there with the family scroll, and it stood guard before the now-peaceful tomb, like the angel of God barring the way to evil.

Toby thought that Isabelle would never quite gauge the full extent of Marie Laroche's love and self-sacrifice; but that she accepted it as her due, quite unself-consciously, because she had always been loved. These days, he could regard her with a cautious regard, and even friendship; he could hardly blame her any more, for she had been a lost child, trying to find her bearings in a strange and difficult world. And she would probably learn, in time, to regard the feelings of others more; experience would teach her and mould her into true and deep beauty, not just the loveliness of face and figure and bearing and speech.

But it was not till more than a month after the events at the cemetery, a short time before Mardi Gras, the end of Carnival itself, that Toby finally decided to pay his promised visit to Klondike. When he arrived at Klondike's house, Tombstone opened the door. Silently, the albino led Toby through the house, to a study on the ground floor. There sat Klondike at a desk, bareheaded, behind him a beautiful painting of the Virgin Mary, whose features reminded Toby greatly of Violette de Castelon.

'Mister Klondike, I'm ready,' Toby said. 'I want to know whatever it is your aunt wanted you to tell me.'

'Very well.' Klondike smiled faintly, and gestured to a chair. Toby sat down, Tombstone beside him.

'I hear everything's going very well at the Terpsichore,' said the gangster. Toby nodded. He hadn't come here for small talk.

Klondike met his brother's eye, swiftly, then said, 'Look, Toby . . . what I'm about to tell you, you may not understand.'

'Try me,' said Toby, tightly.

Klondike shrugged. 'My aunt Marie, she was a good woman, but a stern one. She never thought much of my way of life, though she was family and never denied me in my need. But she was straight as an arrow, and true, do you know what I mean?'

'Yes,' said Toby.

'She thought a lot of you, you know,' Klondike said.

Toby felt a lump come to his throat. 'She hardly knew me,' he said softly.

'She could see truth when she met it. She said you were straight as an arrow, too.'

'She was mistaken, I think,' said Toby, thinking of those strange bright eyes. 'She . . . I think she reminded me a little of my mother,' he blurted out, and looked away, so Klondike wouldn't see his emotion.

'I can understand that,' said Klondike gently.

'It was such a pity . . . such a pity she never had children of her own,' cried Toby. 'To always have to look after the children of others, to never—'

Klondike put a hand to his forehead. Toby saw he was sweating. 'She did have a child, but she had to give up all claims to her. Her name . . . her name was Violette.'

Toby started up from his chair. 'What!'

'Violette was the natural daughter of Marie Laroche and her childhood friend, Count Henri de Boishardy,' said Klondike, in a strange, stern voice. 'Marie had been brought up on the Boishardy estate, with the Count himself; they ran wild as children, together. I think they loved each other dearly, when they were young. But he was a Creole noble, and she was a coloured servant's child, daughter of an ex-slave. There was no way they could ever be together, openly. The Count married, into another proud Creole family. But his wife was barren, and sickly into the bargain. And so . . . he returned to Marie. His wife didn't mind; as long as she had the title and the money and the position, little did she care what her husband was up to. And when Marie became pregnant, the Countess made Marie an offer: her child would be brought up as a Boishardy, if she gave up all claims to maternity. She could stay on as the child's nurse, and thus bring her up in reality; but she must never breathe a word of it to anyone.'

'But that's monstrous!' said Toby, white to the lips.

'It was a good offer,' said Klondike coldly, 'and Aunt Marie knew it. The Countess could have had her thrown off the estate, and Marie and her child would have starved. This way, the Countess promised that Violette would never want for anything, would be brought up as a member of the elite, and that her real mother would also always be provided for. Aunt Marie knew the Count was a weak man, and his attention was straying from her, anyway; there were always new, lovely young servants on the old plantations, you know.' His lips pursed, and he looked almost fierce. 'So it went, and so it was done. Aunt Marie did her deal with the Devil, and willingly, for her sweet daughter's sake. A few weeks after the birth, the Countess died; and it was put about she had died as a result of complications of childbirth.'

'So that was the burden that lay on you . . .' Toby whispered, thinking of the desolate voice, the haunted face. 'Oh, how I wish . . .'

'You don't need to wish anything,' said Klondike. 'Aunt Marie knew what she was doing; and she did not regret it, ever.'

'How couldn't she . . . I mean . . .'

'You don't understand,' said the man, shaking his head, 'just what it can be like, to be . . . in our situation. Aunt Marie did the right thing, for her child. As to the Boishardys . . . well, they could have turned her out, too, they could have just kept the baby and got rid of the nurse. But they kept to their part of the bargain, in full honour; and the Count never touched Marie again, but treated her with unfailing courtesy. For those old families, issue was everything; a son would have been better, of course, but Violette was an enchanting child . . .' His voice broke a little, then, but resumed more strongly, 'And so it ceased to matter, that she wasn't a boy, especially after she made a brilliant marriage to

Armand de Castelon. Everything was fine, in fact, until . . . until that Malpence fellow went ferreting, after Armand turned him out, and found out. Heaven knows how; but it destroyed everything.'

Toby stared at him. 'You mean . . .'

'I mean this is the hold Clarence Wilson – or William Malpence – had over Armand,' said Klondike, his mouth stretching in a mirthless grin. 'He found out Armand's wife had a touch of the tar-brush, as they say, and thus was subject to Jim Crow laws; and what was more, that she was illegitimate, that she was not really entitled to the Countess's fortune which had come to her along with the Boishardy lands. He knew that the revelation of it would not only cause a major scandal in New Orleans, one that the Castelons could never live down, but that it would completely destroy the family. It is a crime to intermarry here, you know. So Malpence bled Armand dry for months over it.'

Toby's skin crawled. He said slowly, 'He was a monster, then. A monster! I thought he loved her . . .'

Klondike got up from his chair. He walked over to the window and looked out. 'Yes,' he said, quietly. '*Mais, que voulez-vous!* He was a tormented monster such as we breed here, and this was truly a tragedy made in Louisiana. Violette . . . anyone could have loved her; she was beautiful, beautiful in ways I can hardly explain to you . . .' He broke off, and Toby, with a surge of pity, thought of the dead girl's photograph in Klondike's bedroom. 'I am sure she did nothing to encourage him; but he was maddened by love, and blind to all reason. Her presence was enough, it made him lose his wits, and sense of everything. And when he was whipped, and driven from the estate, his love turned to burning hatred. It consumed all that was good in him . . . except this one thing; that he kept his promise, and never revealed Violette's parentage.'

Toby thought of the millionaire's white face as he looked on what he thought was the ghost of his dead beloved. He'd said, 'It didn't matter to me what you were . . . but he cared.' Perhaps, in some twisted, perverse way, he really had loved her more than Isabelle's father had done . . .

Tombstone said, speaking for the first time, 'He didn't have to win. The Baron could have damned him to hell; could have refused to pay, and damn the consequences. Or he could have killed him; it would've been easy.'

'Truth is,' said Klondike, 'the Baron was ashamed; ashamed of his wife's ancestry. He did not repudiate her, oh no; he loved her dearly, despite his womanising, and he respected Aunt Marie. But he was still ashamed; so much so he did not even tell her what was happening . . . he did not want her to know, for you see, she had no idea herself. He did not want the shame to be obvious to both of them. And so he paid, and paid, and paid, till Malpence made him understand it was never going to stop, not while he was alive; and so he blew his brains out. He was a weak man, Toby. In the end, he, as much as Malpence, caused his family's ruin.'

'But he could have been protecting them all,' said Toby, gently, thinking of that pale, speechless ghost he'd seen in the St Louis cemetery. 'It could have been love that drove him, after all. Love, and honour.'

'Words,' said Klondike, briefly. 'Small words, to set beside deeds.'

Toby stared at him, at this strange, surprising, disturbing man who had revealed such unexpected things. He said, very gently, 'Why did Madame Laroche do nothing about it?'

'She didn't know. Not then. Armand told nobody. He let it be understood he was losing heavily at the gaming table, much more heavily than it appeared. It was, after all, a common way for an aristocrat of an old but decaying family to go. Aunt Marie did not learn the truth till a year or so ago – when I told her.'

'Does Isabelle know?'

'Not this, no. Only that Malpence was blackmailing her father. She thought it was over some woman.'

Tombstone gave a harsh bark of laughter. 'She wasn't all that wrong. Only she didn't know which woman, did she?' He looked at Toby. 'Take care, kid, if you are thinking of telling her. Isabelle is . . . not always strong.'

'I could tell Gabriel,' said Toby quietly. 'He will find the right words; he loves her, and is to marry her, and take her far from here. He will be glad to learn that Madame Laroche was her grandmother, for he respected and admired her greatly.'

'Do as you wish,' said Klondike, turning back to the window. 'I think maybe you will find the right way, Toby. And I am glad for Isabelle, that she has found a true man to love her, a man who will not be bound by the ways of Louisiana.' He paused. 'Her mother and grandmother will be looking down from heaven, most relieved, I think, me.'

Toby stared at his back. He shot a look at Tombstone. He swallowed, cleared his throat. 'Thank you. You have been . . . . most kind. God bless you.'

'It's been a long time since anyone asked God to bless us, eh, brother,' said Klondike humorously, turning back to Toby; and all his teeth were bared in that intimidating golden grin.

Tombstone's diamond teeth flashed. 'And I'm not sure God would approve, brother.'

'But thank you, anyway, Tobias Trentham,' said Klondike. 'You've a kind heart, and a true one. You'll be all right, you.' He paused, and ran a hand over his brilliantined hair. 'Now, if you'll excuse us,' he went on in quite a different voice, 'we have Mardi Gras preparations to make. I presume you'll all be going to the big parades? I'll wager it's like nothing you've ever seen, anywhere.'

'Wouldn't miss it for the world, sir,' said Toby quietly, and taking his leave of both of them, he went out of the room, out of the house, and into the busy street outside.

As he walked along, deep in thought, he heard the familiar rumble of a wagon behind him, and a familiar voice calling out, merrily, 'Hey, mister!'

Toby turned. 'Louis!' he said, as the child jumped off the coal cart. 'Haven't seen much of you, lately!'

'I been practising, sir,' said the boy, excitedly. He held up a horn that looked a bit battered and worn. 'This is mine, sir! Mr Karnofsky bought it for me! Listen!' And he blew a note, and then another, and another, then another. It was a little ragged, his playing, but it had a verve and an energy that made Toby's blood jump. 'You going to do good, Louis!' he said, to the beaming child. 'You're going to be just like Bunk Johnson!'

'Oh, even better, mister!' said the child. 'That I've decided, in my heart!'

'I'm sure you will be,' said Toby, smiling, and would have said more, but at that moment, the boy darted off after the rumbling cart, with a cheerful, 'Goodbye! And good luck, mister!'

'And good luck to you too,' said Toby, out loud, looking after Louis' busy little figure. 'Good luck indeed, my friend.' Please, God, he thought fervently, let him have good luck, truly, and not be trapped into nightmare by Jim Crow like so many others, too many others . . .

After a moment, he turned his steps slowly homewards, towards the Magnolia and the supper that awaited him. And as he went, his mind, occupied by thoughts of the tragedy he had been witness to began drifting to his notebook, and to the story he might tell. And slowly, insistently, it began to take shape in his head. It would start like this, he thought: *It was a rainy night, the rainiest night that was ever seen, and the wagon of the travelling actors struggled through the Mississippi mud . . .*

Afterword

Twelfth Night is one of my favourite Shakespeare plays, and this novel is greatly influenced by it. The quotes at the beginning of each Act come from that play, and some of the characters' names. But I plundered the names for Gabriel Harvey and Thomas Nashe from two of Shakespeare's contemporaries. Anyone who's interested in the original namesakes of these characters (who were bitter rivals) should have a look at the website maintained by Rita Lamb at *http://www.members.tripod.com/sicttasd*. Theo Trentham's play, *Malvolio's Revenge*, is, however, my own invention!

I was also inspired by one of my favourite childhood books, the wonderful nineteenth-century French historical adventure novel, *Capitaine Fracasse*, by Theophile Gautier, which I read many, many times! This rollicking, romantic novel, set in the seventeenth century, tells the story of a group of travelling players who fetch up at a crumbling castle in the South of France one stormy winter's night. The young owner of the castle, the Baron de Sigognac, joins the troupe as 'Capitaine Fracasse' and leaves with them on their travels because he's fallen in love with one of the actresses, the beautiful, sad and mysterious Isabelle. Many wonderful, suspenseful adventures result . . .

Most of all, though, the inspiration for the novel came through a trip I made to New Orleans and Louisiana country, in 2001. The extraordinary atmosphere and bloody, tumultuous, tragic and exciting history of the city and its surrounding countryside made a profound impression on me, as did its ghost stories, stories of voodoo, and tales of colourful characters, as well as the sad history of its race relations.

The references to the Jim Crow segregation laws relate to the system of legal apartheid that existed in the United States, especially in the South, from the late nineteenth century to the 1960s and the birth of the civil rights movement. Racial categories were severely delineated; even one-eighth black ancestry could classify a person as 'coloured' and thus subject to segregation laws, which ranged from the mean and petty to the extremely oppressive and cruel. These laws were known popularly as 'Jim Crow' after a black character in a nineteenth-century minstrel show.

* * *

New Orleans is, of course, the birthplace of jazz, and of the greatest jazz musician ever: the extraordinary, multi-talented singer and trumpeter Louis Armstrong, who had a fascinating, colourful life-history, and a most engaging personality, as well as enormous talent. My descriptions of this period in his childhood, when he was employed by the Karnofsky family – Lithuanian Jews who owned a shop and a delivery business – are based on Louis' own autobiography about his early days in New Orleans, *Satchmo*, as well as several biographies. The Karnofskys quite early on recognised Louis' natural talent, and encouraged him to play on a cheap little tin horn to attract customers, later helping him to buy his first trumpet. His role in the action of *Malvolio's Revenge* is, of course, pure invention!

Incidentally, one of my parents' most treasured memories is seeing the great Armstrong playing at a massive Independence celebratory concert in Ghana, West Africa, where they were working for a couple of years. We, who knew Louis Armstrong's gravelly voice, lively style and extraordinary trumpet-playing only through records, could only envy them!